CARA IV

Books by BERNARD STOCKS

THE GUARDIANS
THE TEENAGE PENSIONER
THE LANNAN PROJECT
THE FAR SIDE OF NOWHERE
THE LANNAN DIARY
HALF ALIEN
A LEAP TOO FAR

CARA IV

Bernard Stocks

authorHOUSE®

AuthorHouse™
1663 Liberty Drive
Bloomington, IN 47403
www.authorhouse.com
Phone: 1-800-839-8640

First published by AuthorHouse   05/26/2011

ISBN: 978-1-4567-8276-4 (sc)
ISBN: 978-1-4567-8277-1 (ebk)

Printed in the United States of America

CHAPTER ONE

Looking back I would say there were three events in my childhood that went far to making me the man I am today. The first occurred when I was five years old: I saw a spaceship for the first time. You may think that this would be a regular occurrence in the year 2224, but in fact the sight of such a ship over Edinburgh was rare in the extreme. Ships entering or leaving the huge spaceport on Rannoch Moor always did so from the north and west. This particular one must have strayed out of orbit or miscalculated in some way. Whatever the reason it had a profound effect on me. From that moment on I decided that I, Alexander Dunsmuir, would be on board one of these silver monsters one day. I didn't care in what capacity. Captain, pilot, passenger or stowaway, anything would do. From the time I was eight and could find my way around Spacenet, the offshoot of the internet that dealt exclusively with space and the conquest thereof, I devoured everything I could on the subject. I knew the names of the dozen or so colonised planets: Paladia, Magna, Persephone, Garant and the rest. I could tell you something of their geography, their current population and how long it took to get to each one. I knew what the inside of a spaceship looked like, the speeds it could travel at and how the crew was made up. I was, in short, space mad.

To let you understand fully the second major event I'll need to give you some of my family history. I was the youngest child of four. My father, George Dunsmuir, was a film producer, much in demand on both sides of the Atlantic. He was seldom home. My mother Alicia was also a remote figure. She was a highly successful fashion designer and regularly based for months at a time in London, Paris, Milan or Madrid. My two brothers were respectively fifteen and twelve years older than I. Both married and left home when they were twenty-one so I hardly knew them. My sister Aileen was nine years older and we never got on. Our relationship veered between open hostility and an uneasy truce, the latter usually short-lived. I think a lot of the trouble between us was caused by the fact that from

1

fourteen onwards she had to give up a considerable amount of her spare time to babysit me. Until I was six I was looked after by a succession of nannies, then my mother's widowed older sister, my Aunt Eleanor, moved in permanently. Not having had children of her own she found a small boy like myself something of a trial but at least I could talk to her and she always treated me like an adult when speaking to me. I appreciated that. A married elderly couple, the Donaldsons, lived in. The husband tended the gardens and carried out any necessary maintenance work. His wife did the cleaning and occasionally cooked as well. They were an unobtrusive couple and I saw little of them.

That second event to which I've just referred came when I was nine and a half. I was having yet another blazing row with Aileen one day. At one point I told her in no uncertain terms that I had as much right to be in the house as she did. Her reply to that was that I was only an accident and shouldn't have been there at all. I had no idea what she meant so I cornered Aunt Eleanor and asked her. Bless her, she tried to explain in words that I could understand. I got a simple version of the 'birds and the bees' lecture and an assurance that my parents still loved me despite the fact that I hadn't been planned. In view of the fact that I hardly ever saw them that was little or no consolation.

It was another couple of years before I fully grasped the implications of being an 'accident'. Somehow it acted as a spur to me rather than depressing me. I realised subconsciously that I was very much on my own and would have to stand up for myself. If there was anything I wanted I would have to work for it and fight for it. The realisation made me very independent. I taught myself to cook simple meals, to take care of my clothing, keep my room clean and tidy and to look after my possessions. By the time I was fourteen Aunt Eleanor had little to do but keep a watchful eye on my comings and goings. Aileen was still at home, but I learned how to keep out of her way and our paths rarely crossed.

I was thirteen when the third major event came round. By this time I was attending a rather exclusive private school close to home. At the start of my second year we got a new biology teacher, a Mrs. McTaggart. She was young, she was pretty, but above all she was a born teacher. Her lessons were always full of interest and she had a way of making you want to learn.

Through her efforts I quickly gained a love for botany and zoology that has stayed with me all my life. 'Taggy', as she was known, was apparently unable to bear children, so her classes became her family. There were six of us in my own form that showed a particular aptitude for the subjects and she devoted much of her spare time to improving our practical knowledge. Often at weekends or on long summer evenings she would take us on nature rambles, to the zoo and to nearby wild life reserves. It was hardly surprising then that in the following three years or so I worked hard on my biology homework and skimped on the rest of the subjects. As a result, when the time came for final exams before leaving school I got an A+ in both botany and zoology and C's and D's in everything else.

The moment I got my results I went round to see 'Taggy' at her home. She never minded us popping in and always welcomed us with soft drinks and snacks. When we were comfortably settled in her living room she asked me why I'd called.

"I'd appreciate some career advice, Mrs McTaggart," I explained. "I want to go into space biology and I'm not sure how to go about it. I'm hoping you can point me in the right direction."

She considered me gravely. "You're aiming high, aren't you?" she said finally. "It's just about the most difficult profession to get into. The standards are very high, the curriculum very difficult and at the end of the day only one in ten successful students get posts in the space biology sector. On top of all that you'll need to go abroad to study and there are no grants available. You'll have to pay your own way."

"I know all that," I replied. "Thankfully money isn't a problem. Maybe I won't succeed, but if I don't try I'll regret it all my life. If I fail it won't be for the lack of hard work, I can assure you of that."

She sat thinking. I watched her face trying to gauge her reaction to what I'd said but her expression gave nothing away. We must have sat silently for a full three minutes before she seemed to make up her mind. "I believe you and yes, I will help you. Luckily I have a contact in the Space Biology Service. My old tutor at university works there now and we've kept in touch. I'll speak to him in the next couple of days and see what the prospects are. Meantime don't get too excited. Despite the lack of opportunities there are plenty of applicants for places in the service so there may be no vacancies at the college in the immediate future. I'll call you as soon as I have some news." With that I had to be content. I thanked her and left. Despite her plea for caution I was on tenterhooks. My whole future was in the balance.

As it happened I didn't hear directly from 'Taggy'. Instead I got a phone call three days later from a Professor McMaster asking me to call at Edinburgh University the following day at ten in the morning. For once in a while I took great care of my appearance. I wore my best suit with a clean white shirt and dark blue self coloured tie, even spending ten minutes brushing my somewhat unruly hair into shape. Of course I arrived far too early and spent the best part of half an hour kicking my heels in his secretary's small office. On the small side, middle aged and fierce looking, she did little to bolster my rapidly fading confidence. My attempts at polite conversation were met with muttered monosyllables as she dealt with constant telephone calls. At last the hands of the clock reached the hour and one minute later the intercom buzzed and I was shown into the professor's room.

He was younger than I expected, probably not much more than forty. Casually dressed in a short sleeved pale green sports shirt and grey flannel trousers he lacked an inch off the six foot mark. His hair was brown and just beginning to recede from the temples. Brown eyes, a straight nose, wide mouth and a firm chin completed the picture. His handshake was strong, though disturbingly he didn't smile as he greeted me. I was invited to sit in front of his desk and he looked searchingly at me for a full thirty seconds without speaking.

"I'm going to fire a whole string of questions at you," he said finally. "Some will be technical, some personal, some general knowledge and some you might not be able to answer. Are you ready?" I told him I was.

For the next twenty minutes or more he bombarded me with a wide range of questions. They came one on top of another, switching subjects without warning. I had no time to be nervous and little time for thought. Despite that I reckoned I'd done not too badly. I'd only had to admit defeat on two very obscure points that he quizzed me about. Eventually he sat back and considered the desk in front of him. Then he raised his eyes and for the first time I saw the hint of a smile.

"I'm impressed, very impressed," he said softly. "Mrs. McTaggart spoke highly of you and I can see she was justified to do so." He opened a drawer in his desk, took out a file cover and slid it across to me. "Here's the application form for a place in this coming year's intake. I want you to take it home, fill it in and post it off to the selection board. In the file you'll also find full details of the course and all other matters relating to it. I advise you to study them carefully before you send the form away. Make sure you can fulfil all the commitments involved, including the financial side. I wish you good luck." He stood up and held out his hand once more.

I wasted no time in going back home and reading the papers he had given me. I knew a lot of the background of course. The first page of the literature accompanying the application form dealt with the history of the space service from the first orbit of the Earth back in the twentieth century. Then came a couple of pages on the current organisation. Over the last thirty years or so the various national space agencies had amalgamated into six giant continental concerns. The European Space Division, ESD for short, had its headquarters in Switzerland. Training for spaceship pilots and crews was centred in Russia and Spain and all matters concerning emigration to the outer planets were dealt with in Norway. Subsidiary matters, including the Space Biology Section, were mainly based in Italy. The course for which I intended to apply lasted three years and would be held at the University of Science. This was situated a couple of kilometres outside the town of Riccione on Italy's Adriatic coast. Accommodation was available at the student hostel on the campus and would cost two hundred euros a week. This did not include food. One sentence near the end pleased me greatly. It stated that the accepted language of the Space Service was English and all candidates would have to be fluent in that language. I'd known this already, but it was comforting to see it in black and white.

My parents had always been generous as far as pocket money was concerned. I had been thrifty while growing up. Most of my outgoings had been on computer equipment and I'd spent far less than my school friends on other items. Unlike them I had had little contact with the opposite sex and no regular girl friend. That was partly because of an inherent shyness, but mainly due to my unhappy relationship with my sister. I couldn't help wondering if all girls were the same. I thus had a savings account standing at just over two thousand euros. Obviously I needed a further source of funding and my immediate reaction was that I would need to find a temporary job to increase my capital.

A look at the curriculum confirmed all that I had been told. The course was difficult. Each of the three years would consist of three terms, with just a fortnight's break between each. Apart from the expected subjects like terrestrial and extra terrestrial botany and zoology I would have to learn about things such as biochemistry, biophysics, soil management, ecology and half a dozen other related subjects. Space geography, first aid and a certain amount of space technology also featured. The working week lasted forty-six hours and included lectures on Saturday mornings. A warning in bold type suggested that much of the rest of the time would be spent in homework and private study. It seemed incongruous that the description of the university itself emphasised the sporting facilities that were available!

Nothing daunted, I filled in the three page application form and after lunch went out and posted it. No matter how hard it might be this was what I wanted to do in life and I was prepared to face all manner of hardships to achieve it. I had one lucky break two days later which made me optimistic about success. Unannounced and unexpectedly my father arrived home that afternoon. I was on my way out to the library when he burst through the front door. He greeted me briefly and made to pass me. I reacted quickly and dared to put a restraining hand on his shoulder.

"Dad, can I have a few minutes of your time, please?" I asked. "It's rather important."

He looked at his watch. "I haven't got very long. I'm flying out to Athens at eight o'clock tonight. Give me time to make a couple of phone calls, ask Eleanor if she can lay on something to eat in about forty five minutes' time and then come to the study." I did as he asked, though to be on the safe side I waited for fifteen minutes before knocking on the study door. When I went in he was standing by the window, but he turned round as I entered the room. Typically he didn't ask how I was, though it had been over a year since he'd last seen me. It was left to me to open the conversation.

"I've applied to join the Space Service as a biologist," I began. "It involves spending three years at university in Italy before I can get a job. Of course I may not get in, but if I do I'll have to pay my own way through the course. I've managed to save a bit and of course I'll find a job for the summer, but it won't be nearly enough. Would you be prepared to give me a loan? If I pass the course I'll be on a fairly high salary so I'd be able to pay it back fairly quickly. Even if I fail the fact that I've done the course will almost guarantee me a decent job in everyday life."

He looked at me as if he was seeing me for the very first time. "What makes you think you've got a chance of getting in, never mind passing?"

"I got the highest marks ever achieved at the school in both biology and zoology," was my reply. "I've been highly recommended by my teacher and have already spoken to an executive of the service. It was he who gave me the application form and was very complimentary."

"Supposing your application isn't successful, what will you do then?"

"I'd like to go to university here and get a degree in that case, but in the meantime I'd keep applying to the Space Service in the hope that they'd take me sooner or later."

"I see." He paused and seemed to be thinking. "I tell you what. Unlike the rest of the family, you've never asked me for anything before. I guess I've neglected you while you were growing up as well. So I'll tell you what I'll do. You have a bank account?" He made it a question and I nodded. "Give me the details. I'll be back in Edinburgh early next week for a couple of days and I'll make arrangements with my own bank to pay you a monthly allowance for the next three years. Let's see. You'll need money just now for clothes and travel and things like that. I'll give you an initial payment of ten thousand euros and two thousand a month thereafter. Don't bother getting a job for the summer. Use the time for studying. By the way, this

7

is a gift, not a loan." I tried to thank him but he brushed my words aside. Instead he asked me about the course. I went and got the relevant sheets and he read them through from beginning to end.

As he handed them back to me he remarked: "I suppose if you pass you'll be heading off to one of the colonised planets?"

"Probably," I answered. "Ideally that's what I want to do. But there are jobs here on Earth as well in research and analysis. I'll just have to take what I'm offered I guess. From all accounts it's just like being in the army. You go where you're posted."

Despite the short notice Aunt Eleanor and Mrs. Donaldson did us proud in regard to a meal. They prepared a traditional Scottish high tea for us. We started with poached smoked yellow haddock, after which came a mixed grill with lamb chops, steak, kidney, mushrooms, black pudding and potato fritters. My father seemed in high good humour. He insisted I repeated my plans in details for Aunt Eleanor's benefit and then regaled us with tales of his life among the good and the great of the film industry. I think that was the most enjoyable meal I ever had. When we finally saw him into his taxi en route for the airport I reflected that that was the longest single period I'd spent in his company in all my seventeen years.

Once he'd left I asked Aunt Eleanor if she would stay on in the house if I was successful and went off to Italy. By this time Aileen had married and left. She looked at me in some surprise.

"Of course I will, dear. I've nowhere else to go. Your parents make me a generous allowance and I live rent free. I've no other income and little in the way of savings, so the best I could hope for if I left here would be a cheap boarding house." Somehow I felt absurdly pleased that she was staying on.

CHAPTER TWO

I had no idea how long it would be before I received a reply to my application. To be on the safe side I took a day trip up to Aberdeen University with the intention of applying for a place on their degree courses in botany and zoology. Before signing on the dotted line I sought advice from a counsellor. I told him quite honestly what my position was and that if I was accepted for the space service that would be my preferred option. He was very sympathetic and assured me that no harm would be done and no inconvenience caused if I withdrew.

Rather than spend the time studying I decided that it would be more useful to learn some Italian. We'd only done French, Spanish and German at school and while the course, should I make it, would be in English I hoped that I would have some spare time to sample the delights of the local community. It took me three days, but I eventually found a private tutor who was prepared to give me three two-hour lessons a week at twenty-five euros a lesson. By this time the money my father had promised me was safely in my bank so I felt justified in being a touch extravagant. Between that and my continuing research on Spacenet I found my days passing quickly and pleasantly. My mother made a flying visit some two weeks after my father returned to America. She spent less than five hours at home before leaving again for Cairo. In the ten or so minutes I was able to talk to her I told her of my plans. She showed little interest.

The news I was waiting for came one Thursday afternoon in mid July. I'd been for an Italian lesson and arrived back home just after three. Aunt Eleanor met me at the door with a large, bulky envelope in her hand. "This is from Italy," she said with barely suppressed excitement as she handed it over.

I took the envelope from her, my heart pounding within me. "I'm scared to open it," I confessed. "My whole future, my whole life depends on what's inside."

"Surely if it was a rejection there'd only be one sheet inside," my aunt pointed out wisely.

I hadn't thought of that. Quickly I tore open the flap and withdrew the contents. There were two or three booklets but I had eyes only for the accompanying letter. My heart rate increased by the second as I read the following.

Dear Mr. Dunsmuir,

I am pleased to inform you that you have been allocated a place on the forthcoming Space Biology course at the University of Science in Riccione. The course commences on Monday the first of September 2236. You will report to Lecture Hall 6 at 0900 hours on that date. Please confirm as soon as possible that you will be taking up this invitation. An email response is acceptable.

I enclose information booklets regarding the University, the Students' Hostel and directions on how to get here. I hope you will find these helpful. If you are intending to take up residence in the hostel it would be advisable to book as soon as possible.

The letter was signed by Rosella Agnella, Registrar. After showing it to Aunt Eleanor I wasted no time in getting on line and emailing my acceptance. Then I settled back to study the booklets I'd been sent. I intended to stay at the hostel, but before attempting to book I researched the airlines to see what my travel options were. I quickly discovered that a small private airline operated two direct flights a week to Rimini from Edinburgh Airport on Tuesdays and Fridays. The holiday resort of Rimini was just a few kilometres north of Riccione. I booked a flight for Friday the twenty-ninth of August and then emailed the hostel to reserve my accommodation from that date. Optimistically I wrote that I wished to stay for three years!

The next six weeks seemed to crawl by. I saw no more of my parents in that time; in fact my only knowledge that they were aware of my existence came in a postcard from my father from the Nevada desert. I had emailed him to tell him my good news. In one brief sentence he wished me well and mentioned he had just started work on a new blockbuster. I carried on with the Italian lessons and by the week before my departure I was reasonably fluent in speech and reading. Writing I found was slightly more difficult, but then I didn't expect to be putting pen to paper in anything but English. I didn't want to load myself down with luggage, so I managed to get all I wanted to take with me into two medium sized suitcases. I knew I'd need a good deal of lightweight clothing but figured I could buy that just as cheaply and easily in Italy. The day before my departure I visited my bank and made all the necessary arrangements for withdrawing cash at a bank in Riccione.

At last the great day arrived. Though my flight was not until eleven o'clock that morning I was up at six. I had found it near impossible to sleep. Aunt Eleanor insisted on coming to the airport with me. As she said goodbye at the entrance to the departure lounge she made me promise to email her at least once a month to let her know how I was getting on. She'd also made up a small food parcel to tide me over lunch time, just in case the food on the plane wasn't to my liking. I was touched by her kindness. It was so obvious that despite her lack of emotion she genuinely cared for me. While I waited along with my fellow passengers for the flight to be called I tried to visualise how different life would have been if she had been my mother and not my aunt.

The flight was only ten minutes late in taking off. It was a dry and sunny day and the good weather persisted throughout the two hours or so we were in the air. It was only the second time I'd been up so even that was an exciting experience for me. Arriving at Rimini I took the airport bus into town and then caught a local bus to Riccione. There I was pleased to find that there was an hourly bus service out to the university. Though I could well have afforded a taxi I didn't see any point in being extravagant. The bus dropped me at the gates. From the literature that I'd been sent I knew the layout of the grounds and where the hostel was situated. A five minute walk took me to the hostel. At first glance it didn't look very attractive. Six storeys high and with a flat roof and built of dull grey stone, it stretched for many metres in each direction from the front entrance. I learned later that it contained nearly five hundred individual apartments, plus several common rooms, two cafeterias, laundry facilities and three or four games rooms. The front door led to a small reception area, behind the desk of which sat a very pretty black haired girl not much older than I. Eager to try out my Italian I introduced myself in that language and added that I had a room booked.

She looked at me in puzzled fashion. "Do you speak English?" she asked in the broadest Irish accent I'd ever heard.

"I should do," I said with a straight face. "I'm from Edinburgh." We both laughed.

After checking my booking she handed me the key to room 365 on the third floor and gave me directions as to how to get there. Thankfully the building was equipped with lifts. Though I wasn't exactly overburdened I'd been hefting my suitcases around for a large part of the day and my arms were beginning to ache. I'd no bother finding the room. I unlocked the door, went in and stood just inside looking around me. This was to be my home for the next three years, all being well. Though it had been referred to as a room it was in fact a tiny flat. The one main room, about five metres square, contained a single bed, a small table, an even smaller desk, two upright chairs and two armchairs. There was also a wardrobe and dressing table against the wall in which the door was set. Leading off this main room was a small kitchenette with microwave and hotplate and a shower room and toilet. All was spotlessly clean. I knew from the booklet that I was expected to keep the place clean myself. Bed linen was changed and laundered weekly by the hostel staff, but all other washing was up to the student.

I put my two suitcases on the bed and unlocked them. Barely had I started unpacking when there was a loud knock on the door. I walked across and opened it. A fair haired giant came bursting into the room. At least he looked like a giant to me. He must have been about six foot four or even five, heavily built, with curly brown hair, blue eyes and a square determined face. A white tee shirt and a pair of khaki shorts revealed muscular arms and legs. He smiled broadly and extended his hand. His grip was firm, but not excessively so.

"I am your next door neighbour in three six four," he boomed in a voice with just a trace of an accent. "Boris Karporov, at your service. I thought it would be a good thing to welcome you."

I invited him to sit, introduced myself to him and we exchanged details. I learned that my new acquaintance came from just outside the town of

Luninets in Belarus. His family had been farmers and forestry workers for many generations and this had inspired his love of nature and of natural sciences. He was a year older than me. His English was good, though at times his phraseology was a bit stilted. Eventually he jumped up.

"I will leave you now to finish your unpacking and settle in," he said as he moved towards the door. "But tonight we will go into town, yes? We will have a nice meal, a nice glass or two of wine and maybe meet two not so nice girls, yes?"

I smiled. "I'm with you on the meal and the wine, but I'm not so sure about the girls."

He looked at me with some alarm. "You're not . . ." he began as he held out his hand and wiggled his fingers suggestively. It took me a moment or two to grasp his meaning.

"Good Lord, no," I burst out. "I'm as straight as a dye. I'd better explain. All my life I've wanted desperately to go into space and to go to one of the colonized planets. I'm not technically minded or good with machines, so the best, possibly the only way I can get what I want is through this course. I am going to work as hard as I can, not just to pass but to get as high marks as possible. I want no distractions of any kind and particularly no girls in my life for the next three years. There'll be plenty of time for that once my future is assured."

"Ah, I understand," said Boris, looking relieved. "It is agreed. Food and wine only and no girls. I will come for you at six o'clock. If our other neighbours arrive before then we will invite them to come with us."

After he left I completed my unpacking, put everything away neatly and made myself a cup of coffee. I changed into sports shirt and shorts. My stay in Italy had begun well. I was settled into a comfortable lodging and had already made a new friend. I had a feeling that I would be seeing quite a lot of Boris over the next year or so. With half an hour to spare before our next meeting I took time to explore the hostel and find out where everything was. Though most of the common rooms and corridors were empty a steady stream of people were arriving at the front desk and the

Irish lass was being kept busy. Promptly at six o'clock I knocked on Boris's door. He was ready and waiting. Before leaving we checked the rooms on either side of ours, but the new tenants hadn't yet arrived.

We walked the two or three kilometres into town, found a restaurant quickly and lingered over a typical Italian meal of pasta, veal escallops and fresh fruit. The one or two glasses of wine expanded into four or five as we learned more about each other. Boris was sympathetic when I told him of my family background and my problems with my sister Aileen. In contrast his family had been very close knit, though as he pointed out, there was only eight years separating himself and his three sisters and two brothers. After our meal we explored the town before deciding to be energetic and walk back to the campus.

On Saturday Boris went off down the coast to Cattolica for the day, while I went into Rimini to do some much needed shopping. I bought another three pairs of shorts, half a dozen sports shirts and a couple of lightweight suits. The evening I devoted to doing a little reading and studying after a meal in the hostel canteen. This was satisfying but not inspiring. Sunday was spent on the beach along with Boris and my new neighbour in room 366. Eva was Polish, small, dark haired and intense. She spelt her surname for me and wrote it down, but I never got to memorise it. Fifteen letters long it was composed mainly of w's, y's and z's with no vowels at all. When pronounced it sounded a bit like two coughs and a sneeze! In the late afternoon the three of us took a look round the university building itself, making sure we knew where to go the following morning. Then we all went back into town to try out another restaurant. When we got back to the hostel we discovered that Boris's neighbour in room 363 had arrived. Boris and I called in to welcome him but received a frosty reception. He was older than us, probably somewhere in his late twenties. We later learned that he was Portuguese, named Jorge, and came from Coimbra. For the rest of our stay he kept himself strictly to himself and made no friends. We just ignored him from that first meeting on.

I rose at seven thirty on Monday morning feeling excited. This was it, the start of a brand new life. After a breakfast of coffee and croissants in the canteen with Boris and Eva we walked across to the main building and lecture room six. Though we were fifteen minutes early some others had already gathered and we had to settle for seats in the third row. At nine precisely a door at the far end of the room opened and a man walked through and up to the podium. He was medium height, slim built and probably in his late thirties with dark hair. He turned and faced us and began to speak.

"Good morning ladies and gentleman." His voice was pleasant on the ear and carried no hint of an accent. "I am Florent Schmidt, doctor of biological sciences, from Brussels. I am the course director and I would like to welcome you all. You will come to know me well over the next three years. Apart from being one of your tutors I will also be seeing you regularly on an individual basis to assess your progress. I'm sure you know already that this is a difficult course and that you will be required to work very hard. I wish you all success. Now to more practical matters. There are forty-eight of you here. You will be divided into four classes of twelve and as we are in Italy we have taken the names of Italian cities for each group. Thus Roma, Napoli, Torino and Milano. You will find your own assignments and where to move to next on the notice board immediately outside this room. There will be four lectures per day Monday to Friday and one on Saturday morning. Each will last from one hour and a half to two hours and will include practical work where applicable. You will also be allocated additional work to be done in your spare time. I'm afraid you will not have a lot of time for recreation, but I would advise you to spend it on sporting activities of some kind rather than lazing on the beach or in the bars. A fit body improves the mind and the capacity for study. Each year consists of three terms. You will have a three week break at Christmas and New Year, two weeks at the end of April and two in the middle of August."

"I wish you all well and nothing would please me more than to see all forty-eight of you complete the course and pass the final tests and exams. While not wanting to depress you I would be failing in my duty if I did not mention that this has never happened before. Regrettably people do drop out during the course, some because they can't take the pressure, some because they are unable to pass the six monthly assessments. On the previous course we lost nine during the first year, seven in the second year and of the remaining thirty-two only twenty gained pass marks at the end."

"Finally, just a brief word on your prospects should you be successful. After the final exams you will only have to wait for three days at the most to get your results. Everyone who passes will be immediately conscripted into the Space Service with the rank of Scientific Officer. After every intake there are a few vacancies for posts in outer space, some with survey teams exploring new planets, some on the colonized planets. Obviously these are the most sought after posts and they will be awarded to those finishing with the highest marks. Previous experience suggests that there could be anything between three and ten of such postings. The remaining successful candidates will be given positions here on Earth in one of the many scientific and research centres or be allocated to the small settlements on Mars and Venus. One or two of you may even stay on here at the university as lecturers. That is all I have to say, except to wish you well once again. Good morning." He turned abruptly and left the theatre by the door from which he'd entered.

There was little conversation as we filtered from the lecture hall and crowded round the notice board outside. I discovered that I was in the Roma group, with both Boris and Eva in the Napoli section. I wasn't sure whether I was disappointed at being thus separated or not. On the one hand it would have been pleasant to be with two people I already knew: on the other I wasn't sure just how seriously Boris would take his studies. I already liked him very much but I thought I could detect something of the playboy in him.

CHAPTER THREE

The next three months were challenging but rewarding ones. For the first time in my life I was really happy. Although the course was as hard as we'd been promised I was studying subjects that I enjoyed and the time flew by. My fears about Boris proved unfounded. He threw himself into his work like a man possessed. Most of the time he, Eva and I worked together on the evening projects and the homework we were set. We made a good team, with our individual strengths and weaknesses well balanced. The only subject in which I tended to struggle a little was biophysics but luckily this was Eva's specialised field. Despite his size and those huge hands of his, Boris had a delicate touch when it came to making up microscopic samples or dissecting plant or animal specimens. He showed us a number of ways to improve our skills in this field. My contribution to the collective was my extensive knowledge of space geography and extra terrestrial biology.

As advised we did not neglect the need for exercise. All three of us put in a half hour session in the gym morning and evening, Eva took up swimming and Boris and I joined the university's small but select tennis club. We were tempted to join one of the football teams as well as both of us loved the game. The possibility of injury put us off, though. We just couldn't afford to miss lectures, so intense was the pressure on us. One rule we made and stuck to. Sunday evening was for complete relaxation. At five o'clock we would change, walk into town and linger over a meal. This was the only time in the week that we touched alcohol at all, splitting a bottle or two of wine between us.

As the Christmas break came close I thought hard about what to do. Boris and Eva were going to their respective homes. Both invited me to tag along but I felt it would be inappropriate. The festive season is a time for families and I knew I would feel awkward and something of an intruder. I was tempted to stay on at the hostel and do some extra studying. In the end I decided to go back home to Edinburgh and booked a flight accordingly. I arrived on the evening of the twenty-third of December to find the house dark and empty. A note on the board in the kitchen informed me that Aunt Eleanor had gone to stay with an old school friend in Perth and the Donaldsons were with their married daughter in Dunbar. Luckily the freezer was well stocked so at least I didn't starve. I spent four lonely and miserable days before leaving a letter for Aunt Eleanor on the hall table and catching a flight back to Italy. There were no direct flights to Rimini over the holiday period, but I managed to get one to Milan and did the rest of the journey by train. My room at the hostel was never more welcome.

The whole campus was almost deserted, but I quickly discovered that four others of the forty-eight on our course had remained. We naturally gravitated together. On Hogmanay we went into Riccione to sample New Year celebrations Italian style. It was quite a bit different from what I'd been used to but I enjoyed myself nevertheless. For the first and to date only time in my life I imbibed a little more wine than was good for me. I wasn't exactly drunk and incapable but I found walking and talking more of an effort than normal. My four companions were in the same state and I wondered next day how we'd managed to negotiate our way back to the campus without mishap!

All too soon the first of our six monthly assessments was upon us. This consisted of four days of written tests and a morning of role play. We were divided into groups of six, given a mock project and required to discuss it and come up with a solution. If it hadn't been so serious it would have been fun. The only information we were given after these assessments was whether we had passed or failed. We were never told what marks we had achieved or how well or otherwise we'd done. I found this disconcerting. Four people, one from my own Roma group, failed and left us within a day of being told.

After that first experience of going home for a holiday I didn't bother returning for any more. Instead I used one week of each break to tour round Italy by train or bus. I was living well within the income that my father had settled on me, so I could afford to stay in decent hotels and eat in really good restaurants. Sometimes I travelled alone, occasionally Boris and Eva or one or two of my other fellow students came along. I made a rule for myself only to speak Italian during these trips and I soon became fluent. The remaining time of the holidays I spent in study. There were times when I wondered if it was all worthwhile, but then I remembered the prize that could be waiting at the end of the course and redoubled my efforts.

By the end of the first eighteen months no less than thirteen of the forty-eight had dropped out for one reason or another. Seven had been from the Milano group alone, so that group was disbanded and the remaining five redistributed. The six monthly assessments came and went. I kept passing. Not knowing exactly how I'd done was frustrating. I believed I was doing well but I had no way of telling and others including Boris and Eva said the same. Time seemed to be passing far too quickly as we approached the final term and the all important final exams. Then they were upon us. We were kept waiting until a couple of days beforehand to learn the composition. When we did we wished we hadn't! There were to be five full days of written tests, two of practical work and two of project work. Obviously our stamina as well as our knowledge was to be tested. We viewed the prospect so gravely that Boris and I even solemnly discussed the possibility of taking some kind of stimulant before and during the period. Sanity prevailed, however, and in the end we decided to rely solely on our knowledge and ability.

I never want to live through such an experience again. Fear of failure and the importance of doing not just well but brilliantly put enormous pressure on me. Two or three times during those nine days I felt on the point of collapse. Only willpower and the support of my two closest friends pulled me through. Eva was an unexpected tower of strength. She seemed to sail through everything with complete calm and her example and encouragement helped Boris and I tremendously. At last it was over. As we left the committee room in which the final project had been undertaken we were told by one of the supervisors that the results would be notified to us individually in three days' time. That Thursday evening we partied long and hard. The thirty-one of us who had made it through to the end took over one of the common rooms in the hostel and sent a deputation into town for food and drink. The festivities lasted till three in the morning and only sheer exhaustion brought them to a halt. Friday afternoon, Saturday and Sunday we spent mainly sleeping and sunbathing and relaxing on the beach, culminating in a huge Sunday evening supper. We took a private room in our favourite hotel cum restaurant and gorged ourselves until midnight.

Though there'd been no prior planning Boris, Eva and I got up early on that Monday morning and were eating our breakfast before eight o'clock. Thereafter we hung around the entrance hall keeping a watchful eye on our mail pigeonholes. By five to nine everyone had assembled. Promptly at nine o'clock a messenger from the main office arrived and solemnly distributed envelopes into their appropriate slots. As soon as she moved away there was a mad rush forwards. I hung back slightly and waited until the melee had resolved itself before going to pick up my own envelope. Suddenly everyone separated to find a quiet corner of their own and the entrance hall went deathly quiet. The silence lasted for less than a minute. One after another whoops, yells and the occasional groan rent the air. I had only just started to read my own letter when the first shout was heard. I put the noise out of my mind as I took in the printed words in front of me.

Dear Mr. Dunsmuir,
I am pleased to inform you that you have been successful in passing the recent final examinations. You have now been inducted as a full employee of the Space Biology Service. Please report to Committee Room 6 between 1000 and 1030 hours to sign the necessary documentation and receive further instructions.

From the general rejoicing going on around me I gathered that most of the thirty-one had received similar good news. Later I learned that eight had failed. I sought out Boris and Eva for joint congratulations.

"Still they haven't told us what marks we got," Boris complained. "You'd think they might have let us know."

There wasn't much I could offer by way of consolation. A nasty thought had just crossed my mind. Maybe only the top few had been so informed and the rest of us would never be told. I wondered if all the letters had been worded the same way. However, there was no way of finding out. The signing on formality a little while later gave me a terrific thrill. Civilian staff of the E.S.D. conducted operations. There were only a couple of forms to fill in. Then we were given warrant cards that announced to the world that we were fully fledged Scientific Officers, plus authorisation to uplift our uniforms from the university stores. We were instructed to wear uniform from that point on whenever engaged in any official business. Most of us did not need a second invitation! Finally I was instructed to report to Doctor Schmidt's office at three p.m. precisely. On comparing notes I found that Eva and Boris were also to report at the same time.

"Maybe we're going to be assigned together," I hazarded. "If, as we suspect, we haven't made the top bracket, it would be a pleasing consolation if we were to work together in the future." The other two agreed enthusiastically. At five to three, spick and span in our new uniforms, we arrived at the door to the office. Two other students joined us. One was a Slovakian girl, Petra Dovcek, and the other a Welsh boy named David Jenkins. We knew them both quite well. To say that we were all excited would be an understatement. Promptly as a nearby clock struck three Doctor Schmidt ushered us into his office and invited us the seat ourselves in the five chairs facing his desk. When we were comfortable he took his own place and smiled at each of us in turn.

"My congratulations to all of you," he began. "I'm delighted to tell you that you are the top five students from the course. As such, you will be assigned to the five posts currently vacant in the outer space settlement programme." I could hardly contain my joy as he said this. I'd achieved my dream. But I had no time for reflection as he continued to speak. "Now the normal way of assigning these posts is to let you choose in the order in which you completed the course. Top marks had first choice of course. However, something unusual has happened. All five of you achieved the same marks, eighty two point five percent. Nothing like this has occurred in the eight similar courses we've run to date. I've therefore decided to allocate the vacancies by ballot." He produced two glass jars from underneath his desk. One contained five small blue balls, the other five of yellow. "Inside each blue ball is a name and inside each yellow ball a posting. I'll not tell you beforehand just where the vacancies are. That will make it more exciting. I'll give them a good shake." He suited the action to the words. "That should ensure a good mix. Now I'll start to take out the balls that will decide your future fate." He smiled broadly as he uttered the words.

Solemnly he took out the first of the blue balls and unscrewed it. "Boris," he announced tersely. Next came a yellow ball. "You are hereby appointed to the science centre on Persephone." Quietly we congratulated him. One by one the balls came out of the jars. Petra was next, with a dream posting to one of the survey ships responsible for discovering, exploring and assessing new worlds for settlement. I would have loved that one. David Jenkins was off to Paladia. Just Eva and I left now. Eva's name came out next and she was to take over as head biologist on Magna following the retirement of the present incumbent. That left me. I wasn't sure if it was my imagination, but I thought Doctor Schmidt looked at me rather strangely as he pulled the final ball from its container. He spoke my name, then retrieved the yellow ball with my posting inside. As he took out the slip of paper his smile disappeared.

"Alex, I'm afraid you've drawn the short straw," he said sympathetically. "You're going to Cara IV." There was a sudden murmur from the others, while I sat stunned.

Cara IV! I knew all about Cara IV. On the face of it an ideal world for colonisation. Almost identical to Earth in many ways. It was almost the same size, with a similar atmosphere and gravity, similar weather conditions and a year only one day longer at three hundred and sixty-six days. There was land and sea, there were mountains and valleys and plains, rivers and lakes. It had everything except one thing. Life! There were no animals, no plants, no birds, no fish, no insects, not even any bacteria. And that was where they were sending me! My euphoria evaporated rapidly and I felt hard done by. But the good doctor was speaking again. "Alex, I'd like you to stay behind for a moment. The rest of you have been granted two weeks' leave, starting tomorrow, before you're due to report for your respective assignments. You'll receive notification of where and when to attend by post, so make sure you leave a note of where you'll be during your leave. We won't meet again, so I wish you all good luck in your careers. I'm sure you'll all do well and be a credit to this university." He shook hands with each in turn as they left.

"Well, Alex," he said when we were alone again. "Not exactly what you hoped for I suspect?" I shook my head, not trusting myself to speak.

He smiled. "I realise that it doesn't seem an attractive prospect at first sight, but really it is a tremendous opportunity for you. You'll be the only qualified biologist in the advance party. If you succeed in bringing life to Cara IV your name will be remembered for hundreds, perhaps thousands of years to come. You'll become a legend in the Space Service and in the history of Cara IV itself. Try and look at the situation from that point of view and it won't seem nearly so bad. Now to business. I'm sorry you won't be able to go on leave immediately. The advance party leaves for Cara IV in just two months' time and there's a lot of planning to be done before then." I assured him that that was the least of my concerns. Apart from Aunt Eleanor I had nothing to go back to Edinburgh for. My parents would almost certainly be absent and in any case were unlikely to place seeing their 'accidental' son high on their personal agendas.

Doctor Schmidt then handed me a large envelope. "All your instructions are in there," he told me. "The project team are based in Castellamare di Stabia, just south of Naples. You've to report at 0900 hours next Tuesday morning to the director, Nils Anderssen, at Casa Garibaldi. Nils is Swedish, from Stockholm and an extremely nice fellow. I've met him a couple of times. He has a reputation of being a first class organiser and I'm sure you'll find him easy to work with. Accommodation has been reserved for you at the Hotel Vista for the next two months. Everything is being paid for by the Service, including meals but excluding wines. It's a five star hotel so you can enjoy a little luxury for your remaining time here on Earth. I wish you good luck and much success." He stood up and held out his hand.

I went straight back to the hostel. Boris was waiting in his room and with his door open. He called me in and told me that he and the other three were proposing to have a celebratory dinner in town that night and hoped I'd be joining them. I liked the idea and said I'd be pleased to, but that I wanted a little time to myself before then. He said he understood. Back in my own room I lay down on the bed, gazed up at the ceiling and pondered all that I knew about Cara IV.

The initial survey had been undertaken eight years previously by the survey ship 'Blue Danube'. They'd spent nine months on the planet altogether, exploring and mapping, compiling climate statistics and other data and taking samples of soil and water. These samples went to one of the laboratories for analysis and experiment. In all they brought back some 400 kilograms of soil, from different parts of the world. It proved to be mostly a rich loam and when sown with a variety of grasses and other plants allowed everything to grow quickly and naturally. The conclusion was that there was no reason why life should not flourish on the planet once introduced. After much discussion, however, the powers that be decide not to proceed with colonisation at that time, on the grounds that it would be too expensive. It was also suggested that it would need fifty years of advance work by a small number of colonists before large groups could emigrate there. Obviously something must have happened within the last year to make high office change its mind. I never did find out what it was.

Our dinner party was a mix of joy and sadness, particularly for Eva, Boris and myself. We had been so close for the previous three years and now were to part, probably for ever. At the same time we had the satisfaction of knowing that our hard work and dedication had paid off and we had made our dreams come true. Surprisingly I found that the others quietly envied me. As Eva pointed out, she, Boris and David would be going into a routine environment and jobs that could well be slightly boring. Petra and I were at least guaranteed something unusual and almost certainly exciting. By the end of the evening I felt a lot better about my fate.

CHAPTER FOUR

I travelled through to Castellamare on the Sunday and checked into the Hotel Vista just after six in the afternoon. I'd been given a large en suite corner room on the fourth floor with a view of the sea from one window. As Doctor Schmidt had predicted the hotel was the last word in luxury. It had been built some twenty years previously. There were indoor and outdoor swimming pools, gym and fitness room, deep pile carpeting everywhere and expensive looking cars in the car park. I felt a bit like a poor relation. I spent an hour or so exploring the neighbourhood after unpacking, then sat down to a sumptuous dinner. On the Monday I spent most of the day wandering round the town and locating the Casa Garibaldi. This proved to be a tall ten storey building in its own grounds some ten minutes' walk from the hotel. I also spent some time in the gym. In those final furious weeks of study I'd rather neglected my physical wellbeing.

At ten to nine on Tuesday morning I walked through the doors of the Casa Garibaldi for the first time. I was wearing uniform. A security guard just inside the front entrance checked my identity card and directed me to Nils Anderssen's office on the second floor. On entering I was met by his secretary, a dark eyed Spanish girl with a name tag pinned to her dress. The name thereon was Ramona. She gave me a flashing smile and a warm handshake, led me to an inner door and told me to go straight in without knocking. I did so and took my first quick look at the man who was going to be my boss for probably many years to come. I saw a big blond man of about forty, over six feet tall and strongly built, wearing simply a pale blue sports shirt and lightweight cream trousers. His handshake was firm as he came away from the window and greeted me.

"Alex! Welcome aboard," was his greeting. "I've been looking forward to meeting you. Take a seat."

I did so and made an appropriate reply, giving him his full title of Mr. Anderssen. He held up his hand in protest. "Please, no formalities. Let's stick to first names; Alex and Nils from now on. It makes for much more pleasant working relationships. You're staying at the Hotel Vista, I believe?" I nodded. There was just a trace of an accent in his speech but his pronunciation and grammar were perfect.

"You'll be joined there sometime on Thursday by Hans Friedland, the chief engineer. The three of us will be leading the advance party and will make all the decisions between us. Now unfortunately I'm going to be tied up for the next three days, so I'm going to have to leave you to your own devices." He opened a desk drawer and took out an armful of files. "This is just about all the information there is about Cara IV, including maps and pictures of the area in which we'll be landing. I'd like you to study them and start to make your own plans. There's one thing I'd like you to do apart from your normal work. We have no architect in the party, so could you design some sort of layout for the site, please? It doesn't need to be anything fancy as long as it's practical. And now I'll need to go as I have a meeting in ten minutes' time. I'll be back in for a very short while about five. If you've any questions you want to ask me I'll try and answer them then. Ramona will show you to your office. Oh, and when Hans arrives would you tell him I'd like a meeting of the three of us on Friday morning at 0930 hours." He swept up some papers of his own and almost rushed out of the office. I followed at a more leisurely pace.

In the outer room Ramona was standing holding a bunch of keys. She led the way down the corridor, past three other doors until she came to the last one. I noticed my name was already engraved on a plate. I felt a sudden surge of pride as I scanned it. Alex Dunsmuir: Scientific Officer were the words inscribed. Ramona opened the door, waved me in, handed me the keys and departed with a flurry of her long skirt. I looked around. The office was about ten metres square. In front of the large picture window sat a leather covered desk. Two other smaller desks were on the side walls. All three carried computer terminals. A door in the left hand corner led to a tiny kitchen with microwave, kettle and coffee percolator. At that point Ramona reappeared.

"Sorry," she apologised. "I should have told you. The toilets are just around the corner. Also, if there's anything you need in the way of stationery or other office materials just let me know and I'll get them for you. There's a canteen in the building on the fifth floor for lunch if you want to use it. It's not bad, though I prefer to eat at the cafe round the corner." She left again.

I made some coffee and settled down to study the files that Nils had given me. The first one I opened was titled 'Geography of Cara IV'. Although the dimensions and other main aspects of the planet were almost identical with Earth the geography was vastly different. There was only one continent, covering around half of the world. Thankfully measurements were shown in both kilometres and miles, which for me was a blessing. (Unlike Europe and the rest of the British Isles Scotland had throughout the past two hundred years steadfastly refused to use metric measures. Like the Americas and Australasia we had kept the old imperial miles and gallons.) This continent measured some eleven thousand miles from north to south and fourteen thousand from east to west. The sea that covered the remainder of the planet was very deep and there were no islands. A footnote to the general description decreed that the initial settlement would be on the east coast of the continent and led me to a separate file.

The spot for our maiden landing was at latitude forty-one degrees north. This was roughly equivalent to northern Portugal or central Italy and presaged better growing conditions than my native Scotland. I made a mental note to include a few tropical plants in my shopping list. Some three hundred and fifty miles inland a mountain range extended for thousands of miles north and south with some of the peaks over twelve thousand feet in height. The area between these and the coast was mainly flat with just a few areas of hilly country dotted here and there. I put the map aside for a moment and spread out the photographs of the proposed landing site and initial settlement. There was a slight ridge separating the land from the sea. Behind this the land was flat for some five to six miles inland, and then rose gradually to about two hundred feet in height for another ten miles. Trapped in this higher ground was a large lake which a note decreed was to be our water supply. Taking a piece of blank paper I drew a square representing five miles north and south of the landing spot. Plumb in the middle a river flowed down to the sea. Referring to the notes attached to the photograph and transcribing metres into feet I learned that this river was ninety-five yards in width at the estuary.

On a separate piece of paper I made a note to ask Nils if we would have any means of crossing that river. That gave rise to a parallel thought. Throughout the twenty-five square miles a number of small streams flowed into either the river or the sea. Some looked narrow enough to jump across; others would also need to be bridged. By this time it was noon and I decided to give the in house canteen a try for my first meal in my new surroundings. I found it to be almost deserted. The menu choice was somewhat limited and mainly Italian, but the food when it arrived was well cooked and I enjoyed it.

Back in my office I took out the statistics file. In the nine months that they'd been on Cara IV the survey team had taken daily temperature readings wherever they'd been and noted weather conditions also on a daily basis. It took a bit of digging to find the ones for our proposed area, but when I did they made agreeable reading. Summer maximum was ninety degrees Fahrenheit, winter minimum forty. That meant frost and snow was unlikely. Rainfall was estimated at thirty to thirty-five inches a year, slightly more than I'd been used to in Edinburgh. In general conditions seemed benign wherever the team had been. The highest wind recorded was around forty miles an hour and that only occurred once during the nine months. Mostly wind speeds were light. They'd seen no thunder or lightning and no evidence of things like hurricanes or tornados or even localised flooding. Next in the file came the analysis of the soil and water samples the team had brought back. The chemical composition of both was similar to Earth soil and water, the soil mainly being the equivalent of a rich loam. Clay was only present in a few selected areas, one about a hundred miles north of where we would be landing.

By this time my eyes were getting tired. I closed up the office and went for a walk to think about all that I'd read and plan my next action. After forty minutes I was hot and leg weary so it was back to the office. There I started to make a list of all the materials I would want to order. Before long it had grown to enormous proportions and I knew there was still much to be added. For the first time that day I began to be a little frightened at the task ahead of me. At five o'clock precisely Nils came in looking frustrated and muttering about politicians in general. He asked if I'd any questions.

"Just two," I told him. "Firstly, will we have any way of crossing that river in the middle of our proposed landing site? I'll need to know that before I can design a layout."

"That point's already taken care of," he replied. "Two sectional bridges have been ordered to enable us to cross the river close to the sea and further upstream, plus another six to use on the lesser streams. Next question."

"How much cargo space will I have? That will determine what I can take with me."

"I can only give you a provisional answer to that. I'm still negotiating on how many cargo ships we can take with us. For the moment assume that you have unlimited space. After all, your shopping list is the most important of all. I'll know for certain by the time we meet with Hans on Friday, but to be on the safe side don't order anything until next week. Now I've a couple of bits of news for you arising out of what I have been discussing today. You've been allocated two assistants. They should be recruited over the next couple of days and be with you some time during next week. They will, of course, be going with us. The second decision that was made today is that the director of each settlement will have the privilege of naming it. That's assuming that colonisation goes ahead. In honour of my own country our town will be called Stockholm. You should use the name from now on, particularly in any official documents. Now if there's nothing else I promised my wife that I'd be back by six o'clock." I had no more questions.

Over Wednesday and most of Thursday I divided my time between the list of things to order and the plan for the layout of Stockholm. When I was finally happy with the latter I made half a dozen fair copies. Just before three o'clock on the Thursday afternoon a knock on the door heralded the entry of a stranger. He was of medium height, probably in his early to mid thirties, with dark, almost black hair and a thin face with high cheekbones. His dress was casual, a rather colourful sports shirt and lightweight fawn trousers.

"Hans Friedland," he announced. "I take it you're Alex?" I agreed that I was and rose to shake hands with him.

29

"Welcome Hans," I greeted him. "Have a seat and I'll make some coffee, then we can talk. I won't be a minute. The coffee pot is hot already."

Hans told me that he'd just arrived that lunchtime from his home in Duisburg. He was married to Gerthe, had no children and his wife was going with him to Cara IV. They were also staying at the Hotel Vista.

"Perhaps you would like to join us for the evening meal tonight," he invited. "If we are going to be colleagues then we should get to know each other as soon as possible." I'd already taken a liking to him and agreed readily. He next wanted to know when he would meet Nils.

"We've a meeting with him at half past nine tomorrow morning," I told him. "I suspect it will be a long one. The impression I got is that he'll want to get down to some serious planning. After all, we've only seven weeks before we leave. Have you got copies of the survey team's files?"

He shook his head. With some relief I lifted them off my desk and into his hands. "This will give you a little light bedtime reading," I grinned. "As a bonus, here's a copy of the plan I've made for the arrangement of our township, which in deference to Nils will be called Stockholm. Let me know if you'd like to make any amendments." He grimaced as he flicked through the files I'd given him and then rose with a sigh.

"I suppose I'd better trawl through these if I'm to make a reasonable contribution to the meeting tomorrow. See you at seven o'clock in the Vista's main restaurant." He went out and into his own office next door.

Dinner that evening was a very pleasant meal. Gerthe was an attractive blonde, four years younger than Hans as I quickly found out. She was also an inch or two taller. The two of them had been married for eighteen months and were obviously very much in love. By the time we rose from the table some two hours later they knew almost everything about me and I about them. My last thought before going to sleep that night was that although Cara IV wasn't exactly the dream posting I would have liked at least I was going to have the best possible colleagues.

There was a small conference room on the opposite side of the corridor to my office. Hans and I were there at twenty past nine and five minutes later Nils arrived with Ramona in tow. I introduced the two men. After welcoming Hans, Nils got straight down to business, mentioning that Ramona was there to take brief notes.

"I finalised details with the Space Service board of directors yesterday," he began, "so I'm at last in a position to tell you exactly what's been agreed. That means we can go ahead and make firm plans. Assuming that all goes well and things will grow each of the first thirty or so settlements will be restricted to two hundred. In our case, however, there will only be forty-eight of us in the advance party. The remaining one hundred and fifty-two will leave Earth a week behind us and travel to Paladia initially. Once we are certain that things will grow and that humans can survive on Cara IV they will then join us."

Hans half raised his hand. "Supposing it's a doomsday scenario and we find nothing will grow. What happens to our forty-eight?"

"The three of us will be brought back to earth for reassignment. The rest will be diverted to another of the colonised planets along with the other one hundred and fifty odd. But I am optimistic and am planning only for success. I'm sure Alex will bring the world to life for us." I kept quiet. I wasn't nearly so confident. There were so many things that could go wrong. But Nils was speaking again. "Our party will consist of ourselves and wives, Alex excepted of course, a doctor and his wife, Alex's two assistants and two farmers. Sorry, I'm not supposed to call them farmers. They're agricultural technicians. Incidentally I've already met them and they're a strange pair. Henri and Jean-Paul Lemaire are French brothers, qualified but not exactly forthcoming. I'd put them in their mid twenties and unmarried. I won't elaborate on what I've said. You can judge them for yourselves when you meet them. The rest of the party will be the various tradesmen that Hans will need: I've a list of them here for you. Three are married, but their wives are also skilled and will work alongside the men. There will be no children in the advance party, but there are a number in the remaining group."

"The Russians are supplying four of the five ships that will be in our convoy. We will be travelling on the *Ural Star*, which will also be carrying five years' food supplies for two hundred people. It will all be dry and tinned food of course. The hope is that by the end of that period we will be producing at least fifty per cent of our requirements, though I feel that's somewhat over optimistic. Three of the remaining ships will be cargo ships, carrying all the materials that you'll both need. There'll be prefabricated houses and other buildings, bridges, transport vehicles and whatever Alex orders. The fifth ship, the Hungarian based *Budapest*, will carry the extra settlers to Paladia. This will have some cargo for that world and some additional items for us. We'll also have a number of the new plastipods. These will be available for storage and can be adapted for use as greenhouses, meeting places and a few other things besides."

The plastipod was a recent invention. Made of a new form of plastic they could be packed flat for carrying purposes and inflated on site. The material of the outer skin could be made clear or opaque at the touch of a switch and the interior could be regulated to any desired temperature from zero to forty degrees Centigrade. Despite being light in weight they were immensely strong and could withstand extreme weather conditions.

Nils turned to Hans. "You know what will be needed of course. Our first priority on landing will be to get the buildings up. After that we'll need power, running water and sewage in that order. Once we've had some lunch we'll discuss the layout that Alex has prepared, settle all measurements and then you can go ahead and order what you require. Remember that if you run out of anything it will take a year to bring it from Earth so as a rule of thumb I suggest you work out what you'll need and add thirty per cent to that figure. This particularly applies to timber as it's going to be many years before we'll be producing our own. Any surplus matter can always be used at a later date by new arrivals."

We spent the rest of the morning going over the timetable for ordering and delivery to the fleet of cargo ships at our disposal. These would be based in Poland during the three weeks before take-off. At twelve o'clock Nils called a halt for lunch.

CHAPTER FIVE

The three of us ate together in the canteen and deliberately talked of other things during the meal. At one o'clock we returned to the committee room where Ramona was already settled. I had a question that I'd been dying to ask Nils.

"As there are only a few of us will we be awake during the voyage?"

Nils shook his head. "I'm afraid not. It will be the usual cryogenic freezing for us. Space ship crews don't like having passengers under their feet all the time. Why?"

I tried to hide my disappointment. "Ever since I was five years old it's been my dream to travel on a spaceship. Now it seems my dream will come true and I won't know a thing about it."

Nils laughed. "If it's that important to you I'll have a word with our captain when we meet. Maybe he'll agree to the three of us being resuscitated a couple of days before landing. Now I'd like to discuss the plans you've made for the landing site."

I handed each of them a copy of my drawing, plus one to Ramona for her files. "I've tried to keep everything as simple as possible. Incidentally, if it's alright with you both I'd like to work in miles for the moment. I'm not too comfortable with kilometres, though I'll add the conversion once you're happy with my design. As you can see I've used the river as a centrepiece. One square mile on either side will reserved for the residential area. If it's possible to place the bridge half a mile inland my idea is that the main street of the eventual town will run from north to south across the bridge. Future shops and offices would be on either side. The remainder of the two square miles will be housing and open spaces with any industrial and storage buildings on the outer edges. I'd like the ships to land on the north side of the town area just outside the one mile. South of the town I propose to lay down another square mile of open grassland. Once we get settled we can use this area for sports grounds and possibly as a picnic area." I paused to draw breath.

"South of that again another square mile will be planted with trees, so that in twenty or thirty years' time we'll have an extensive forest there. Once the ships have left, the north side of the river would be similarly laid out with a square mile of grassland and a square mile of forest. The only difference between the two is that the southern forest will be of deciduous trees and the northern one conifers. Of course these won't be the only forests. We'll plant more inland as soon as possible and scatter as many trees as we can throughout the immediate vicinity. Again as you'll see I've left a half mile gap between the western edge of the town area and the land that the glorified farmers or whatever they call themselves can start work on. That should take care of any future expansion needs. Incidentally, although I'll do the ordering I propose to leave them to deal with most food bearing trees and bushes. That includes various nut trees."

Both Nils and Hans seemed quite happy with my plans and I was next quizzed on my prospective timetable. I'd given a good deal of time to thinking about this though I hadn't as yet put anything down on paper.

"Obviously the first priority is grass," I began. "If grass won't grow it's unlikely that anything else will. I'll probably spend the whole of the first two days scattering grass seed over a large area to the south and east of the town. We have one advantage. We don't actually need to plant it properly. With no birds or insect life we can leave the seed on the surface to germinate. Once that's done I'll make a start on the tree planting. Which reminds me, Nils. Ideally I'd like to take at least two hundred young trees in pots to give us a flying start. Will the crew of the ship be willing to keep them watered?"

"I'll make sure of it," Nils said emphatically. "From what I've heard boredom is the main problem for the crews on long space flights. I imagine they'll welcome something extra to do. Once you've planted the young trees, what then?"

"Sorry," I apologised. "I'm getting ahead of myself. I'll be bringing several drums of plankton, other aquatic algae and water weed. Before I start on the trees I intend to dump most if not all of this into the sea, the rivers and streams and the lake. With no natural enemies it should multiply very rapidly and spread out. After the young trees are in I'll go on spreading grass as far afield as I can, simultaneously planting out trees from seed or stones. I intend to order a large quantity of those."

"Forgive my ignorance," said Nils hesitantly, "but aren't bacteria essential to the growing process?"

"They're not vital," I explained, "though they help in the conversion of the chemical elements in the soil and the breaking down of dead material. That's one reason why I'm taking potted young trees. The bacteria present in the soil of these will proliferate and spread rapidly in all directions. In a couple of years we'll have all the bacteria we need for hundreds of miles around."

"How long before we can bring in animals and fish?" Hans wanted to know.

"Difficult to say," I answered. "So much depends on how quickly things grow. I haven't even begun to think of that yet. There'll be a lot of precise calculations to be made as we go along. One thing I will not do is try and rush things. Nothing in the way of livestock will come on to the world until there is more than sufficient food and facilities to sustain it. Ask me the same question in eighteen months' time and I'll be able to give you a more accurate assessment." Both my companions seemed quite happy and we left it at that.

"Just two more things then before we close," Nils announced. "Firstly some of your more senior assistants will be joining you over the next week or two, Hans. Alex, your two assistants will be reporting to you next Wednesday morning. If you're not happy with them let me know and I'll arrange for more possible candidates to be sent. Secondly, once you've both ordered whatever you need and arranged deliveries to the ships matters will be out of our hands. The captains will handle the receipt of goods and decide what goes where. I suggest that you each take a couple of weeks' leave. As you probably realise it will be a long time before we get a chance to come home. In fact it is very likely that we will never come back to Earth. I'm sure you'll both have things to settle and people to say goodbye to. My wife and I will be taking time off to go back to Sweden, even though we haven't lived there for many years. We both have family there." I nodded, but I wasn't sure if I had anything worth going back home for other than to make my farewells to Scotland itself.

I spent the next few days making out the lists of things to order. Once I was reasonably happy that I'd left out nothing important I started sorting out potential suppliers. I put in a few hours on both the Saturday and Sunday that weekend. My physical fitness had been neglected since my arrival at the Casa Garibaldi, so I went for a long walk each day, vowing to make that a daily part of my routine. I also put in a couple of rigorous sessions in the gym. Tuesday I spent most of the day on the phone placing orders. I ordered as much of what I needed as I could from Scotland. This was not only good for my country's economy, but also meant I could work in tons and hundredweights instead of metric measure. I made notes as I went along. There was little practical help that my soon to be present assistants could do, so dealing with the written confirmations and other paperwork would keep them occupied. First thing Wednesday morning Ramona laid two personnel files on my desk.

The newcomers were to be two young women I discovered. I wasn't sure if that was a good thing or not. One was an English girl, Julie Browning, twenty-four years old. She'd been to an upmarket girls' school in the south of England and had done well academically. The other was a Maria Zambretta, Italian, twenty, from the small town of Corella in the shadow of the Appalachian Mountains. The name Zambretta rang a vague bell at the back of my mind, but it took a few minutes before the penny dropped. They were a well known family in winemaking circles. They had the reputation of being extremely wealthy and I wondered why a member of the family would want to leave such prosperity behind and head for the wilderness of outer space. Once I'd digested the two files I rang through and asked Ramona to send in the two girls together.

A hesitant knock on the door announced their arrival. I invited them in, offered them chairs and made a quick appraisal. The first adjective that sprang into my mind as I looked at Julie Browning was 'sturdy'. She wasn't fat by any means, but was solidly built, with a square determined face, fairish hair cut short and hazel eyes. She was simply dressed in a light blue blouse and black skirt. Her face and her bare arms were covered in freckles and she looked younger than her twenty-four years. I could just picture her on the hockey field tearing down the wing. Maria Zambretta fell just short of being beautiful. Her nose was a little too long and her mouth a little too small. She was slim, quite tall and her outstanding feature was her long raven black hair. Her eyes were a very dark brown and held more than a hint of humour in them. She was wearing a plain dress of deep cream, belted at the waist.

"I've really only one question to ask each of you," I said quietly. "Why do you want to give up a comfortable life here on Earth and eke out a Spartan existence in outer space? Julie?"

I expected the English girl to have a deep gruff voice, so I was surprised when she answered in a well modulated tone. "I want some excitement in my life. I'm the youngest of the family, with three older brothers. I love them to death, my parents too, but they've always tended to protect me from hardship. I want to stand on my own feet now. For the last couple of years I've toyed with the idea of emigrating to one of the new worlds, but this project has really captured my imagination. I want to be part of it. I've had outdoor jobs, worked on a farm and in a garden centre, so I'm used to hard graft."

I made no comment and turned to Maria. "Am I right in thinking you're part of the Zambretta wine family? If so you've surely got a job for life?"

She nodded. "My grandfather is the president and my father general manager. But there is no place for me in the organisation. I have four brothers and three sisters. Apart from my oldest sister who is married they are all employed in the company in some capacity or other. My father has made it clear that he can take on no more staff. There are no other jobs around locally. To find work I would need to go to a big town or city and I don't want that. I'm a country girl and I don't like built up areas. Mama's no help. All she can think about is getting me married off. That doesn't appeal to me either. I want to do something worthwhile with my life and this is the perfect opportunity."

I looked searchingly at them both before speaking. "You do realise, I hope, that this mission will be no picnic. You talk of excitement, Julie, but there'll be little of that. It will be hard physical work, mostly outdoors in all weathers. There'll be little or no social life, none of the amenities we all take for granted and the food will be monotonous to say the least for some years to come. Realise too that it may not be possible for any of us ever to return to Earth or to go to a more civilised colony. I'm not trying to dissuade you, but I want to be sure you're both fully aware of all the drawbacks. If you want some time to think it over or discuss it with each other I can give you the rest of the day to do so."

"I don't need to think it over," Julie spoke strongly. "I understand all that you say, but it just makes me more determined."

"The same for me," Maria emphasised. "I considered all the options for a long time before I applied. I want this job."

I sat back and smiled. "Good. You're hired. Go and give all your details to Ramona so that she can arrange for your salary to be paid from today. Then come back, take a desk each and I'll give you some nice boring paper work to break you in. Oh, one thing, Maria. I take it your grapes are often grown from seed. Would it be possible for you to get hold of some to take with us? I'd like as many different varieties as you can get. Who knows? You might own a vineyard and a winery yet!"

"No problem," she answered. "I'll get it organised when I go home this weekend. As to owning a winery or a vineyard I guess I'll give it a miss. I've been too close to them all my life so far. It will be good to get away."

The rest of the week passed quietly. I was well up to schedule with all my orders placed and deliveries direct to the cargo ships arranged. My two assistants were kept occupied with the resultant paperwork and I also discussed my provisional plans with them. By Friday we had developed a good working relationship. Strange though it may sound I was relieved to find that I harboured no romantic attraction to either of them. For the foreseeable future I wanted my mind free to concentrate on my work. Maria was as good as her word and returned on the Monday morning with two dozen or more bags of grape seed donated by her father. We parcelled them up and put them aside for delivery to the cargo ships.

On Tuesday morning the two agricultural technicians came to see me. As they very soon became known as agtecs I'll refer to them thus from now on. The Lemaire brothers were a strange pair, as Nils had foretold. Though there was three years difference between them they could have been taken for twins, so alike were they. Henri, the older brother, had a faint scar above his left eye and that was the only way I could tell them apart. They were below average height, slim and with sallow complexions. Their faces were long and narrow and always seemed to be set in a frown. Throughout our two hour meeting they never once smiled. I told them of my plans, they described theirs and we made amendments wherever the two overlapped. They informed me brusquely that they had ordered all the materials that they would need for their own activities. I was also told in no uncertain terms that they were not farmers. Their job was to experiment with food crops of all kinds and to pass on the results to the real farmers who would follow. They did, however, adopt one suggestion of mine. I advised them to take a number of trees and bushes in pots, explaining as I did so about the need to introduce bacteria to the soil. Despite their insistence on taking control of anything to do with food production I included some fruit trees and bushes plus a considerable quantity of vegetable seed in my own requisitions. I had an idea at the back of my mind, one that I wanted to keep to myself until I'd seen the conditions on Cara IV at first hand.

By the end of that week there was little more to be done and I decided after all I would take some leave and go back home for ten days. My two assistants could handle any minor matters that might crop up and they had my phone number should there be anything urgent. My motives for spending a few last days in Scotland were twofold. I wanted to say my goodbyes to Aunt Eleanor and I wanted to spend three or four days up north. I'd always loved the Highlands on my occasional visits there and in view of my immediate future I thought it might be good conditioning to spend some time in a virtual wilderness. I didn't expect to see my parents: the best I hoped for was a phone conversation with them separately. As it happened I was pleasantly surprised. When my father learned that this

Bernard Stocks

was my farewell visit he flew in specially from San Francisco to spend a day with me. We lunched at an expensive restaurant, just he and I, then at his suggestion went for a long walk through the old town and up to the castle. We talked mainly of the work I was about to embark on.

Leaning against one of the cannons he regarded me thoughtfully. "I want you to know that I'm very proud of you and I'm sure you will be successful in all you do. You should be proud of yourself as well, because everything you've accomplished has been done by you alone. I know I haven't been a very good father to you, but when I look at you now I think that has been the reason you've done so well. Before we part there's something I want you to ask of you. Please don't feel bitter towards your mother for her indifference to you. As you know, your birth wasn't planned and it proved a setback to your mother in her career. It was also a very difficult birth and she was in great pain for several weeks both before and after. It left her distressed and traumatised for a long time. I have to say, too, that despite having had four children she is not and never has been the motherly type. Changing the subject, will you be coming home on leave at any time?"

"I really don't know, Dad," was my honest reply. "So much depends on the progress we make and on availability of transport. The service doesn't encourage settlers to return home so they make it as difficult as possible. I'm resigned to the fact that I'll spend the rest of my life away from Earth. If our efforts on Cara IV are successful I suspect I'll be there for the rest of my life."

He shook his head sadly. "That's a pity. I'm thinking of retiring in three years or so. I've made enough money to last me for several lifetimes. I planned to buy a country cottage up north and spend my time fishing and playing golf. I would have liked to think there would be things we could do together."

I smiled. "Never say never. I might yet land on you for a few months, especially if we fail. Oh, by the way. I'm getting paid now so you can stop my monthly allowance. But I want you to know I'm eternally grateful for it. Without your help I would have had to take a part time job and I wouldn't have done nearly so well in my studies."

His flight back to San Francisco was at five o'clock. I saw him off at the airport, fairly certain that I would never see him again.

40

CHAPTER SIX

I arrived back in Castellarana ten days before we were due to fly to Poland and board the *Ural Star*. Hans and Nils were still on leave and Julie had gone to England to say goodbye to her family and friends. The only item of importance to arrive during my absence was a memo from headquarters to inform us that all service personnel headed for Cara IV had been paid a year's salary in advance. We were further instructed to visit our banks before leaving, close our accounts and collect a credit note for the remaining balance. I assumed from this that there would be some kind of banking system set up soon after our arrival on the new world. Ramona confirmed this when I mentioned the matter to her. I also discovered for the first time that she wouldn't be going with us, but instead would be redeployed once we'd left. We would all miss her, Nils especially. She'd been a tower of strength in her role as his secretary. Meantime I had one more task to perform.

Taking Maria with me I paid a visit to a large garden centre just outside of Naples. We spent more than two hours there buying up hundreds of packets of flower and vegetable seeds. In fact we took just about every variety they had in stock. Though my first priority was to provide vegetation for animal feed and trees for timber I saw no reason why I shouldn't also bring some additional colour to the new world. My intention had been to take them away with us, but when I saw the size and weight of the resultant package I quickly arranged for it to be sent direct to the spaceport. Then it was off to the bank to close my account. When I saw the amount on the credit slip I realised with a shock that I was on my way to becoming rich! For the past three years I'd lived well within my monthly allowance. Now I had a year's salary on top of that and I'd be spending nothing for the eleven months of our journey to Cara IV. It seemed unlikely that there'd be much to buy on the new world for many years to come so my financial future looked rosy.

Nils returned three days after me and Hans the day after that. We had one final meeting to go over our preparations and make sure we hadn't left out anything important. Nils had one piece of good news for me.

"I've spoken to Captain Petrovic of the *Ural Star*," he told me. "He's agreed that you can be resuscitated two or three days before we land. Apparently they have a couple of spare cabins so it won't be a problem." I was overjoyed at the news. I'd still have liked to stay awake for the whole journey but at least I would have the experience of being in space to remember for the rest of my life. Both Nils and Hans had been in space before so they were quite happy to sleep for the full time.

We left Naples airport at ten o'clock on a Thursday morning, having said our farewells to Ramona. Our transport was a recently built 'jetship' as they'd been christened. These additions to the flying world were half spaceships and half conventional aircraft. Taking off almost vertically they rose to some fifty miles above the surface and travelled at high speeds. All forty-eight of the advance party were on board, plus half a dozen Space Service officials on some business mission or other. The journey to the spaceport in central Poland took just over an hour. On landing we were immediately taken across to the *Ural Star* by hoverbus. Although I'd seen ships close up at the spaceport at Rannoch Moor back home the sheer size still took my breath away. All deep space passenger and cargo vessels were built to roughly the same dimensions and design. In shape they resembled a gigantic whale, nearly a mile long and two-fifths of a mile wide. We had little time to stand and stare, however. A crew member quickly ushered us inside, led us through a maze of corridors and delivered us to the cryogenic chamber.

Although I was familiar with pictures of these chambers this was the first that I'd seen at close quarters. Row upon row of plastic sided cubicles lined the walls, apart from a central control desk covered in dials and switches. Each cubicle was a perfect cube with seven foot sides. Inside was a padded bunk above which hung a pulley with a number of tubes hanging down. Three medical staff, two women and one man, were in attendance. The man explained the procedure to us.

"Please take off your outer garments and put on the gowns provided. You'll each receive an injection, then go straight into the chamber and lie on the bunk. You'll lose consciousness in less than a minute and the next thing you know will be when you wake up in eleven months' time. The freezing process takes place very quickly. Within ten minutes the cubicle will be at minus fifty degrees Centigrade. You'll receive small quantities of liquid and vitamins through the tubes above to keep you hydrated and prevent organ damage and muscle wastage. Because your metabolism will be low it will take very little to keep you alive and fit. Probably for the first ten minutes or so after resuscitation you'll experience a bit of cramp but that soon wears off." Stripped to vest and shorts I donned the gown provided and stood in line waiting for my injection. Then I went into the cubicle and lay down. I just had time to discover the bunk was surprisingly comfortable before the darkness descended.

I have a feeling that I dreamed during that long sleep, but no memories remained once I'd awakened. My immediate impression was that I'd simply had a good deep eight hours. A Second Officer was standing at the open door of my cubicle. Once he saw that I was fully alert he put out his hand and helped me to my feet. I felt a little bit wobbly at first but soon the strength came back and I was able to walk.

"Captain Petrovic's compliments, sir," were his first words. "I've to take you to the guest cabin where you can wash, shave and change, then to the canteen for breakfast. After that you have an invitation to join him on the bridge. I'm Bert Larrabey, by the way, originally from Australia but I've lived in Wales from the time I was seven until joining the Space Service."

I learned from Bert that we'd been travelling for just under eleven months. My next surprise, when I reached the cabin and looked in the mirror, was to see that I only had a couple of days' growth of hair on my face. After a quick wash and shave I changed into my uniform and we headed for the canteen. I found I was hungry and I was disappointed to find that only continental breakfasts of coffee and croissants were available. I'd have given a lot for a good old-fashioned Scottish fry up. Then it was time for the moment that I was looking forward to, my first sight of outer space. Bert led me through a maze of corridors and on to the bridge, or the control cabin to give it its proper name. Captain Petrovic came forward to greet me with hand outstretched. He was a tall heavily built man in his early to mid forties, with dark brown hair just beginning to turn grey at the edges.

His most prominent feature, however, was a great hooked nose beneath humorous brown eyes. Far from detracting from his appearance the nose gave him the appearance of great strength and character.

"Welcome, Mr. Dunsmuir," he greeted me in a deep booming voice. "I understand that you've been looking forward to your brief time in space. Frankly we all find it incredibly boring, but I hope you will enjoy the next two days."

"I have indeed been looking forward to it, sir," I replied. "And I intend to savour every minute. It may be the only time I will have the experience."

He looked searchingly at me. "Surely not. You'll be entitled to home leave, won't you?"

"There's been no mention of that. In any case, I've not too much to go home for. I've family, but we're not close. No, unless we fail and I'm reassigned I expect I'll settle here permanently."

Our conversation had been held just inside the cabin door and behind a screen. Now the captain took me into the cabin proper. It was smaller than I'd expected, about the size of an average living room. The dominant feature was the ultra strong plexi-glass screen at the front. This gave a panoramic view stretching through one hundred and eighty degrees. I was somewhat disappointed. All I could see was blackness relieved only by numerous tiny pinpricks of light. These, of course, denoted distant stars. Three people were present apart from the captain and myself, the pilot who was a Second Officer, my guide Bert and a First Officer standing behind the pilot. One other thing I was aware of. Though we were presumably travelling at more than twelve million miles per hour there was no sensation of movement. Captain Petrovic led me to the front and unerringly pointed out one of the pinpricks in the centre of the screen.

"There's our destination, the sun Cara. By tomorrow evening we will be able to see it as large as a football and receive some of the light it sheds. I take it you know the make-up of the planetary system around it."

"Just the basics," was my answer. "There are thirteen planets in orbit around Cara, but only the fourth is suitable for humans."

"That's correct," said the captain. "Cara III is too hot. It has an average temperature of more than eighty degrees Centigrade. Cara V is too cold. The thermometer there can go as low as minus forty."

At this point I noticed two digital clock calendars on the left hand wall of the cabin. They were showing different dates and times. The one on the right recorded July 28, 2240 and 1340 hours; the other April 3, 2240 and 0915. Captain Petrovic saw the direction of my gaze.

"The one on the right is the Earth date and time; that on the left the Cara IV equivalent. We were able to calculate the latter fairly accurately from the data supplied by the survey team. The difference is the main reason it was decided to start the mission last September. You're arriving early in spring at the start of the growing season."

The next eighteen hours may have been boring for the crew but it was exciting for me. I spent long hours in the control cabin just gazing out into the void. Then came the thrill of the first real sight of the sun Cara late on the second afternoon. Slowly but surely one of the microscopic specks of light began to grow. By ten that evening it was just as the captain had predicted and the blackness around had become a dark grey. My friend Bert was in the pilot's seat at this time and he turned to me.

"There won't be much more to see tonight, so I suggest you get some sleep. By six our time tomorrow morning you'll get your first look at your new home. Landfall will be at about eleven our time, just before seven on the surface. The rest of your group will be resuscitated between seven and eight. According to the instructions Mr. Anderssen gave before we took off you'll all meet for breakfast and a briefing at eight thirty."

Reluctant as I was to tear myself away I realised the sense in Bert's advice and returned to my cabin. I set my alarm for a quarter to six next morning. The next day would probably be my last ever experience of space flight and I wanted to enjoy it to the full. Excited as I was I still managed to fall asleep within a couple of minutes. When the alarm went I rose immediately, washed, shaved and put on my uniform. I arrived on the bridge at five minutes past six. A Ukranian girl that I knew slightly was in the pilot's seat and Captain Petrovic was standing slightly behind her. They both turned and greeted me.

"There you are," said the captain as he pointed to the screen. "There's your new home."

My first sight of Cara IV was disappointing. Over the years I'd seen many pictures of planets taken from space. They'd all been multi coloured with bright greens and blues predominating. The image in front of me was about the size of a large water melon. Almost half of the surface was a uniform light grey, the rest brown with patches, spots and lines of a darker grey. Even the clouds which obscured parts of the surface were a dull grey in colour. I'd expected the sea at least to show up blue. The grey bits on the land were almost certainly mountains and lakes.

"We're going into our first orbit in about three quarters of an hour," Captain Petrovic informed me as he pointed again. "Round about here is where we'll be making our landfall and where you will be setting up camp. Unfortunately dawn hasn't come there yet, so you won't be able to see any detail for two or three hours yet." The image was growing in size as I watched and I saw light spreading once we'd orbited half way round.

I spent the next two hours with my eyes firmly fixed on the growing planet. By the time I was due to join my newly awoken companions for breakfast we'd made one complete orbit of the world from east to west and back again. It would be another hour or more before we entered the atmosphere for our final orbit. I set off for the canteen in high spirits. Our whole group of forty-eight were already seated and eating. Quickly grabbing what I wanted from the hot plates I joined Nils and Hans, after saying hello to Julie and Maria and nodding to others in the team.

"I take it you've already had a look at our new home," was the greeting from Nils.

I nodded. "A vision in brown and grey," I said with a grin. "I just hope we can transform it."

"Any idea what the weather's like?" asked Hans with his mouth full.

"We're not close enough as yet," I replied. "There's a fair amount of cloud about, so I suspect it will be raining somewhere. I saw our landing area. It's clear there at the moment but still dark."

Once everyone had finished their meal Nils asked us all to gather round. "Schedule for the next few days," he began with a smile. "Now the original plan as laid down by the commission was that we would wait in the ship while Alex and his helpers planted sample patches of grass and other things. Only when these began to show signs of growth were we supposed to start setting up our community. In the meantime we were supposed to sleep in the ship, on the floor with sleeping bags because there are no cabins available. But I'm an optimist and I'm going to assume that all will be well. Therefore we'll begin right away. If the worst comes to the worst it will only take us a few extra days to pull everything down again. The first of the cargo ships is due to touch down about an hour after us. This is the one that contains the housing packs. Our first task therefore will be to unload some of these and set up our own housing requirements. Everyone will play their part in this, even before Alex starts his given role. I'm told these houses are easy to assemble and that with practice a team of four can get one up and ready in half an hour. After that's done and the basic furniture installed — and if there's enough time left — the various units can start on their own jobs."

"I've agreed with Captain Petrovic that in exchange for us handing over part of our own food supply his crew will provide meals for us all until Hans has power, water and sewage requirements up and running. Once that's done you'll be expected to do your own catering. I'll go into the matter of food allocation at a later date. There's one other thing to tell you just now. The remaining one hundred and fifty-two settlers who'll complete our community will arrive on Paladia in two weeks' time. As soon as the first signs of growth appear they'll be notified and will join us within a couple of months. Now I've had instructions duplicated for the assembly of the houses and in the next hour or so I'd like you all to study them. Hans and three of his assistants will demonstrate the first one to us all once the sections are unloaded. There are also copies of the layout of the houses on the ground, so please study that too. For the moment I suggest you split up into groups of four."

I'd have much preferred to return to the bridge and watch our approach, but I realised I ought to set a good example. My own group of four was made up of Julie, Maria and a shy young Spanish plumber named Pablo. The assembly of the houses and other buildings didn't look too difficult. I'd had a Lego set as a youngster and the only difference that I could see was in the size of the pieces. Just before eleven, ship's time, Nils called us all together again.

"We're just about to touch down," he reported. "I'll be first to set foot on the surface, followed by Hans and Alex. The rest of you line up behind us. Once we're all on the ground I'll say a short prayer. One of the crew will then bring out a supply of pegs and while we're waiting for the cargo ship to arrive we'll mark out where the houses are to go."

CHAPTER SEVEN

There was the slightest of bumps as we landed and a brief shudder as the ship settled on the surface. About a minute later the exit door facing us slid back. Nils pressed a switch and a flight of steps emerged smoothly and silently from just beneath his feet. Quietly we followed him down the steps and on to the ground. Nobody spoke as we looked round then formed a circle around our leader. Solemnly he knelt down and kissed the bare brown earth. On his knees he intoned these words.

"Oh Lord, we ask Thy blessing on our mission. Guide our footsteps in all we do and help us make this barren place into a land fit for habitation. Amen."

He rose and beckoned towards the ship. Immediately four of the crew emerged, each carrying a sack full of metal pegs. While these were being distributed I had time to look around me. The view was depressing in the extreme. To my left was the ocean, a vast slate grey expanse. Most of the rest of my horizon consisted of bare brown soil. Beneath my feet this was loosely packed but damp, indicating that there had been rain not long before our arrival. Overhead the sun was rising in a sky relatively free of cloud. Turning to my right I got my first sight of the higher ground to the north-east that masked the lake. I had little time for further appraisal as the parties of four were beginning to move off towards the square mile on this bank of the river that was to accommodate half our town. Each group had a plan of the layout and a metal tape. Unfortunately from my point of view this measured in metres. Thankfully someone had taken the trouble back on Earth to add metric measurements in brackets after my own annotations.

The town area was slightly back from the seashore and on a ridge some five yards or four metres above sea level. I'd planned the first line of ten houses to start three times that distance from the edge of the ridge and facing the sea. We marked those out first, then three more rows behind number one. These were facing each other with a twelve metre gap between them. The first of the houses was a good fifty metres from the river bank, leaving a walkway beside the river. Each house measured either eight metres by six or eight by eight, depending on whether they were of two or three apartments. Married personnel were allowed three apartments; single persons two. There was a front garden four metres deep and a back garden fifteen metres deep to each house. The gap between each property was ten metres. For simplicity we'd named the four streets thus formed as First, Second, Third and Fourth Avenues. Barely had we finished when the first of the cargo ships came over the horizon and in to land. Nils told us we could have an hour's break while the housing units were unloaded. Julie and Maria joined me in a walk along the shore to the mouth of the river. The sand was firm and a brownish colour without any shingle or pebbles. Julie commented that it would make a good bathing beach in the years to come.

"So what do you both think of your new home?" I asked them.

"Not a lot," said Julie frankly. "But I can see the potential."

Maria was more thoughtful. "It's like a blank canvas before the artist starts to paint. We're the artist and what we do in the months and years to come will decide what kind of picture emerges. In my mind I can see it turning green. I can see the rows of houses with neat front gardens filled with flowers and children playing on the beach. You know, I was really depressed when I first stepped down from the ship, but now I'm beginning to get excited."

Crews from both ships took on the task of unloading the house sections. Once sufficient numbers had been stacked up on the ground Hans and three of his assistants explained the function of each section. The base units were either four by four metres or four by two. These were some fifteen centimetres thick, made of a light metal alloy outer case filled with a newly invented plastic foam that was water resistant. At each corner of these base units was a metal spike about twenty-five centimetres long. These would be driven into the ground. Each unit interlocked in various ways with each other. The walls, with doors and plexi-glass windows already in place, were four or two metres wide by three metres high and locked into the bases. Once locked they were then bolted on. The roofs were similar to the floor units but without the spikes. Small flaps in walls and floors indicated where water and power pipes would be fed in and waste pipes would go out. Every section was light to handle and could be carried easily by four people. Once Hans was satisfied that we all had grasped the principle he and his assistants demonstrated the method of erection. Then he gave a beaming smile and told us to get on with it.

It took Maria, Julie, Pablo and I over an hour to put our first effort together. We weren't the slowest. All around us we could hear laughter and the occasional outbursts of bad language as things didn't go according to plan. By the time we got to our final house we'd got the hang of things and completed it in forty minutes. Before that we'd had a welcome one hour break for lunch. By three o'clock all fifty houses were finished and we found our furniture and fittings unloaded and ready for collection. These were basic in the extreme. Everyone had a table and four chairs, two cupboards, one double bed, one microwave oven and a small selection of crockery, cutlery, bedding and linen. Married couples had an additional bed and cupboard and two extra chairs. At this point we had no bathroom fittings or kitchen hob. Hans and his team would install these once power and other essentials were available.

By six o'clock we were all installed in our new homes and had collected our personal belongings from the ship. Nils and Hans had both opted for a house on First Avenue facing the sea. I'd taken one on Fourth Avenue facing east and nearest the river. By that time I'd been able to take a good look at the river and satisfied myself that there was little possibility of it bursting its banks and flooding the surrounding area. Julie and Maria had settled for adjoining houses further along Fourth Avenue. After a much needed supper we were left to our own devices. The third cargo ship had arrived a couple of hours previously and this was the one containing all my materials, plus most of the transport. I managed to persuade the crew to unload a fully charged hover car and a couple of bags of grass seed. I decided against calling the girls to help as there was little we could do until we were able to cross the river where most of the planting would be done. I drove along the seafront distributing seed thinly here and there, then turned and traversed the riverside walk. Here I scattered the seed more thickly. I reasoned that there could be a fair amount of foot traffic towards the sea, but very little along the river at this point. I still had half a bag of seed left over so I then headed four miles north before spreading the remainder of my supply. This was beyond the area where the final cargo ship was due to land on the morrow. In all locations the ground was damp, and the seed stuck easily. There was no point in trying to cover it. After all, there were no birds or insects to eat it! Feeling well pleased with my evening's work I returned the hover car to the ship and went to see Nils and his wife, Ingrid.

I wasn't surprised to see Hans and Gerthe already there. From somewhere Ingrid had got hold of three large thermos flasks of coffee. I was immediately offered a cup and invited to sit. I mused that it was a good job married couples had the two extra chairs! While the two ladies drifted into a corner and started a conversation of their own Hans, Nils and I discussed the day's progress. Nils seemed pleased. I asked what came next.

It was Hans who answered. "Our first job tomorrow will be to get the parts of the main bridge across the river unloaded and then we'll assemble it and put it in place. That will be another case of all hands on deck. I reckon we should have it in place by mid afternoon which will give you a chance to get across and get some planting done on the open space beyond the south side of the town. After that our agtecs—I'm calling them that from now on, their proper name's too much of a mouthful—will start unloading their stuff and get to work. If we've sufficient time I'll take my crew up to the lake and start laying plans for the water and power supply. I intend to put the wind turbines up there on the higher ground. It means extra cabling, but there'll be more wind up there and thus a more reliable source of power."

I asked Nils if he was planning to have another general meeting in the near future. He said he was intending to have one just after breakfast next day and wanted to know why I'd asked.

"If it's O.K. with you I'd like to say a few words," I told him. "I want to make some suggestions about the use of the gardens. Although we've got an ample supply of food there'll not be any fresh items on the menu for at least a year. I included a few hundred packets of vegetable seeds among my purchases and I thought that everyone could use their back gardens to grow some of their own food. I've also got a fair quantity of flower seeds for the front gardens. If you're happy with the idea I can hand them out tomorrow some time and everyone can use an evening or two planting them. I'm not proposing to plant grass around the houses."

Nils approved of my suggestion and I duly made my little speech the next morning. It seemed to go down well. Then we got down to setting up the bridge. Although my part in the operation was simply to push and pull whenever I was told to I was fascinated with the way it was done. First out of the cargo ship came four heavy metal bars long enough to span the river at the designated point and to overlap by some fifteen yards on either bank. At either end spikes like an inverted letter 'V' would anchor these to the ground. One of the life ships from the *Ural Star* carried these across the river one at a time, dropping them neatly in their intended places. Four men went across with the life ship to the opposite bank, made sure the bars were exactly positioned and then drove in the spikes. The top of these bars formed a capital 'T'.

Next came the bridge itself, in two parts. Though each part had a wheeled undercarriage it proved difficult to push the mile or so needed to get it to the river and it took the combined efforts of more than two dozen of the bystanders more than an hour. Eventually both sections were in place. The underside of each section of the bridge carried slots which attached to the top of the bars, which had been heavily greased. Once in the right position it proved a relatively simple matter to push the bridge part across. The second section followed the first and by lunchtime our bridge was in place. Now we had the means of crossing the river on foot via a narrow pathway on each side plus two lanes for our hover cars and lorries. Hans was given the honour of being the first to cross and I followed close behind.

Now that the bridge was in place I got down to some serious work. First I carried half a dozen sacks of grass seed by car to the far side of the river. Collecting Julie and Maria we set off along the edge of the beach scattering seed thinly. We were using the trip meter in the hover car to measure distances. Unfortunately this was calibrated in kilometres so I had to adjust all my linear measures. With no need to do this exactly I simply converted one mile to fifteen hundred metres. When we reached the point at which the parkland was to start we traversed the whole area in parallel lines some twenty yards apart spreading the seed much more thickly. I drove as slowly as I could while the girls threw handfuls of seed from each rear window. It probably wasn't the most scientific method of doing the job but it was quick and effective. Whereas I'd used quick growing rye grass for the river bank and beachside areas, here I planted much finer grass, suitable for the tennis courts and bowling greens that would come at some time in the future. This would also be suitable for football and hockey pitches. Lady Luck was with us that day. No sooner had we finished than the rain started to fall, just what was needed to embed the seed and encourage growth.

While we were thus engaged Hans had abandoned his original plan to make a start on the power supply. Instead he switched his troops to setting up the desalination plant which would initially provide our water supply. This was at the request of the space ship captains as they were anxious to improve the quality of their stored water. Although everything on ships was recycled, after a long journey the water became tasteless. Once our regular water supply was ensured and the ships serviced this plant would be used to provide salt.

It was that evening that I started to keep a diary. It had been agreed that the date of our landing was Monday the sixth of April 2240. I still have that first ever diary and have continued the practice right up to the present day. My entries were always short. For instance that for the seventh of April simply read: 'Bridge put in place, planted parkland grass."

CHAPTER EIGHT

Wednesday dawned overcast but dry and warm, ideal for our purposes. Although we'd only been on the planet for two days it was already apparent that we had a first-class team. Everyone toiled from dawn to dusk and worked with a will. Even Nils and our doctor, who had no specific daily tasks other than directing and looking after our health respectively, put in a full day's hard graft. The doctor was Rumanian, Nico Lupesku by name. He had graduated in Edinburgh and married Jennifer Love, a nurse at the hospital in which he had studied. Their connection with my home city brought the three of us together and much of what spare time I had in the coming weeks was to be spent in their company. Jennifer was tall, blonde and willowy with china blue eyes and with a really traditional posh Morningside accent. She was a wonderful mimic, however, and she could imitate faithfully various accents from all over Britain and Europe. The task the four of them set themselves was to erect the non domestic buildings we would need. These included a school which would double as a meeting hall, four or five shops, purpose unknown at that point, a bank and three or four small offices. One of the latter was for me; a three roomed structure which allowed for storage and laboratory space.

An appeal to Captain Petrovic secured me the use of one of the lifeships and a pilot for Wednesday morning only. With the initial planting on land completed I felt I should turn my attention to the sea. Although there was nothing specific for them to do on this trip Julie and Maria came with me for the experience. They did contribute usefully by helping to load the drums of concentrated plankton and other microscopic marine life. Our pilot was a young blonde Ukranian second officer called Evita. On my request she headed out to sea for about three miles then turned due north. Once we had covered sixty miles Evita brought the craft down to hover some ten metres above the waves. I gingerly opened the small trapdoor on the underside of the ship, rolled a drum across to its edge and unscrewed the stopper. While the ship hovered I slowly poured the drum's contents through the trapdoor.

"Go forth and multiply," I said quietly as I poured. It wasn't a very original remark but it was all that I could think of at the time. At least it made the girls giggle.

From that northerly point we zigzagged southwards down the coast with the furthest distance out to sea set at eight miles. At each point of the zigzag another drum was heaved into the ocean. By the time the last drum was empty we had travelled some sixty miles south of Stockholm. Now all I could do was wait and hope that conditions would be right for the plankton and other material to multiply quickly and spread widely. There was every reason why it should. For the foreseeable future it would have no natural enemies. That job done we went back to base, loaded the fifteen drums of assorted waterweed and 'seeded' the river and the inland lake.

"Apart from occasional sampling and microscopic analysis we can forget about the waterways of the world for at least a couple of years," I reflected when we'd finished.

A quick break for lunch and then we got down to the afternoon's task. Half of our potted young trees had been unloaded — the deciduous ones — and I wanted to get them planted as soon as possible. Loading the car with the pegs that had been used to decide the placing of the houses we drove across the bridge and over to the proposed start of the eventual forest. Again the car's trip meter came in handy. The plan was to plant ten rows of ten trees one hundred and fifty metres apart. After that we would take some of the seeds that we'd brought and plant them at intervals between the young trees. I'd debated bringing them on in pots in the plastipod greenhouse that we'd be getting, but reasoned that with summer fast approaching they would grow nearly as fast in the ground. That would leave the greenhouse free for other things. It took us less than an hour to get the pegs in place, so we went back to base, borrowed a spare lorry and took half the trees back to the site and planted them. Hans had mentioned the previous evening that his team had a number of offcuts of metal piping for which he'd no use. Taking seven or eight of these I drove them into the ground far enough so that their tip reached the exact height of some of the young trees. In this way we would be able to measure their growth.

We completed the tree planting next day and then scattered some more grass seed over a couple of square miles beyond the proposed forest area. The girls were keen to go even farther afield but I restrained them. I felt it more sensible to wait and make sure grass would grow before using up too much of the seed.

On Saturday morning Nils, Hans and I held what our leader was pleased to call a progress meeting. This, he told us, was to be a regular weekly affair. We reviewed all that had been done in our first week. Hans and his team had completed the desalination plant and had started work on erecting the wind turbines that would provide us with power. One section of his gang was busy laying the pipes that would bring the water from the lake via a purification plant into the town. For the first time Nils gave us an outline of the financial measures that would be put in place once the remaining settlers arrived.

"Obviously there'll be no inflation on this world, at least for the foreseeable future," he told us. "Salary for everyone will be constant therefore, with no annual rises and no deductions. We won't be introducing taxes for some years yet. Before we left Earth I had some discussions with the man who will head the bank when it's set up. The unit of currency will be the crown, which will be equal to one euro. Salaries to everyone will be credited to their bank accounts on the last day of each month. It will be compulsory for all, even young children, to have a bank account. The banker will bring an adequate supply of notes and coins with him. Most if not all of us will become rich fairly quickly I would think. Everyone will have to pay for food and clothing, etc., but other than that there'll be nothing to spend on for a considerable time. To change the subject, I've been wondering whether we should rename our world; call it Europa or New Europe or something. What do you both think?"

Hans looked at me with a grin on his face. "What Nils really means is that he'd like to call it New Sweden." Nils protested loudly.

"If it comes to a vote," I said slowly, "I'd prefer to stick with Cara IV. None of the other colonised worlds has a name and a number so it's distinctive.

As far as a reference to Europe is concerned it might upset some people. Although the majority of settlers will be European in origin there will be some who have connections outwith Europe."

Hans agreed with me, so Cara IV it would remain. "We'll all be Carans, then," Nils remarked. "But I am going to claim one privilege of rank. The lake hereinafter will be Lake Gothenburg and the river the river Sverige. That's the Swedish name for Sweden in case you didn't know."

Apart from that meeting Saturday and Sunday were normal working days. While the settlers had been engaged in their various occupations the space ship crews had worked equally hard unloading cargo and setting up a number of the huge plastipods. The weather remained kind to us with a mixture of clouds and sunshine interspersed with the occasional light shower. By Sunday morning our greenhouse was erected and we started using the pots that previously had held the young trees for planting a variety of other things. We used native soil for this. Whether that would prove wise or not time would tell, but I hoped that there would be some bacteria alive around the inner surface of the pots. That weekend and the following few days were anxious times for all of us. Every day I scanned the riverside area where I had planted the quick growing seed. By the Wednesday of our second week my confidence was beginning to take a tumble. Niggling doubts persisted. In my diary that night I entered the terse comment: 'not a sign of green anywhere'.

Throughout this time I'd been keeping a close eye on my two assistants. Despite their enthusiasm at their initial interviews I still worried that they would not settle to the hard life that Cara IV promised. Also in my mind was that apart from the eighteen-year-old Pablo and myself they were the youngest of all of us. I was both relieved and delighted to see them going about their daily tasks with vigour and humour. In fact they seemed to revel in everything they did, no matter how menial. They also proved to be a lot stronger physically than I'd expected. Julie was the more muscular of the two and could heave hundredweight sacks of seed around just as easily as I could. Maria, being more slightly built, hadn't quite the same strength, but she did her share of the lifting without complaint. I thought that there might have been overtures from some of the single men, but I saw no sign of it in that first couple of weeks. Mind you, with everyone working a minimum twelve hour day there wasn't really any spare time for dalliance.

On Friday morning I had just finished washing and shaving and was ready to head for the *Ural Star* and breakfast when a loud knocking took me to the door. Maria and Julie were standing there impatiently. "Come and look," was all Maria said as the two of them turned and walked rapidly towards the river. I followed them quickly and when we got close to the bank the girls pointed seawards. Looking along the length of the river walk I blinked and refocused. My eyes weren't deceiving me. At least six patches of green could be seen. The largest was circular about the size of a small garden pond and the smallest about two feet square. Giving a whoop of joy I led the way carefully along the very edge of the river bank to look more closely. I was still slightly worried that it might be nothing more than a form of moss but my doubts vanished on closer inspection. There were indeed tiny shoots of grass to be seen. I think the three of us danced rather than walked to the *Ural Star* for breakfast. I took Nils aside and told him the good news.

"Great, well done," he enthused. "I'll send a signal to Paladia for the rest to come."

I'd been thinking about this. "I'd rather you left it for a few days," I told him. "We need to be cautious. It's unlikely, but something may yet happen to kill everything off. If that happened we'd look rather silly having to cancel when the ship is en route. Tell you what. I'll check on Tuesday morning. By then the grass should have grown noticeably. I'll inspect the trees as well to make sure they're healthy. As soon as I've done that I'll let you know and then you can send your signal." He seemed disappointed, but reluctantly agreed to my proposal. He insisted on telling all of our group though. There were happy faces all around as everyone set off to work. Although I tried to avoid looking at the grass for the next two or three days my eyes were inevitably drawn to it whenever I was close to the river.

Little had been seen of the two agtecs, the Lemaire brothers. They set off at dawn to their area inland and returned at dusk. They kept themselves strictly to themselves at all other times and I don't think they'd spoken a single word to anyone since our arrival, not even Nils. On the Monday morning I determined to pay them a visit. I had a good excuse for doing so. Now that our initial sowing of grass had been successful I proposed to start spreading seed inland. I needed to know what areas they had earmarked for crops and where they planned eventual grazing grounds. Taking one of the two cars that had been allocated to us I headed inland for a couple of kilometres. At first I could see no sign of life, but two plastipod greenhouses stood side by side and when I explored the first I found the two of them planting seed of some sort in pots. They'd obviously brought a supply of empty pots with them, something I wished now that I'd thought of.

Trying to get information from the two of them was like drawing teeth. They volunteered nothing and simply answered direct questions as tersely as possible. It took me more than an hour to establish exactly what they had done so far and what they had in the pipeline. They were planting extensive areas with wheat, maize, barley, potatoes and green vegetables. Little of this though would find its way into cooking pots: it was mostly intended for generating a future supply of seed. A similar fate awaited the tomatoes and other salad vegetables they were currently sowing in the plastipods. After a great deal of discussion between them in French, of which I understood not a word, we agreed on where the future grazing areas should be.

"You realise," I said as I was leaving, "it will be two or three years before there'll be enough grassland for us to bring in any sheep and cattle."

Henri shrugged. "No concern of ours. We'll be gone by then."

"Gone," I exclaimed. "Gone where?"

Another shrug of the shoulders. "Who knows? Our contract is only for two years. When the second or third lot of settlers arrive we will go back to Earth on their returning ship and be reassigned. Our work here will be over long before then. As we keep saying, we are not farmers. We simply experiment and advise; set things up for the farmers to take over."

This was news to me and I was fairly certain would be to Nils as well. I knew that there were a couple of farmers among the remaining colonists for Stockholm, but I had assumed they would take up separate areas from the Lemaires. In a way the information pleased me. They were a strange pair and I couldn't see them integrating into the tightly knit community we were becoming. I got back to base just in time to see the first of the cargo ships lifting off for departure. This was the one that had brought all the building parts and had completed discharge the day before.

On her own initiative Julie had started keeping a detailed daily weather log. Looking back at it later I realised just how fortunate we had been. Temperatures for that month of April had been in the high sixties Fahrenheit and reached seventy-one on the twenty-fifth. In other respects it had been reminiscent of a typical Scottish April with frequent short sharp showers and light to moderate winds. There'd been no protracted downpours to interrupt outside work. That meant perfect growing conditions for us and ideal conditions for Hans and his men and women.

As promised I made my first task on the following Tuesday an inspection of the grass. The green areas had spread widely, both along the river bank and also the seashore. A close look at the early growth showed that the stems were already about a centimetre high and were looking extremely healthy. Even more pleasing was the sight of a sheen of green across the proposed parkland. Our young trees hadn't increased in height but they too showed every sign of having bedded in. I conveyed the news to Nils and then gave the girls their instructions for the rest of the day. We now had two cars at our disposal.

"I want you to take a car, load up half a dozen or so bags of seed and head south," I told them. "Once you get a kilometre south of the far edge of the forest area head inland for five kilometres, then turn south again and start sowing. Whichever of you is driving keep to about fifteen to twenty kilometres an hour. The other sits in the back seat and throws handfuls of seed out of the window. This should result in small patches at intervals over a wide area. Go as far as the next main river, which is about sixty-five kilometres from here. The turn inland again for another five kilometres and make your way back, still spreading the seed thinly. I've had a word with the duty cook on the *Ural Star* and she'll have a packed lunch ready for you to collect." They set off happily.

Bernard Stocks

Picking up a packed lunch in my turn I took the other car and headed north on a similar mission. I'd hoped to find someone to take with me but everyone was engaged on some task or other. Once I reached my start point I set the controls at due north and fifteen kilometres an hour and put the vehicle on automatic pilot. With a bag of seed on the passenger seat it was easy to pull out handful after handful and throw each out of the open window as I rolled along. It sounds boring, but I was more than content. It was a warm sunny day with just a light breeze and I occupied my mind by visualising the land as it would look in two or three years' time, covered in lush green grass. The next main river was over sixty kilometres to the north and the planned site for the third township to be set up. One or two smaller streams meandered down to the sea between the two wide rivers, but they were narrow enough for me to hop the car over them. I reached my destination just before one o'clock and ate my lunch sitting on the river bank admiring the view. The layout was fairly similar to that at Stockholm. There was a range of low hills some eight kilometres inland, but no handy lake. Water supplies here would have to come from the river or the sea.

The return journey took me nearly three hours. My first call on getting back to Stockholm was on Nils. I learned that he'd sent the signal immediately after I'd spoken to him in the morning.

"Our remaining complement will be lifting off from Paladia the day after tomorrow," he reported. "They're due to arrive here in ten weeks' time. I've also relayed the good news to our masters back on Earth. They got a message back to me half an hour ago, strictly formal and no attempt to congratulate us. They have the next two hundred settlers picked out and hope to have them on their way inside a month. That means they will be here in just under a year's time."

CHAPTER NINE

Just over a month from our first landing Hans announced that the supply of electricity and running water to all existing buildings had been completed. According to my diary the exact date was Wednesday the thirteenth of May. Nils called a meeting in the school hall that evening.

"Starting on Friday everyone will take over their own catering," he announced without preamble. "We will finish stocking the food store at lunchtime tomorrow. We'll make the afternoon a holiday for us all to enable you to draw your first week's rations. Until the bank is set up everything is free: after that you'll need to buy your requirements. We've set the rations as follows and by weight rather than by the number of tins or packets. Each person will receive five hundred grams of meat and the same weight of poultry and fish per week. The issue of vegetables includes potatoes and is set at one kilogram. Flour and yeast is available for bread making, the weekly quota per household being one kilogram bag of flour and one packet of dried yeast. Incidentally, there will be a professional baker among the new arrivals, so you'll only have to make your own for three or four weeks. Other quantities include one kilogram of fruit, dried or tinned, three packets of soup powder, five hundred grams of tea or coffee powder, eighty grams of sugar and the equivalent in dried milk of three pints."

There was a murmuring among the assembled ranks. Nils held up his hand. "I know it doesn't sound a lot and it does mean a bit of belt tightening. But Dr. Lupesku assures me that it is perfectly adequate and healthy for everyone, even those doing the heaviest of manual labour. Those of you who haven't already done so can supplement your diet very easily by following the advice given you by Alex regarding the use of your gardens. You keep everything you grow yourselves. As a suggestion, it might be a good idea to form small communes with each member concentrating on one or two items and dividing the results between you. However, that's up to individuals to decide. The motto's the same: the more you grow the more you eat."

After the meeting Nils called me aside. "Can you use another greenhouse?" he asked. "There's one of the smaller plastipods to spare. I can find another use for it if you don't want it."

"I'll certainly take it," I replied. "In fact I could take another two or three if they were going begging." Hans was still around and I wanted to see him. I had a job in mind for him and his gang that wouldn't take too much time and would be a tremendous boon. It didn't take much persuading to get him to agree to lay on a supply of water to our existing greenhouse and the one Nils was giving us.

"After all," I said to him, tongue in cheek. "You'll have a lot of spare time on your hands now the main services are installed."

He gave me an old-fashioned stare. "Don't you believe it. We've the rest of the houses to erect and fit out, plus the extra shop units and other buildings. On top of that we've to finish unloading the ships. The *Ural Star* is leaving tomorrow and the other two within the week."

On my way back to our office I formulated plans for the coming month. There was still much to be done. Maria and Julie were both engaged on paper work when I went in. Settling down in my chair I outlined our programme. "Get your sleeves rolled up," I warned them. "We're in for a busy time. We're getting a second greenhouse in the next day or two, so there'll be planting to be done. The ships are leaving in the next few days, so we can sow the northern park area and the coniferous forest. When that's done I want to scatter grass seed over a wide area inland. On top of all that I think we should plant up the gardens of the other one hundred and fifty houses that Hans and his crew will be putting up. It will be the middle of July before the new colonists get here. That's a bit late for them to get any benefits from their gardens this year."

The *Ural Star* left the next morning. Captain Petrovic came to say goodbye. "Next time I come I want to see a huge area of green in my visiscreen as I approach to go into orbit," he said as we shook hands. I told him that we'd do our best. The remaining ships left over the next seven days. Hans had given me a temporary loan of the Spanish youngster Pablo, who was surplus to requirements for a couple of weeks. This raised something of a minor problem. It was obvious that Pablo was smitten by Maria; it was equally obvious that Maria wasn't the slightest bit interested in him. Because we were working mainly in pairs that meant I couldn't put the two of them together. It would have been too awkward for them both. Normally Pablo paired with me, though on the odd occasion I'd put him with Julie.

It took us three days to plant the second area of parkland and the coniferous forest. Heavy and prolonged showers of rain on two of the days hampered our progress. By now daytime temperatures were well into the eighties and coupled with high humidity made working conditions uncomfortable. To compensate everything grew quickly. Our early grass was now six or seven inches high and the trees in the southern forest had shot up more than an inch. Most of the gardens that had been sown were turning green. Hans and his gang were still busy laying on electricity and water to the newly erected houses so the next task we tackled was the planting trip inland. There was still plenty of grass seed left so I planned to use two days for this. On the first day the girls took one car and Pablo came with me. They went twelve kilometres south; we went the same distance north. Starting some eight or nine miles from the coast we headed due west scattering seed thinly for over ninety kilometres before turning and going north, south in the case of the girls. At the thirty kilometre mark we turned and headed back east to the coast. If the grass spread as I hoped it would a large inland area would be created for grazing within three years.

After that burst of effort we took things a little more easily. The pots the conifers had come in filled the remaining space in our original greenhouse. For the second one we beat a path down the middle and planted directly into the ground. I'd brought a lot of odds and ends with me from Italy. From the time I'd been appointed to the expedition I'd been saving up seeds and stones from all the fresh fruit I'd eaten. Thus I had a motley collection of plum, apricot, peach and cherry stones along with seeds from oranges, grapefruit, apples, pears, soft fruit and the like. These were all planted haphazardly. Experimentally I'd also brought a dozen each of hydrangea and rhododendron shoots. These I'd put in plastic bags with a minimum of damp soil. My reasoning was that they would be easy to maintain, gave plenty of colour when grown and could be propagated very easily. These all went into gardens including Julie's, Maria's and my own.

CHAPTER TEN

Time flies when you're busy and it seemed no time at all until word spread round the camp that the ship carrying the remaining colonists was less than a week away. Nils had more detailed information when we arrived for our regular Saturday progress meeting.

"I've been in radio contact with Captain Stovini of the *St. Matthew*," he informed Hans and I. "That's a Paladian ship. I'd thought that they would have been coming in the ship that took them from Earth to Paladia, but apparently they were transhipped. The *St. Matthew* is less than half the size of the regular ships so it shouldn't do quite so much damage to your grass, Alex. There's additional cargo coming as well. There's half a dozen self assembly small factory units, some sports gear and two hoverbuses among other things."

"What do we need hoverbuses for?" Hans wanted to know.

"They're more for the future than the present," Nils replied. "Once other towns spring up there'll be a demand for a linking bus service. For a start they'll be a fair amount of toing and froing on official business. Once each town settles down everyone will have more leisure time and we'll encourage people to visit other towns. After all, there won't be much else for them to do in the early days. Knowing the human race as I do I expect that within two or three years there'll be a football league, tennis tournaments and maybe one or two other sports. Which reminds me, Alex. Over the next year or so you might give some thought to the possibility of laying out one or two golf courses."

It was ten in the morning of Friday the third of July when the *St. Matthew* made landfall. Everyone was gathered at the edge of North Park as the ship sank slowly to the ground. Nils and Hans walked forward to greet the new arrivals. They would take them to the schoolhouse, give a short welcome speech and hand out the keys to the houses. Once settled in there would be a formal lunch on the ship and Nils would make a longer speech. From a short distance away I watched with interest as the ramp came down and the first of our new townsfolk emerged. There were several families to start with, then some obviously married couples followed by a group of seven or eight young women. They were all passably good looking but right away I only had eyes for one. She was about five feet seven, slim with a freckled face and a small mouth and nose. But her crowning glory was the mane of red hair that hung down nearly a foot below her shoulders. I don't know whether or not she felt the intensity of my gaze, but she looked my way for a second and caught my eye. She gave me a flashing smile, then looked away and started speaking to one of the others in the group. I felt a gentle hand on my shoulder.

A voice said softly: "Put your eyes back in your head, Alex, or they'll fall out." I turned to find Nico, our doctor, standing just behind me and smiling. "I agree though, she is quite a sight for sore eyes."

"Was I that obvious?" I asked, somewhat shamefaced. He just laughed.

The official party for the formal lunch consisted of Nils, Hans, Nico and their wives plus myself. I sat next to Nico and Jennifer. The latter had been doing some detective work and was able to tell me that the name of the red headed vision was Donna Mallory, that she was Irish, unattached and accompanied by her younger sister Teresa. Unfortunately she was sitting towards the bottom end of the table and on the same side as myself so I wasn't able to feast my eyes. There was a small dais at one end of the dining area and after the meal I had to join Nils and Hans there. Nils repeated the official welcome, Hans detailed most of the work that had been carried out to date and I gave my own little contribution and encouragement to take up gardening. Once the speechmaking was over tea and coffee were served and the seven of us began to drift among the crowd. Without making it too obvious I fairly soon manoeuvred to the spot where Jennifer was already talking to Donna and her sister. After introducing me Jennifer diplomatically moved away.

Close up I thought that Donna was even more beautiful than I'd first imagined. I noted for the first time that she had green eyes. She was wearing a simple dark green dress that set off her red hair to perfection. Teresa, her sister, was attractive in her own right but very different in appearance. Her hair was shorter, darker and a shade of auburn and she had a fuller figure than her older sister.

"So what brings you both to this outpost of civilisation?" It wasn't the greatest of chat up lines but it was all that I could think of at the time.

"I guess we both wanted something more adventurous than the daily round back home," Donna replied in a warm and slightly husky voice. Over the next few minutes I learned they came from Sligo, that Donna was twenty-three and Teresa two years younger, that their parents had split up and that since leaving school they'd worked in call centres. Both had been keen amateur cooks since childhood and they were going to open the baker's shop. Soon Teresa drifted away to speak to someone else, thus earning my eternal gratitude, and Donna started to question me on the work I'd been doing. She seemed genuinely interested so I made up my mind to be bold.

"I understand you're having your evening meal here on the ship," I said. "After that I'd be only too delighted to show you around if you like." She indicated her agreement and we arranged to meet at her house at eight o'clock.

The rest of the afternoon seemed to drag by. I wanted to be alone so that I could think exclusively about Donna, so I found some jobs for Julie and Maria and made the excuse that I wanted to check on the forests. I needed time to analyse the events of the past few hours. Girls had never played a significant part of my life up to then. I'd dallied here and there, been to bed with one or two, but I'd been far too intent on building my career to take anyone seriously. I'd always known that love had been absent from all my relationships. Certainly I'd never experienced the feelings that engulfed me from the moment I saw Donna. By the end of the afternoon I knew without doubt that I was in love at last and that she was the only girl for me.

The sisters had chosen a house across the river, one on the sea front. I was there at five to eight to find Donna ready and waiting for me. She'd changed into a simple white cotton blouse and dark blue satin trousers. I'd half expected Teresa to be tagging along, but was delighted when I learned she had gone off to visit someone. At first I felt somewhat tongue tied, but Donna quickly put me at ease. She complimented me on the gardens which in truth were looking trim and green. There were even one or two flowers beginning to come out here and there. Soon we were chattering away like old friends as I took her over the park towards our embryo forest. By now the grass was almost six inches high and Donna asked if I was proposing to cut it.

"Not this year," was my response. "I want it to grow strong and spread, plus there are some bare patches needing reseeded. We're planning to lay down football and hockey pitches plus a couple or three tennis courts next year, so we'll make the first cut then."

Changing the subject abruptly she asked me about my childhood. I gave her a quick resume without putting too much emphasis on my parents' continual absences. It seemed to strike a chord with her.

"I can sympathise," she said slowly when I'd finished. "Ours was never a happy home, either. Most of my memories are of constant rowing between my mother and father, usually fuelled by drink. There were six of us children. Maureen and Seamus were twins and the oldest; they're five years older than me. Then came Michael, me and Teresa and the youngest is Patrick who's just eighteen, or was when we left. Maureen was a gem. It was she rather than my parents who brought us up and looked after us."

"Is that the main reason you decided to come to Cara IV?" I asked.

She thought for a moment. "I suppose it had something to do with it. But I meant what I said this afternoon. We both wanted some adventure in our lives and the chance to do something more worthwhile than sitting at a computer or hooked up to a telephone all day. Life at home generally had too many problems as well. Pollution, even in Ireland, is rife, there are food shortages and crime is rampant. It's not safe to walk the streets at night so we had very little social life. It may sound silly, but I thought that there would be more chance here of meeting a nice young man."

There was a smile on her face and a dimple in her cheek as she said this, and I couldn't resist the opening. I turned to face her. "I hope you already have," I said softly.

The smile left her face. "Maybe," she murmured. "But let's not rush things. We've a lifetime ahead of us."

I wanted to take her in my arms, hold her tight and shower her with kisses and it took an effort to restrain myself. But I realised that she was right. We'd only met for the first time nine hours previously and while I was sure of my own feelings she would need time to adjust and analyse hers. I changed the subject slightly.

"You realise that life isn't going to be a bed of roses here," I pointed out. "Hard work, long hours, same old food day in day out. No TV or radio, no cinemas. No fancy clothes and no make-up and nothing much to do in whatever leisure time we do get."

"Of course I thought of all that before I signed up," she replied a trifle scornfully. "I'll survive. I'm used to hard work and long hours. TV bores me, I'm not clothes conscious and I've never used much make up. I'll miss the radio, though," she concluded with a smile. When I left her at her door just after ten she gave me the briefest of kisses on the lips before turning quickly and going inside. I took that as a good omen.

The Mallorys weren't the only representatives from the Emerald Isle among our new townsfolk. The two farmers in the group were also Irish and lifelong friends. Sean Flannigan and Eamonn O'Shea were in their early forties and had worked adjacent farms just outside Limerick. Both were family men, Sean with two sons and a daughter and Eamonn with a son and daughter, all above school age. Eamonn specialised in cereals while Sean was a dairy farmer. Until some animals arrived they intended to work together. The morning after their arrival they came to see me and ask if I would take them up to the prospective farmland to meet and talk with the Lemaire brothers.

"Of course I will," was my response. "But be warned. They're a strange pair who keep themselves to themselves and seem to actively resent people knowing what they're doing."

We set off just after ten and found the Lemaires working in one of their greenhouses. I didn't particularly want to talk to them again, so after making the introductions I wandered off for a walk and left the four of them to it. I kept within sight of them all the time, but it was over an hour before Sean signalled me that they were ready to go back to town. Once we were moving I asked them how they'd got on.

"Not too bad in the end," it was Eamonn that answered. "They're going to turn the whole farming operation over to us from Monday. As far as we could tell from their expression they seemed quite pleased about it. Once we've taken over they're heading south and west for a few miles to experiment with growing cotton, sugar beet and sugar cane. I must say, though, that they've done a pretty good job up here. Everything's in first class order."

Many of the new arrivals were tradesmen or professional people and had brought specialised equipment with them. This included a fully equipped baker's shop for the Mallory sisters. By the following weekend Stockholm began to resemble a normal small town or village. Apart from the bakery and the bank we had an electrician and a plumber, a dentist, a combined barbers and ladies hairdresser and even a hypnotherapist. By far the most important new member of the town was our banker. Given Switzerland's centuries old expertise in the banking industry it was no surprise that he came from that country. Hermann Klost was in his fifties, a solidly built man with iron grey hair and moustache. He brought with him a staff of three, a young male accountant and two teenage girl tellers. Along with Nico, our doctor, he was invited to join what Nils called our committee of management and the two of them attended all our progress meetings from that time on. I was very much in the dark as to how our monetary system would work and I sought out Nils on the Friday evening before the first meeting of the newly enlarged committee.

"I'm not sure that I fully understand it myself," Nils confessed. "From what I've gathered everyone will need to have a bank account into which those of us who are salaried will have their wages paid monthly. Herr Klost has brought with him a large supply of banknotes and coins, enough according to him to last for the next twenty years, by which time we should be able to manufacture our own. In any case further supplies will be sent from Earth from time to time. Each banker for each new township will do the same. Nominally the Space Council allocates a capital sum to us annually. In fact they don't pay us anything, but that nominal sum is credited to the budget of Cara IV. From that our wages are paid together with those of everybody who basically works for the community. Private traders generate their own income. That, I believe, is a simple explanation. In practice it's a lot more complicated."

We now had a police force, made up by an experienced male sergeant and two rookie constables, one male, one female. Personally I thought that was somewhat excessive and in fact they had little or no work to do. Two men set up a refuse collection service and oversaw the collection of items for recycling such as glassware and paper, levying a small charge for the service. Though people had little time for bathing Nils also appointed a full time lifeguard who was also responsible for looking after the beach and the river banks. Religious needs were now in the hands of two churchmen. The Protestant minister was an Austrian, Fritz Holman and the Catholic priest an Italian, Guiseppi Latto. Only one building had been set aside for religious purposes and we were worried that this might cause friction. Our fears were groundless. The two men immediately became fast friends and quickly agreed on sharing the somewhat austere premises they'd been allocated.

One of the things that surprised me was that all the two hundred who had come to Stockholm were pure bred Europeans. Even the three Russians among them were from the extreme west of that country. I put the point to Nils.

"I gather that was deliberate policy," he confirmed. "This first settlement was deemed so important that the powers that be wanted every possible chance for harmony among the colonists. You'll find that when future groups arrive there'll be more of a mix, with a significant number of black, Asian and Chinese among them."

By the end of August our town had settled down to a regular routine. Most of us still worked through all the hours of daylight, but we were beginning to reap rewards from our efforts. Front gardens were now a riot of colour. With little else to do in what little spare time they had people took a pride in caring for their property. The first of the home grown vegetables were ready for harvesting, thus improving our daily diet. In the early days I'd become friendly with Nico and Jennifer, the Edinburgh connection forging a bond between the three of us. I'd been in the habit of spending three or four evenings a week with them, talking or playing card games, scrabble or monopoly. With Donna's arrival the threesome became a foursome. Donna and Jennifer took to each other immediately much to my satisfaction. My relationship with Donna was progressing slowly and by the time the first month was over I was sure that she cared for me. I was very careful not to press matters, content to let her set the pace. Physical contact was restricted to a chaste goodnight kiss on her doorstep.

One evening at the end of August Donna invited me to a meal with her and Teresa at their home. They'd prepared a fairly straightforward dish of tinned chicken and tinned vegetables with tinned fruit salad to follow. I can't remember how it started, but while we were doing the washing up Donna and I got into an argument over cooking. She contended that men were less capable than women. It was all very good natured, but it ended with me inviting the two of them to supper with me the next night. Teresa called off as she was meeting friends. My childhood days had given me plenty of experience in making my own meals and I'd always been imaginative in preparing them. For this challenge I took some carrot thinnings and baby potatoes from the garden along with two or three outside cabbage leaves. I made gravy with some oxtail soup powder, put this with the vegetables into a casserole dish, switched the microwave oven to low and simmered at medium heat for just over an hour. Then I added a tin of beef stew and left the oven on low heat for another thirty minutes. For dessert I opened a prized tinned steamed pudding that I'd been keeping for a special occasion.

Donna looked lovelier that evening than I'd ever seen her before. Her hair shone like fire. She was dressed very simply in an emerald green blouse and maroon skirt and for the first time since we'd met was wearing nylon stockings and high heels. When I opened the door to her I was thankful I'd made the effort and changed out of my working clothes into something a bit more presentable. We talked idly of the day's happenings through the meal and the washing up. Going back into the living room I sat down on one of the chairs and looked up at her.

"What would you like to do?" I asked "We can sit and talk, go for a walk or go round and see Nico and Jennifer. You're the guest, so it's your choice."

Very deliberately she came across and sat down on my lap. "This is what I want to do," she said softly. Her arms went round me, she pulled me to her and kissed me passionately. I responded in kind, stroking her lovely hair as I did so. Her fingers caressed the back of my neck. After some ten minutes I drew back slightly.

"Where do we go from here?" I whispered.

A wonderful light stole into her eyes. She stood up and pulled me from the chair. "We go to bed, silly," she whispered back. I needed no second invitation.

Much later, as she lay soft and warm in my arms, I heard her give a suppressed giggle. "What's so funny?" I asked.

"I was just wondering what we're going to call the baby," she replied in a matter of fact tone.

Startled, I put my hands on her shoulders and gently pushed her away from me. "What makes you think there'll be one?"

She giggled again. "Well, it's that time of the month when I'm most likely to conceive, I'm not on the pill and you weren't wearing a condom. I'd say it was a fifty-fifty chance."

"Aren't you worried?" I asked.

"Not in the least," was her reply. "Are you?"

I didn't answer that directly. More abruptly than I intended I said: "Donna, will you marry me?"

"You don't have to marry me just because I might be pregnant," she replied with a tiny frown across her forehead.

"My darling, I don't care if you're having one baby or a hundred or none at all." I said hotly. "I want to marry you because I love you with all my heart and with all my soul and I've done so from the first minute I set eyes on you. I want to marry you because life without you would be unbearable."

She kissed me. "In that case of course I'll marry you. I can't say that I fell for you as quickly as you fell for me, though. It took me two whole days before I realised that you were the only one for me. Now let's stop talking and make doubly sure that baby's on the way."

CHAPTER ELEVEN

We were married three days later. Much to my surprise I learned that despite her origins Donna wasn't a Catholic. In fact her religious views were very similar to mine. We both believed in a divine power but preferred to worship privately rather than as part of a congregation. In a diplomatic move we asked both the minister and the priest to conduct the ceremony jointly. I wore my uniform and Donna looked breathtaking in a dress of the palest blue. We were blessed with a cloudless, sunny and warm day. All our immediate friends packed the small church cum chapel, but the whole community gathered outside and listened through the open door. I heard someone saying as I walked in to await my bride that they weren't going to miss such a historic occasion. Teresa and Jennifer were the bridesmaids and Nico was my best man. The service itself was short but poignant, lasting just over twenty-five minutes. Afterwards a meal had been laid on in the schoolhouse, Nils having authorised a special issue of food off the ration. Though ingredients were in short supply Teresa had somehow managed to bake a large wedding cake and there was enough for everyone in town to have a small piece.

Any sort of honeymoon was out of the question but we wanted to do something to preserve the old traditions. Thus we took one of the cars, drove south for some thirty miles and spent the night making love on a beach. Thankfully it was a warm and balmy night and we'd taken a sleeping bag with us anyway. It may not have been the traditional week or more beside the Mediterranean or on some tropical island but we both agreed that it was a memory we'd always treasure. When we returned to Stockholm the next day we found that Hans had cemented our new status. Another room had been added to our home.

Apart from the fact that we were blissfully happy married life made little difference to either of us. There was still plenty of work to be done. Donna still rose at four o'clock each morning to go to the bakery and I still worked from dawn to dusk. As September gave way to October, however, and the nights began to draw in rapidly we had more and more time together. Though content with our own company we kept up our routine of exchanging visits with Nico and Jennifer. One evening when our wives were engaged in some sort of feminine discussion in another room I asked Nico why he had come to Cara IV. I'd learned that he had had a promising career as a surgeon in Edinburgh and thought it strange that he should abandon what would have been a comfortable life for the wilderness of outer space.

"Putting it simply, I wanted to be a real doctor," was his reply. "Medicine is so far advanced on Earth now that doctors are really little more than computer operators. Nearly all diagnoses and operations are done by machines and robots. Basically anybody that can read and write, remember all the parts and functions of the body and work a computer can be a doctor nowadays. Here I have to rely entirely on my own ability and skill. Perhaps my only regret is that there is so little to do. Physical work and exercise, a clean atmosphere and healthy though basic food equals general good health."

"How well are you equipped to deal with an emergency?" I wanted to know.

"I've got a supply of the most vital medicines that should last until we can manufacture our own. Because there are no native bacteria or viruses concerns such as blood disorders, cancer and respiratory ailments will be rare. The operating theatre is modern and well equipped. Broken bones, which are likely to be the most frequent problem, are easy to deal with. With Jennifer's help and nursing skills I'm confident I can handle anything short of an epidemic. Just to be on the safe side I'm going to run courses in basic first aid through the winter. My only worry is that five or six women decide to give birth at the same time, but I judge the odds against that are pretty high."

In the third week of October Donna left the house one afternoon without telling me where she was going. I was deep in calculations of some kind and my mind barely registered the fact. It was nearly an hour before she returned and when she did she looked more radiant than I had ever seen her.

"I've got some news for you," she announced.

"Good news, I hope," was my response.

"The best there is. I've just been to see Nico and he's confirmed what I already suspected. I'm two months pregnant. Are you pleased?"

My heart was too full for words. I simply took her in my arms and hugged and kissed her. When I did find my voice I was husky with emotion. "Of course I'm pleased. I'm over the moon." I did a quick calculation. "Let's see. That makes it sometime in May, doesn't?"

"I hadn't thought that far ahead," she confessed. "I'll take your word for it. But there's one disappointment. I was hoping our baby would be the first to be born here, but it won't. Nico told me that Jennifer is nearly three months ahead of me and there's someone else just a month behind her. We won't be making history after all."

"We've already made history," I pointed out. "We were the first to get married."

The end of October heralded a spell of strong winds and near constant rain. Little could be done out of doors. I took to giving Donna and Teresa a hand in the bakery. Though it meant a drastic change in my routine I wasn't too displeased as it gave me more time with Donna. After a week or so of this unpleasant weather Nils called our committee of management together. He was concerned about the onset of boredom and had one or two ideas to maintain morale. His plan was to canvass the whole population and unearth any entertainment skills they might have. This initiative brought almost instant reward. Several of the incomers had brought musical instruments with them and in a short space of time we discovered an Austrian man who played the melodeon, an Italian lady fiddle player and two guitarists. There were also two or three would be drummers. Hans managed to make up two drums using spare materials and hey presto, we had ourselves a band.

From there it was a short step to putting on a regular Saturday night dance. The first one was held in the school, which could hold no more than sixty people. So many were turned away that we cleared out one of the medium sized plastipods and thereafter used that for all functions. Practically the whole community attended the dances. These were great fun, especially in the first few weeks. With so many nationalities having their own traditional dances, we set aside an hour every week to learn new ones. Thus our repertoire gained polkas from Hungary, folk dances from Spain and Russia and many more. Jennifer and I played our part, introducing the Gay Gordons, the St. Bernards Waltz and the Eightsome Reel into the mix. One of the older German men had been a square dance caller back on Earth and was soon encouraged to pursue his art. The popular dances of the day when we'd left Earth weren't neglected. The two main ones were the la-la, a sort of cross between an old fashioned conga and military counter marching and the heydal. The latter could be danced solo or with a partner and involved a somewhat complicated coordinated series of body movements.

By Christmas we had also set up a weekly concert on Wednesday evenings. There were a number of fine singers in our midst, all with a seemingly endless repertoire of popular songs and folk songs from their respective countries. Donna and Teresa formed a trio with Sean Flannigan's oldest daughter Kathleen. They sang a mixture of recent pop hits and old Irish favourites. All three had fine voices and took solo spots, but their greatest attraction was their close harmony singing. Before we knew it seven or eight people had formed a small repertory group, writing their own short plays and performing them from time to time at the concerts. These usually lasted no more than fifteen minutes and became very popular.

There was much discussion around the middle of December as to how Christmas Day and New Year's Day should be celebrated. Nils had declared that both would be a public holiday. Cards and presents were out of the question as were any sort of decorations. I regretted not having included holly and mistletoe among the plants I'd brought. As both days fell on a Saturday the usual weekly dances would go ahead. The general opinion was that most people wanted to spend the daylight hours in their own homes or in small groups rather than try to organise one big communal meal. Nils authorised the release of a three pound tin of turkey for each household on top of the normal rations.

The early arrival of darkness from the beginning of November onwards brought one unforeseen problem. There was no street lighting. Most nights were cloudy, which meant little or no moonlight. Though we all had torches it was unnerving for many, so Hans and his team got to work. Out of the spare material that was available they provided two streetlamps for each street. Though they didn't shed a great deal of light they were a comfort to us all and brought a semblance of normality to the town. Living was still austere to say the least. We were thankful to have running water and electricity, but our homes were very bare. We had no carpets or curtains, no lampshades, pictures or ornaments. There was no paint to brighten up the unrelieved metallic grey outside and inside. Armchairs and couches were conspicuous by their absence and it took a long time to adapt to there being no TV sets dominating the rooms.

For Christmas we spent the whole day with Nico and Jennifer. Teresa and her then boy friend, a young Pole named Jan, were also invited. We pooled our rations for the occasion. At the dance that evening I watched closely, but everyone seemed to be in high spirits. There was one other Scot in our community besides Jennifer and myself, a former beekeeper named Alastair Baird who was in his mid forties. The three of us insisted on inducting our families into the customs of Hogmanay. Despite the absence of such things as whisky, coal and black bun we honoured the tradition as faithfully as we could. I showed Donna how to make shortbread and with this we solemnly first footed each other. My only regret was at not hearing the sound of the pipes.

As the dance on New Year's Day was coming to a close Nils made a short speech. After wishing everyone a happy New Year he went on to review the year past.

"I am amazed at how much we have accomplished in nine short months. We have turned a considerable part of this barren waste into a productive and colourful environment. We have established a strong and vibrant community. This has been done thanks to the hard work put in by each and every one of you and I thank you all. I have decided that everyone's contribution must be remembered by future generations. To this end I have discussed with Matthew Van Klees, who as I'm sure you know is a sculptor, the preparation of a suitable monument. In the next few weeks we will search for and bring to town a block of stone. On this Matthew will engrave the names of all two hundred of us. We will then decide on the most appropriate place to erect it. In this way those that come after us will be able to pay their own homage to the first settlers on this world."

As Nils left the platform to great applause Hans jumped up on the stage and held up his hand for silence. "All that has been achieved to date could not have been done without the right leadership. I think you will all agree that Nils Anderssen has given us that leadership. If you had glasses in your hand I would ask you to raise them to him. As it is I would ask you for another round of applause for the man who will surely go down in history as the father of Cara IV, Nils Anderssen." This time there was a massive cheer and more than three minutes of clapping. Nils simply looked embarrassed!

It was a very mild winter. Reference to Julie's log shows that the lowest overnight temperature was five degrees Centigrade (forty-one in Fahrenheit terms). During daytime fifty to sixty degrees was the normal reading, though in mid January we had a couple of days of a heavy mist that kept the mercury down into the forties. Thanks to this growth in the grass, trees and other plants continued, though on a much reduced scale. To compensate for the time I was spending in the bakery I turned control of the greenhouses over to Julie and Maria, leaving all the decision making to them. They kept the temperature of both in the low seventies and right through the winter continued to supply the likes of lettuces and tomatoes to the recently opened greengrocer's shop. The farms, too, were able to supply much more than we'd expected, including a considerable quantity of grain. Bashful though they may have been the Lemaires had obviously done a first class job. Donna reckoned that more than a quarter of her purchases of flour came from the farms, thus eking out the supply that we'd brought with us on the cargo ships.

As it had been for more than three centuries whenever a group of men get together, one of the first desires was to play football. A supply of balls along with other sports gear had been included in our cargo. I came under great pressure to cut sufficient grass to lay down a pitch on one of the parks. My refusal wasn't popular, even though I promised there would be one by the end of the following summer. I believed my resistance was justified. Though growing well the grass was still not fully established nor producing enough seed to ensure spreading. To cut it at that time would have weakened it. Eventually the enthusiasts settled for a half sized pitch on a suitable area of beach and got some sort of five-a-side competition going. I assume that I was forgiven in the end, for after a week or so I was invited to join one of the eight teams.

Throughout the winter I made an inspection of the surrounding countryside at least once a week, with forty mile trips north and south once a fortnight. I was pleased with all that I saw. Much of the early grass had seeded and with the prevailing easterly wind there was evidence in the small patches of young grass that the seeds produced had spread over a wide area. The young deciduous trees that we'd brought had doubled in size and all those that we'd planted from scratch were showing above ground. Even the conifers had grown by some fifty per cent, though there was no sign as yet of the ones that we had planted since our arrival. We'd used most of our second plastipod greenhouse for planting fruit seeds and stones. These were coming along nicely and some were as much as six inches high. In the initial planting of the front gardens I'd included bulbs for winter flowering. When the first snowdrops came into bud on the second day of January it gave everyone a boost. These were quickly followed by crocuses, hyacinths and daffodils. By mid March these gardens were a riot of colour.

As is always the case there was a downside. We had used up nearly all the seeds and other things that we'd brought. I spent more than two days going round each household personally imploring everyone to collect and store as much seed as they could and instructing them on how to split and store their bulbs at the end of the growing season.

Though I was mostly concerned with what was happening on land I didn't neglect the aquatic side of things. Our male and female constables were both keen rowers and willingly agreed to take monthly samples of the ocean for me. It wasn't safe for them to go more than a mile out to sea, but that was sufficient for my purposes. By the end of October inspection under a microscope showed that plankton in reasonable quantities had reached that far and by Christmas had even spread into shallow water. The water weed in the river and lake was also healthy and growing fast. I revised my earlier estimate of six years before we could bring in fish to five and then to four.

CHAPTER TWELVE

Saturday morning meetings of the committee of management had by now become standard. Mostly these lasted for about an hour or so and we discussed progress, dealt with the few problems that arose and made tentative plans for the future. I think it was the second one in February that Nils had some news for us.

"I've just been in radio contact with the ship bringing the next two hundred colonists," he announced. "It's one of yours, Alex, the *Caledonian Cavalier*, under Commander Craig. The next settlement will be on the river south of us. It wasn't a very clear line, so I didn't get too much information. The director is a Minos Sousopolis, Greek of course, and the town will be called Athens. Their estimated date of arrival is Saturday April the twentieth. Commander Craig will contact us two or three days beforehand to give us an exact landing forecast."

I had mixed feelings about the news. While it would be exciting to welcome new settlers there had been something very satisfying about being the only group in the world. In a rather twisted way I'd have been quite happy to have kept it that way. I realised that this was rather a selfish view to take but it persisted. Mind you, I was still very much in love with Donna. I suppose I would have been even happier if there was just the two of us playing at being Adam and Eve! I didn't have much time for reflection as Nils turned to me.

"I've been getting enquiries about the possibility of pets, Alex," he said. "I suspect that's your province. When do you think we'll be able to bring some in?"

"You can probably answer that better than I can, Nils," I replied. "By pets I take it you mean cats and dogs. That means additional calls on our meat and other rations as there's no pet food among the stores. Do we have enough reserves to feed animals and if so how many?"

Nils turned the tables on me. "It's back to you again. When do you anticipate we'll be producing our own meat, poultry and fish?"

"It's still very much a guestimate rather than an estimate," was my reply. "For meat and poultry, say five years minimum and then only a very limited amount. Ten years until we have a surplus. Eight to ten years for fish. If you think our stores can stand it I suggest bringing in six cats and six dogs. Remember though that they'll multiply; the cats fairly rapidly unless you bring in all one sex. Canaries, budgies and birds generally are out for the moment. We need all the seed we produce and will do for at least the next couple of years. Rabbits are definitely out. You only need two of them to escape and we'll have a plague of them within two years."

Nils seemed optimistic that we could feed the number I suggested and we decided to ask for them to be sent by the next ship to leave Earth. We agreed that we could only feed fairly small dogs so we asked for a pair of Pekingese, a pair of Cairn terriers and a pair of cocker spaniels. To provide a varied future cat kingdom we requested one each of black, white, ginger, grey, tabby and tortoiseshell, any three to be male.

More and more my workload was changing from physical activity to oversight and decision making. Without the intensive planting schedule of the previous year Maria and Julie were well able to handle the day to day chores. The three of us had a short meeting each morning to decide what needed to be done and then I left them to it. I checked progress at regular intervals and occasionally bore a hand with the daily routine, but continued to help out in the bakery. Donna had begun to show and I didn't want her doing too much heavy lifting.

The discussion about pets made me realise that the whole question of livestock needed to be resolved. My first meeting to this end was with Alastair Baird, our beekeeper. I didn't expect any of our food bearing bushes and trees to flower that year. If a few did then hand pollination wouldn't be too time consuming. But by the following year there was a real prospect of considerable blossom.

"You've seen what we had in the way of flowers last year," I put it to Alastair. "It's likely there'll be the same or more this year and a yearly increase in the future. Is there enough to sustain bees and if so how many? Remember it will be another year before they get here."

He gave it considerable thought before replying. "Yes, I think there is. As for quantity we should start with three hives only. It's probable they will multiply naturally; if not we'd need another few hives at a later date. I take it there's no problem in transporting them?"

"None at all," I reassured him. "They've had more than twenty years of practice with the other colonised worlds. They cryogenically freeze the hive just after the bees are born. That way they stay at the same age until resuscitated. If I order them now they'll be here for next spring at the same stage of development. I'll get Nils to send the signal through."

A couple of days later I visited Sean and Eamonn. Sean had quizzed me from time to time as to when I was going to provide some livestock for him. Now I had a question for him.

"Nils will be ordering one or two things in his next report to Earth. I'm thinking about getting a few cows in if conditions permit and maybe one or two other animals. You've a far better idea than I have about how much grazing is needed, so what do you think? Remember it will be a year before they arrive. My only stipulation is that you concentrate on milk, butter and cheese production. We can worry about beef cattle later on."

Sean had obviously done his homework and needed no time for reflection. "I'd say there's enough pasture now for eight cows and a bull. Maybe by this time next year it could be more but let's be cautious. A cow produces around three gallons of milk a day, so that will give us half a pint per person per day plus a small surplus for making butter and cheese. I've included a bull for reproduction purposes. That way the herd can grow naturally and when we do bring in more it won't be quite so many. Can I suggest some other things. By next spring we'll have enough corn to support a couple of dozen chickens. Although they eat grass as well their consumption is small. Twenty-two hens and two cockerels should be the right balance. A year from now would also be the right time to introduce some pigs, maybe a dozen or fifteen. I've been doing some calculations and reckon we could feed them without draining the human rations.

The only things I'm reluctant to take on would be sheep and goats. Their grass requirements would be too high." I liked all his ideas and made the necessary mental additions to my list for Nils. Before I left Eamonn had a suggestion to put to me.

"I don't know if this is feasible or not," he began rather diffidently, "but I was wondering if we should set up a kind of seed market. Storage out here is a bit of a problem and we'll be producing more and more seed as time goes on. My idea is to appoint someone to set up a shop in the town. We'll sell all our seed to him or her at a low price, they'll store it until it's needed and then we'll buy it back at a slightly higher price. You and your two girls are producing seed as well so you could do the same. With nearly everyone growing fruit and vegetables in their back garden whoever takes the job should be able to make a decent living out of it." I thought the idea had merit and promised to bring it to the notice of the committee at the next meeting. There it found unanimous support. A suitable candidate was found and the seed shop set up within the week; another addition to our expanding main street.

Jennifer's baby arrived on the eighteenth of March, a fine healthy boy weighing just over eight and a half pounds. They named him Stefan Andrew after Nico's father and Jennifer's brother. One month later to the day twins, one boy and one girl, were born to a Norwegian couple. Nico reported that all the births had been routine and reassured Donna that neither mother had suffered much in the way of pain. Donna was showing very plainly by now and early in April we felt the baby's first kick. We started counting the days. Our marriage was proving all that we'd hoped for and I was blissfully happy. Of course we had our little disagreements from time to time but never a serious quarrel. I think the nearest we came to it was when Donna wanted to have her hair cut short. Needless to say I protested long and loud. One of my greatest joys was to wake up every morning and see that glorious mane spread across my chest. After our most heated argument to date she agreed to compromise by only taking nine inches off. Even that was a sacrilege I considered.

That was early in April, two days before we received confirmation of the arrival of the *Caledonian Cavalier*. As expected the ship would land on April the twentieth, round about ten thirty our time. Its three companion cargo ships would touch down at one hourly intervals thereafter. It was decided that Nils, Hans, our banker Herr Klost and I should drive down to welcome them. Preliminary discussions between each of us and our opposite numbers were highly desirable and lines of communication needed to be set up. One of the plans that had been put on the back burner after our own arrival had been the setting up of a telecommunication system. Hans was working on that at the time and hoped to have some form of radio link set up by the end of April.

One other event of note occurred around this time. April the sixth was the anniversary of our first setting foot on Cara IV. We'd hoped that the monument might be ready, but Matthew was still working on it. We'd had to amend our earlier plan to have the two hundred names inscribed as Hans hadn't been able to find a big enough block of stone. Instead, and with the approval of a large majority, the names of the first forty-eight would go on the stone and attached to it in an ornate case would be a scroll carrying the names of the rest of the two hundred. We therefore simply held a short service of thanksgiving after which Nils said a few words and then declared a public holiday.

We set out to meet the next group of settlers just before nine on the morning of the twentieth, arriving at the site at ten past ten and parking on the beach to avoid getting in the way of any of the incoming ships. Hans and I were both in uniform. At twenty past we had our first sight of the *Caledonian Cavalier* high in the sky. Fifteen minutes later she touched down gently a mile north of the river and about half a mile inland. As we walked across to meet her the exit hatch on our side opened and the steps rolled down. First out was a portly male figure, almost certainly Minos Sousopolis. He looked a good bit older than Nils and I later learned that he was fifty-two. Just as Nils had done a year ago he knelt down and kissed the ground before turning and beckoning towards the ship's hatch. At that point the new arrivals came pouring out and gathering in small groups close to the ship. Everyone was looking around eagerly. The four of us made our way towards Mr. Sousopolis but halfway there I spotted a woman in uniform and broke away. When I got within fifteen yards of her I noted the acorn flash on her epaulettes, the insignia of a Science Officer. This was obviously my opposite number.

She was talking to three other people as I approached and that gave me time to study her. She was tall, around the six foot mark I guessed and heavily built. Even from a few yards away I realised that her bulk was made up of muscle and not fat. She was also older than I expected, probably around thirty. Her fair hair was cropped close to her head and she had very pale blue eyes. At that point she broke off her conversation, saw me, smiled and walked towards me. It struck me then that she looked vaguely familiar. I mentioned the fact as I introduced myself.

"Kristina Olsen, originally from Copenhagen," she announced herself. "You probably have seen me before. For the last seven years I worked in the labs at the University in Riccione. You've likely seen me in the canteen or around the corridors."

"Were you in the hostel?" I asked.

"Good heavens no," came the reply. "I shared a flat in the town with three other girls. I didn't really fancy the hostel. Now to change the subject. I have an hour to spare before the cargo ship lands and there's so much I want to ask you. Do you mind if we walk along the beach while we're talking? I love the sea. Perhaps I should have been a marine biologist."

I agreed readily. Her voice was low pitched and pleasant to listen to, and her English held just a trace of an accent. Once we were on the beach I told her to ask her questions.

"First of all I have to thank you," she began.

"What for?" I asked.

She laughed. "For making my job so much easier." I looked puzzled and she went on to explain. "When I was appointed to this group the first thing I did was to dig out all the notes you made. After I'd read them I realised that I couldn't improve on them, so I've just copied all that you ordered plus one or two additional things that I want to experiment with. It was the same with the town planning. Ours will be very similar to yours. There'll be a park on either side with woodland beyond that. Also I have to thank you for doing some of my work for me. I saw the grass to the north as we came in."

"We've planted for sixty miles north and south of Stockholm," I told her. "That way I figured you could concentrate to the south and east, possibly eighty to a hundred miles in each direction. You mentioned that you'd brought something to experiment with. Can you tell me, or is it a secret?"

"It's no secret," she responded. "I want to try out some tropical trees along the shore. It should just be warm enough for them to grow, if not flourish. I've brought four each of small potted date and coconut palms and banana trees. If they don't do well there's no harm done. I'll simply pass them on to the next colony south. They're due to arrive in six months' time."

Kristina seemed to know quite a lot about future plans and I pumped her for information.

"The next colony will be to the north of you in Stockholm," she informed me. "They will be here three months from now. The final influx for this year will be in six months' time and will settle about a hundred and thirty kilometres south of us here in Athens. They will be concentrating on tropical and sub tropical production, including sugar cane and cotton. Incidentally I'm going to try both of the latter myself in a small way."

"You'll need to come and visit us," I suggested. "Hopefully that will give you some ideas, and you can also talk to our two agtecs. They've been playing about with sugar and cotton growing for the last few months. Maybe you can learn something from them. I expect you won't have much time for the first week, but come whenever you like. Everybody knows everybody in Stockholm by now, so if I'm not in my office someone will be able to point you towards me. I take it you've got assistants."

"Oh, yes. Two young eighteen-year-old boys. They're enthusiastic but not very knowledgeable. Never mind, I'll soon knock them into shape. Before I forget, I'm under strict instructions to consult you and get your approval for any new projects I might be dreaming up, so I may need to visit fairly often."

"I don't think you need to worry overmuch about that," I smiled. "I'm sure your judgment is as good as mine, if not better. Go ahead with anything you feel like, but let me know about it at some stage. I might learn something worthwhile myself."

For the rest of our walk the conversation turned to personal matters. I learned that she was married to Olaf, an electronics expert, and that they had two children, a boy aged six and a girl of four. She too had taken the course at Riccione, but some five years before I started. She hadn't made the top group and was assigned to a laboratory post. When word had come round about vacancies for Cara IV she had volunteered immediately. Like myself she'd long had the ambition to head for the colonies. All too soon the first of the cargo ships appeared over the horizon and we had to get back.

On the way back to Stockholm we discussed our various meetings and it seemed that all had gone well. As Nils remarked, it was important that we should work closely with all new arrivals and ensure some uniformity throughout our new world. My one final memory of the outing was a remark made by Hans as we neared home.

"I'm thinking it's a good job all our transport is on the hover principle. Just imagine the work involved if we had to build roads."

"It's a good job too that all our transport is battery operated and we don't need fuel," Nils remarked drily. "Otherwise we'd have no transport at all."

CHAPTER THIRTEEN

For the next few weeks I found it hard to concentrate on my daily round. Donna's time was getting near and I was worried, though without any reason. She herself was in fine form, constantly joking about her increasing midriff and revelling in the occasional kick the baby delivered. On my insistence she stopped doing any work at the bakery though she came along most days to advise and supervise. We brought in a girl friend of Teresa's to keep things ticking over. At three in the morning of the seventeenth of May Donna shook me awake.

"I think the time has come," she said calmly. "Will you take me over to see Nico, please?"

I hurriedly got dressed and bundled her into the car. Though it was only two minutes' walk to Nico's house and adjacent surgery cum hospital I wasn't taking any chances. It took a good ninety seconds of knocking before a sleepy Jennifer came to the door, babe in arms. When I told her why we were there she thrust the baby at me and went to wake her husband. Nico got dressed hurriedly, Donna was put to bed in the tiny ward and the waiting began. We didn't talk much during the hours of waiting. Donna was in some pain and was sweating a lot. Every so often I had to gently wipe her face and hands. At eleven o'clock she went into labour. I held her hand tightly and made encouraging and probably inane remarks. Nico wanted her to have a pain-killing injection but she refused. Round about quarter past one her contractions became more frequent and fifteen minutes later the baby arrived, a beautiful girl child. Less than five minutes later I was holding her in my arms and breathing a prayer of thankfulness. At my request Jennifer weighed her in pounds and ounces: the result was seven pounds three ounces.

We'd long been agreed on names, whether for a boy or girl. Thus our new arrival was Moira Louise. Like all babies her features were indistinct but to my proud eyes she already looked more like Donna than me. The wisp of hair that could be seen had a distinct reddish tinge and she had Donna's eyes. Nico insisted that mother and daughter must stay in hospital for at least another twenty-four hours, so at four o'clock I left reluctantly and spread the news around. I'd several offers of hospitality but I turned them all down. I wanted to spend a while on my own to adjust to my new status, so I went home. Only then did I realise I'd had nothing to eat all day. By seven o'clock I was back at the hospital and stayed until ten. Despite my lack of sleep I was on hand at the bakery at four the next morning and still walking on air.

Meantime Nils had made contact with the next group of impending arrivals. They were coming in on a Spanish ship, the *Viva Espana*, under Commander Sanchez and were due in mid July. This was the group that would settle at the next major river estuary north of us. Their director, Saku Nimenen, came from Finland and their new home would therefore be named Helsinki. My opposite number would be an Englishman, Roger Beasley. I remembered him vaguely. He'd been on the same course at Riccione, but in a different group. I recalled him as a rather intense and serious young man who seldom laughed. I wondered whether his selection for Cara IV would have lightened his mood in any way. I would soon find out. Truth to tell my mind wasn't fully on my work at that time. My world centred round my wife and daughter. I soon got used to disturbed nights and getting up every four hours to feed Moira. Donna was still feeling a little weak after the ordeal of giving birth and I tried to spare her as much of the parental duties as I could. She wanted to go back to the bakery, but for once I put my foot down and forbade her. Once again an argument ensued, but when she saw how determined I was she gave in meekly. That alone told me she wasn't a hundred per cent.

We did make one major change after Teresa made a suggestion. Instead of baking in the early morning we switched to doing so the evening before. By starting about six we could have the morning's requirements finished and ready by ten or shortly after. This made life easier for Teresa and myself and would suit Donna better once she returned to full time duties. I found this much more satisfactory as it enabled me to concentrate more fully on my main function. Maria and Julie were doing a first class job, but there was still plenty left for me to occupy myself. The trees and bushes we'd planted in our second greenhouse were coming on well and by mid April most were over a foot high. I therefore passed the word round that we would be planting a fruit tree and two fruit bushes in each back garden. This was obviously a long term project, but with the warm climate and hopefully absence of frost I calculated that everyone would have some fresh fruit of their own well within five years. In ten years' time they should have a big enough surplus to sell and exchange.

Checking through our store room one day in mid May I came across a couple of sacks, one half full of horse chestnuts and another half full of acorns. These had been surplus to our requirements for the deciduous forest area and I'd forgotten we still had them. There seemed no point in hoarding them. A few days later, after a spell of drizzly light rain I took one of the cars, a packed lunch and the two sacks and headed inland. Once I'd gone about twenty miles I started planting. At a rough calculation I had about two hundred of each variety. Initially I stopped and planted one nut every half mile or so, then as I got farther from base I started planting small copses of twenty or thirty. Then I reverted to the odd tree here and there. By the time I'd finished and started for home I'd covered around three hundred miles. In fact I almost overdid it. I arrived back at our office with a little over five minutes' life left in the battery! As well as planting trees I took note of the progress the grass was making in these far inland areas. Though large areas of bare brown earth persisted I was pleased to see grassy patches all over the landscape, many of them nearly a foot high and seeding profusely. To my surprise I also spotted one or two wild flowers here and there, buttercups and dandelions mainly. Obviously the grass seed we'd been given had not been one hundred per cent pure.

The 'economy' of our little town had been growing steadily and by the end of May less than a dozen people were still unemployed. A Norwegian man in his mid forties who'd been a bus driver back on Earth set up a public transport company. He bought the two hoverbuses on a hire purchase agreement and then negotiated with his opposite number in Athens. The result was a regular bus service between the two townships with two buses a day in each direction. I see from my diary that the return fare was twenty crowns. Sean and Eamonn were rapidly extending the land under cultivation and took on half a dozen temporary workers. With a bumper grain harvest in prospect a small milling factory was being set up.

With Jennifer much occupied with their baby and more pregnancies being announced Nico took on two extra nurses. The first flush of enthusiasm for gardening having died down a gardening business made its appearance. Once Hans and his troop had the radio telephone system up and running a small communications company came into being.

Although we were not directly involved Nils and I sat in on the meeting to discuss the numbering system to be adopted. Many ideas came forward and it proved a lively debate. In the end agreement was reached, grudgingly in some cases, on a seven digit allocation. The first three digits formed the town code. Thus Stockholm became 001, Athens 002 and the future Helsinki 003 and so on. Individual numbers started at 1001 and in view of his position Nils fell heir to 001-1001. Numbers were allocated to individuals and not houses as it would be a mobile setup. Hans captured 001-1002 and I was given 001-1003. Donna was well down the list at 001-1125. Initially calls would be free, but handsets had to be purchased at ten crowns apiece. After a year there would be a small charge imposed on each call. In due course an emergency system was added with the number 333.

The *Viva Espana* arrived on the fifteenth of July. Once again Nils, Hans, Herr Klost and I went to meet and greet them. It meant a five a.m. rise for us as the ship was due to land at 7.30. In fact it was even earlier and we arrived after the settlers had disembarked and were gathering in small groups nearby. As with those at Athens they looked a pretty diverse lot at first sight. Ages ranged from late teens to late fifties, with half a dozen or so younger children. As I had been at Athens I was pleased to see black, Asian and Chinese personnel among them. I spotted Roger Beasley right away and made my way over to him. We shook hands and spent a few minutes catching up on news from back on Earth. Roger had been assigned to a research unit in Portugal after finishing the course and told me he was delighted when his application to come to Cara IV was approved.

"Don't get me wrong," he assured me. "The work I was doing in Faro was interesting and rewarding, but like you and most of the others on our course my real wish was to head for space." I noticed that he was still as serious looking as I remembered him. Like Kristina at Athens he'd based his orders on my original work, but as he went on to explain had had one or two additions more or less thrust on him.

"One of the groups coming next year will be sent to the Oval Lake," he said. "Their job will be to make a start on setting up a water distribution system for the whole of the area this side of the mountains. The powers that be want me to grass the area around the lake and so I've been given double the amount of seed. I also plan to scatter seed thinly between here and the lake."

For a moment or two I didn't quite understand. I'd never heard of the Oval Lake. Then I recalled the survey ship's map and realisation dawned. Due west of us and some two hundred and fifty miles inland lay the largest lake on the planet. I remembered now that it was almost a perfect oval, which accounted for the name that it had now been given. In metric terms it was around one hundred and sixty kilometres long and one hundred and twenty at its widest point. It was also very deep. Soundings taken by the survey ship showed that in its central area the depth was just under two kilometres.

"It will be a time consuming job," I remarked. "It will take you three and a half hours just to get there and the same to get back. Even with the long hours of daylight you're going to be limited as to how much planting you can do each day."

He smiled for the first time. "I've thought of that and I've managed to organise some help. Commander Sanchez has agreed to let me have the use of a lifeship and pilot for as long as the *Viva Espana* remains here. The ship will take me out to the lake in half an hour and leave me there for the day. The seats can be removed easily and the space created will carry a van with the grass seed in it. I'll be in radio contact and half an hour before I decide to finish up for the day I can radio in and they'll come and pick me up. Also, I've had a chat with the Chief Engineer. They're going to adapt two of the portholes in the lifeship. They'll replace them with a kind of chute. On the way to the lake and back I can drop handfuls of seed into the chute. While I'm doing that my two assistants can take care of the routine planting around the town."

"You're off to a good start," I complimented him. "Tell you what. How would you like some company on the first day? I'd quite like a trip that far inland and we can get the job done quicker with two of us working."

He seemed to like the idea and we settled on the following Monday. There was one other thing to discuss. "The three directors will be meeting on a regular basis, probably starting a month from now. I think it would be a good idea if we three biologists did the same. If we arrange our meetings to coincide with the directors it'll ease the transport requirements." He agreed enthusiastically.

Just as we were leaving one of the Stockholm lorries arrived carrying the Lemaire brothers and all their belongings. Apparently they were due to leave on the *Viva Espana* but true to type had told nobody of their plans, not even Nils. In truth we were not sorry to see the back of them. They had done excellent work but they'd never fitted into the community. While the rest of us became a tight knit and happy group they had steadfastly remained aloof.

Another who didn't mix well was Herr Klost, but for different reasons. Basically he was a very shy man and one who took his responsibilities seriously. In a way this was understandable. Hans and I were in the fortunate position of knowing exactly what we had to do and how to do it. The only real decisions we needed to make was in the order and timing of our respective functions. Herr Klost carried a heavier burden. The whole financial future of the planet rested upon the measures that he was setting up. One wrong decision on his part could have disastrous consequences for coming generations. He worked long hours, even longer than we had all done the previous year and I often saw the light burning in his cabin late at night and early in the morning when going to and from the bakery. His wife, Erta, also kept herself to herself. Unusually in this day and age she had very little English, which put her at a disadvantage with all except the German speakers among us. I must stress though that there was nothing remotely unpleasant in their attitude and they were always polite to everyone. The nearest they had to friends were Hans and his wife with whom they shared a common native language.

On the way back home Nils filled us in on future developments, expanding on what Roger had told me earlier. "There'll be one more group of two hundred arriving this year," he informed us. "They'll locate some one hundred and twenty kilometres south of Athens. Although it will be the end of September before they get here the warmer winter temperatures in that area should enable them to get established and get things growing. Next year there will be three groups arriving. The first will be six hundred strong and will settle a hundred and sixty kilometres north of Helsinki, where the mountains taper off and come down close to the sea. Their main function will be to start mining operations for metals and other minerals. A small part of that group will be specialists in oil exploration and development and they'll start drilling a few kilometres north in an area yet to be determined. About a month after this group arrives another four hundred will land at Oval Lake. They'll make a start on setting up a water distribution system which eventually will provide a mains supply for the whole of this eastern seaboard."

"Finally one more township of two hundred will arrive, probably in late April, and settle at the river delta roughly halfway between Helsinki and the mining unit. All this is very much in line with the plans that were laid down before we ourselves left Earth. After that most decisions will be taken by the governing body here. That's one of the reasons we want to get an embryo parliament up and running. Let me give you an example of the things we have to consider. It's expected that four more groups of two hundred will be coming the year after next. Should we set up four new towns inland and if so where? Should we spread further north and south along the coast or should we double the size of our existing towns? All three options have their advantages." We discussed the matter amongst ourselves for the rest of the journey and found complete disagreement reigned. I favoured moving inland, Hans preferred to spread along the coast and Herr Klost opted for existing towns to be enlarged. I began to see the problems Nils and his fellow directors would be facing.

I arrived home to find Donna putting baby Moira down for the night. By now she was developing features and personality. She had Donna's red hair and green eyes but I insisted that her nose and chin were beginning to resemble mine. There was no doubt now that she recognised us. We had little trouble with her. She rarely cried and usually only awoke once or twice during the night. I found fatherhood a strange and slightly terrifying role. One part of me couldn't wait for her to grow up while another wished she could stay as she was forever. Over our evening meal I told Donna the gist of the day's events. Then it was her turn and I learned she had been busy.

"Sean Flannigan came down from the farm to see me this afternoon," she announced. "He and Eamonn have made a rough calculation of the amount of wheat they'll have available for flour making in the autumn. He reckons that even if we give some to the other communities we'll still have a fairly large surplus. I've done some sums of my own and it looks as though we'll be able to take bread off the ration come September. Now that raises a problem. Quite simply we won't have enough yeast. After Sean left I went over to the stores section and checked the stock. I estimate we'll run out by February next year. From what you've just told me it's obvious we haven't time to order more from Earth."

"I suppose we could always switch to unleavened bread," I said slowly. Then inspiration dawned. "Wait a minute. You know that middle aged Austrian couple that showed us how to dance the polka last winter. Fritz and Helena. I can't recall their last name, but I'm sure he was an industrial chemist back on Earth and that his wife also worked in a laboratory. I'll look them up tomorrow and see if they can come up with a solution."

I was as good as my word. After checking with Maria and Julie that there was nothing urgent to be attended to I went looking for Fritz. He and his wife were not at home, but I learned from one of their neighbours that they were working part time on the farm. I finally ran them to ground in the orchard to the north where they were hand pollinating fruit trees. Without saying why I asked Fritz if it would be possible to set up a permanent yeast factory.

"Given a suitable quantity of yeast to start with and a reasonable supply of sugar the answer is yes," was his reply. "Though we'd also need a factory unit. We couldn't do it at home. There isn't enough space and the smell might upset the neighbours."

"The factory unit's no problem," I assured him. "We've still got three or four that are not in use. I don't know what you consider to be a suitable quantity of yeast but we have nine months' supply of dried yeast in hand. If you can guarantee a sufficient regular supply you could take at least half of that. Sugar might be difficult though. There's little or none to spare from the supplies we brought with us. But there is one suggestion I can offer. Before they left us the Lemaire brothers laid down two large areas of sugar beet. Why don't you take those over and manage them as well? That way you can produce your own sugar and by harvesting seeds from the existing plants you can keep the supply going permanently. It would make a nice little business for you both."

Both he and his wife were keen on the idea. I promised to talk to Nils and also to make arrangements for Hans to discuss with them their requirements in the way of equipment.

I was quite excited when Monday came round and I set off for my appointment with Roger Beasley. Despite the late nights at the bakery and the occasional attention to Moira's needs during the night I seemed to be thriving on less sleep than I was used to. Before coming to Cara IV I'd always reckoned on seven to eight hours a night, but nowadays I seemed to be functioning perfectly well on five. I got to Helsinki just after eight on a drizzly and humid morning. Roger was all set and ready to go, as was our lifeship and its pilot. Natasha was young, fair haired and Russian. She was fluent in English but spoke with a thick accent, almost as if she was talking with a mouthful of treacle. Proudly she showed us the adaptation that had been made to the ship. One porthole on either side had been removed and been replaced with a backward slanting funnel. The plan was that Roger and I would take one each and alternate in feeding handfuls of grass seed into the funnel beside us. Even though the ship would be travelling at over two hundred miles an hour that would still give us a reasonable spread of seed.

We took off and Natasha climbed to about two hundred feet. The drizzle showed no signs of relenting and there was a gentle wind. Conditions were perfect for sowing and at our height and with the wind each handful of seed that we tossed into the chute would scatter widely. We waited until we'd been travelling for ten minutes or so, then Roger and I took up our stations by the chute. At first we shouted to each other each time we released a handful but we soon got into a rhythm and remained silent thereafter. Where we were in the ship meant that we couldn't see the countryside beneath us, which was disappointing. All we knew was that whenever the ship rose or fell we were traversing higher or lower ground. We stayed on a level keel for about twenty minutes, then we rose steadily. Minutes later we dropped again, only to rise shortly afterwards and stay at a higher level for at least a quarter of an hour. Then we began to fall again and Natasha shouted back to us that the lake was coming into range. We each fed one more handful into our chutes for luck and moved forward to take in the view.

It was a breathtaking sight. We were headed towards the mid-point and widest section of Oval Lake. Despite our height we could not see the other shore, but grey and bleak in the very far distance the mountain range thrust up into the sky. The drizzle had stopped and the light had improved though there was no glimpse of the sun. As we passed over the shore Roger disappeared back into the rear of the ship and I heard him moving things about. Though curious I was too fascinated with the sheer beauty of the lake to investigate. He was back in five minutes.

"I brought along three drums of plankton and water life of various kinds," he explained. "That will get things started off in the lake and once we start to introduce fish to the world we can stock it with trout and maybe one or two other freshwater fish." We simply emptied the drums through the chutes as we passed over the watery expanse.

Natasha speeded up and the far shore soon appeared on the horizon. After a smooth landing we unloaded the hovervan with its stock of seed and arranged for Natasha to pick us up on the eastern side at six that evening. We would be in radio contact with the *Viva Espana* and could notify her of our exact position before she set out. Roger had made some quick calculations and reckoned that we would complete half the circuit of the lake by the deadline. The lifeship took off again and we watched as it faded into the distance before getting down to the job in hand.

"This is the latest model of hovervan," Roger said proudly. "It can travel over just about any terrain and best of all has an automatic pilot. That means the driver has his hands free, so we can scatter seed from both sides. I'll set the speed for twenty kilometres an hour. Allowing half an hour for lunch that should get us half way round by the time Natasha comes to pick us up. I'll do the other half tomorrow with one of my assistants. The following day I want to plant some trees on this side, so the other assistant can get a jaunt as well."

We got organised and set off just as the first glimmer of sunlight broke through the clouds. Every so often Roger adjusted the auto pilot to compensate for the curve in the shoreline. We set our line at roughly a kilometre from the water's edge. At first I was entranced by the view. As the sun grew stronger the lake's surface changed from grey to blue. Gentle waves lapped against the shore. Much of that shore comprised sandy beaches and I could picture the scene in thirty or forty years' time. There would be boats on the water, bathers and sun worshippers on the beaches and anglers fishing off the shore and in their boats. Here and there we saw small rocky outcrops and just before we reached the southern tip a larger area of rock and low cliffs. After an hour and a half we changed places to ease the strain on our 'throwing' arms.

I could happily have taken a break any time after twelve, but Roger wanted to reach the southern end before lunch. We made it at two minutes after one. By now it was a lovely sunny day with the temperature well into the eighties. Apart from the view the most noticeable thing about our surroundings was the complete and utter silence. We positioned the van to give us maximum shade. This meant that we were sitting sideways on to the lake and with a great view of the distant mountains. Halfway through our meal I had an idea.

"How easy is it to get the use of the lifeship?" I asked Roger.

"No problem at all," he replied. "Commander Sanchez seems more than happy to lend it and a pilot to us as long as they're here. Why?"

"If you can spare the time it would be a worthwhile project to cross the mountains and scatter some grass seed on the other side. I know it will be at least fifty years before any attempt will be made to settle or even visit there, but if we can get some growth started it will be a real boost when they do. There'll be pasture lands for sheep and cattle ready and waiting for them."

"I like it," Roger approved. "How about going one better? When I was on my pre embarkation leave I took my two young brothers and spent three days in local woodland. We gathered up all the acorns, horse chestnuts and maple nuts that we could find and I brought them with me in addition to the stuff I ordered. I've got twice as much as I'll need around Helsinki. While we're sowing grass we can land every so often and plant trees as well. In fifty years that will give the first settlers a source of timber as well as pasture." He thought for a moment, then added: "How does next Monday suit you?" We agreed there and then.

After a break of half an hour we set off again. By now the whole operation was getting boring, but we stuck gamely to our task with only two short stops during the afternoon for refreshment and toilet needs. Just before five Roger radioed back to Natasha to give her our approximate position. Her voice came cheerfully back telling us that if she didn't spot us right away she'd patrol the shore in each direction until she found us. In actual fact she landed a few hundred yards in front of us dead on six o'clock. Roger was happy; we'd completed the full half circle. Before I left to drive home Roger got confirmation that a lifeship would be available for us the following Monday.

Two days after my excursion to Oval Lake Kristina made her long awaited visit to Stockholm. On arrival she apologised for not having come sooner, pleading pressure of work back in Athens. I understood. I'd been in a similar position the previous year. After introducing her to Donna and of course Moira Louise we set off on a tour of what she called my kingdom. She was loud in her praises of the progress we'd made and frequently took notes in a small diary. After visiting the farm and talking at length to Sean and Eamonn we went back home for lunch and then out to the area where the Lemaire brothers had been experimenting with cotton and sugar beet. By great good luck Fritz and Helena were on site and engaged in lifting some of the beets and Kristina milked the two of them for information. However, it soon became clear that their knowledge of cultivation was limited to say the least. She spent nearly an hour studying the two large fields of cotton. These looked healthy. Sadly all my learning seemed to have avoided any lessons in the raising and harvesting of this particular plant, so I wasn't much help. Kristina seemed satisfied, however, and after taking some samples stated positively that cotton would certainly be a viable proposition for Athens and probably for us too. I made a mental note to find someone to take charge of the fields and extend them. Though we invited her to stay for an evening meal Kristina declined, saying she had work to do that evening and the family to feed. Before she left I told her about proposed meetings of the respective biologists whenever our directors got together. She thought it was a good idea.

On top of their normal duties Julie and Maria had been developing projects of their own. The latter had called upon her experience of wine growing, taken over an area some four miles south of our southern woodland and started a vineyard. A married Italian couple who'd also had wine growing expertise was helping her. With the strong possibility of a regular supply of yeast the three of them were working on plans to start a small winery within the next two years. I'd cleared it with Nils and was surprised to discover he was enthusiastic.

"Although nobody has complained," he explained, "I know that many people miss the solace of alcohol. Yes, I know it can cause problems, but taken sensibly it provides relaxation and improves morale. No doubt if wine and later on spirits become freely available there'll be some who'll take it to excess, but we'll keep an eye on it and clamp down hard on any abuse. There's always the fear too that if we forbid it some bright sparks will start making home brew and probably poison themselves in the process."

Julie's main focus was on the weather and its patterns. From somewhere or other she'd begged, borrowed or stolen enough equipment to set up a proper weather station on the edge of South Park. One wall of our small office was covered with graphs and charts of all kinds. A month or so after New Year she'd started issuing daily forecasts and after a shaky start she soon achieved a high degree of accuracy. She did, however, take a lot of ribbing from Maria and I whenever she got it wrong. It was just as well she was easy going and good natured. The two of them were a real pleasure to work with and highly efficient in whatever they turned their hands to.

CHAPTER FIFTEEN

I couldn't wait for that Monday to come around. The prospect of a trip into the unknown was as exciting as anything I'd done up to that point. I'd taken the trouble to study the maps that the original survey team had provided so I knew roughly what to expect. Beyond that vast range of mountains lay a huge plain spanning nearly eight hundred miles in each direction. In centuries to come this would be the farming heartland of the more central part of the continent. According to the maps most of the open area was over a hundred feet above sea level, so dangers of flooding were remote unless weather conditions became extreme. So far there had been no signs to indicate the possibility of continuous torrential rain. The plain was well watered, with half a dozen large lakes and numerous rivers and streams flowing through.

Despite the fact that I was twenty minutes early in getting to Helsinki the lifeship was ready and loaded and Roger was standing by. Natasha was our pilot once more, cheerful as ever.

"What are the orders, boss?" she asked me with a cheeky grin.

I tried to look severe and probably failed. "Less of the boss, young lady," I reprimanded her. "I'm an adviser, nothing more. This is less an order than a suggestion for your and Roger's approval or otherwise. Fly out due east as fast as possible until we're over the mountains and on to the plain itself. Then cut back to your lowest safe speed and fly in a random pattern of curves for a couple of hours. After that we'll start landing at points some distance apart and we'll plant groves of forty or fifty trees at a time. What do you both think?"

"O.K. by me," said Natasha. "I'm just here to do what I'm told. Can I help with the tree planting?"

Bernard Stocks

"By all means," I replied. "It'll speed things up. Roger?"

"Just one thing to add," said that worthy cheerfully. "I've brought along half a dozen drums of plankton and aquatic life. I thought we'd 'seed' one or two of the lakes and rivers while we're there. Then once we start bringing in fish we can stock up. By the time people start settling over the mountains there'll be more fish than they can cope with."

It was a fine dry morning when we took off, though a touch on the chilly side. It was encouraging to see the frequent patches of greenery over the first thirty or forty miles. Then the bare brown soil took over the landscape. As we approached the Oval Lake Natasha took the ship higher to give us a panoramic view of the complete expanse of water. It was a breathtaking sight. Nearing the foothills of the mountains we climbed again to around thirteen thousand feet. I'd had a vague thought that we could at sometime in the near future plant some grass and trees in places along the lower slopes, but looking at the ground beneath I realised this just wasn't an option. I'd expected to see pockets of soil here and there but there were none. There seemed nothing but bare rock in all directions.

I was watching the dials on the control panel in front of the pilot, trying to work out the extent of the mountainous area. By my reckoning and converting from kilometres it was around twenty to twenty five miles. In between the towering peaks were long valleys, many of them boasting small lakes. But wherever I looked all I could see was bare grey rock. I looked, too, for possible passes. There were a few, but all were narrow, winding, steep and hazardous. I saw none over which a hover vehicle could be taken safely. Unless there was easier access somewhere to the north or south any future travelling between the two sides of the range would need to be by air or round by the north end. Snow covered more than a third of the slopes and on some of the higher lakes the sheen of ice was visible.

Roger broke in on my thoughts. "We ought to name these mountains while we're here. How'd you like to imprint your name on this world and call them the Dunsmuir Mountains?"

"No thanks," I responded. "I'm not a glory hunter. Let's borrow from Earth and call them the Rockies, or maybe the Urals in honour of Natasha." In the end we decided on the former. It transpired that Natasha had done some of her training in the Urals and been less than impressed.

"Tell you what, though," said that young lady. "When skiing finally reaches here there are miles upon miles of fantastic slopes. I bet in a hundred years' time this will be a paradise for winter sports."

The first thing we saw once the peaks began to recede was the large lake that I'd seen on the map. Unlike the Oval Lake the shoreline was irregular and very few of the beaches were sandy. It was probably about two-thirds of the size of Oval Lake and would certainly provide an ample supply of fresh water to a large population. As soon as we crossed the nearer shore Roger asked Natasha to slow down while he emptied two of the drums of aquatic concentrate through the side chutes. Beyond the expanse of water the plain stretched unendingly, bare and brown. It reminded me of the sight that had greeted us when we first touched down in this world. Once over the lake we settled down with our bags of seeds while Natasha flew in a series of curves north, west and then south again. At half past twelve we landed and had a leisurely lunch. Before taking off we planted forty or so trees, Natasha joining in enthusiastically.

During the afternoon we landed seven or eight more times to plant trees, finishing off along the western side of the lake with a line of trees stretching over four miles. Roger still had a third of a sack of acorns left over, so on the way back once we crossed the mountains we dropped them through the chutes at random. As we came in to land I turned to the other two.

"It's unlikely that we'll still be alive to see the benefits," I said, "but we've done a good day's work today. When the time comes to extend across the mountains the first settlers there will thank us for giving them a head start." Then jokingly I turned to Natasha. "Are you sure you want to stay a lifeship pilot for the rest of your days? We could use you here."

She gave her usual infectious laugh. "Thanks for the offer, but no thanks. I've enjoyed today but I wouldn't want to stay here forever. I'm a space girl through and through, wild and free."

By the end of August Donna was ready to resume full duties at the bakery. I'd rather she'd taken a little longer, but she insisted. No one had thought to include prams among the supplies we'd brought with us from Earth, but I improvised a kind of carry cot from a stout cardboard box and we carried Moira to and fro in that. She seemed to be quite happy in the bakery and fascinated by all that went on. I still spent a fair portion of my day there. With the increased supply of flour and yeast bread had been taken off the ration and the demand had more than doubled.

The next big event was the arrival of the fourth group of colonists in mid September. Their director was an Italian, Salvatore Celli. He'd been in post somewhere in Castellamare during my time there and had stayed in the same hotel. I'd met him briefly several times and shared a dinner table with him on a couple of occasions. He was in his fifties, bald, portly and jovial. He hailed originally from Verona and his town would be named similarly. The leading lights at Helsinki declined the opportunity to welcome the newcomers on the grounds of distance and pressure of work. Nils, however, was adamant that we should be there, so once again the four of us made the journey. It was a long one this time, over a hundred and thirty miles. We left Stockholm at six in the morning for the near two hour trip, arriving a good half an hour before the ship was due. In a way I was quite pleased as it gave me the chance to study the site.

Verona differed from the other three settlements in one big respect. There was no river. Water supplies would have to come from a desalination plant to be set up close to the seashore and a small lake eight or nine miles inland. In one way the absence of a river was an advantage as it made movement within the town easier. The difference in temperature was very noticeable suggesting that growth would be possible throughout the winter. On our way down I'd noticed that patches of newly growing grass were frequent: Kristina had obviously been working hard. She'd seeded the area around the town quite thickly and when I worked out the likely time since it had been planted it was apparent that it had grown twice as fast as that around Stockholm. The Athens contingent arrived just as the ship, a German one, drifted in to land.

As was becoming customary Salvatore Celli was the first to disembark. It seemed to me that he'd put on even more weight than when I'd last seen him. He came straight over to where we were standing and shook us all by the hand.

"Alex. It's good to see you again," he said as he came to me.

"Likewise," I replied. "I'm flattered that you remember me."

He gave one of his booming laughs. "It would be hard to forget you. You're something of a hero back on Earth. They call you the man who brought life to a dead world. Every time there's a mention of Cara IV on TV, the internet and in the papers it's your picture that's shown. Poor old Nils here hardly gets a mention. We must have a long talk later. Meantime Nils and I have much to discuss, so please excuse me."

As the two of them drifted away I wondered to myself what my family were making of my unexpected fame. I knew Aunt Eleanor would be pleased and I thought my father would too. My mother probably didn't even know about it: her reading was always strictly confined to the fashion magazines and she took no interest in current affairs. My siblings, Aileen especially, would no doubt be mortified that their 'accident' of a younger brother had managed to outshine their own achievements. At that point Kristina roused me from my reverie.

"Denise is in the ship checking over her supplies," she informed me. "Come and meet her." On the way she told me a little about our newly arrived biologist. Denise Mofara had been born in France of Ghanaian parents and was in her mid twenties. When we finally ran her to ground in one of the holds I got quite a surprise. I'd met and mixed with a number of black African girls during my time in Italy and they'd all been big strapping lassies and outstanding athletes. Denise was small and slim, probably around five feet five and I doubt if she weighed more than seven stone soaking wet. She was beautiful and when she smiled at me as we were introduced I was reminded of the sun emerging from behind the clouds on a dismal day. Without the slightest hint of disloyalty I realised that if I hadn't met Donna first I could easily have been smitten.

"I'm so glad to see you, Alex," she said in a soft husky voice. "I've been given my instructions of course, but I've been told emphatically that I must clear everything with you first."

I was beginning to get annoyed with the powers that be back on Earth insisting that I approve everything. Roger, Kristina and Denise were all well qualified to make their own decisions and I said as much. I suggested that in future they worked under their own steam and only contacted me if there were any urgent problems.

"Once things settle down we'll all be meeting at regular intervals," I told the two of them. "Time enough then to tell me what you've been doing."

Denise was inspecting the young trees stored in the hold and gave me a rundown of the orders she'd been given. "I've to grass up the areas to the south and west in the same way that the rest of you have done. The rest of my planting will be different. I've to concentrate on tropical stuff. Among the two hundred young trees in here nearly half are walnut, to provide both nuts and in time timber. There are other trees that will eventually give us timber plus things like oranges, lemons, grapefruit, figs, date and coconut palms. I'll be growing bananas, pineapples, mangos, lychees and similar fruits. And Kristina, I've been given ten small mulberry trees to pass on to you. The suggestion is that Athens will eventually become the centre of the silk industry in this part of the world."

I spent a very pleasant four hours with the two girls. In the main we talked about our work, and Denise brought us up to date with all that was happening back in Europe. We were treated to lunch in the ship's canteen and it was a real joy to sit down to roast beef and Yorkshire pudding after more than two years of tinned meat. Just before we set off for home I managed to get a few minutes with Salvatore Celli. He had news of some mutual acquaintances and was interested to hear of the work I was doing.

Within a couple of weeks our embryo phone service was extended to Verona. A week later a regular bus service was introduced and the existing one amended. Athens became the focal point, with services running north and south to Helsinki and Verona respectively. Initially there were still only two journeys a day on each route as demand was low. The intention was that after the first flurry of work settled down there would be increased services at weekends. This was a suggestion from Nils, who insisted that morale would be improved by visits to other townships.

There was one more important event in that year of 2241. At least it was important to me. In the second week in December Donna announced that she was pregnant again. Needless to say I was overjoyed. We'd talked often on the subject of family and were both agreed that we wanted at least four children. With the proviso that Donna's health didn't suffer we also agreed we wanted them fairly close together. We knew that it wouldn't be easy bringing up a large family in the very basic conditions we lived in, but we were prepared to take the chance.

The previous year's festive celebrations had been so successful that we repeated them almost to the letter. Donna and I hosted the Christmas Day luncheon with our closest friends. I think the presence of the two babies gave a more joyous atmosphere to the occasion. Much of the talk centred around the future when the children would be running about. We were all resolved to try and find some sort of presents for them, even if we had to make them ourselves. The dance at night was again a huge success. About ten o'clock, after a particularly vigorous polka I went outside for a moment or two to cool off. There was no moon, but the glow from inside the plastipod provided a shadowy light for some distance around. To my surprise I saw Nils standing motionless and gazing at the sky. I deliberately made a little noise as I approached to avoid startling him. He turned as I reached his side.

"You know, Alex," he sighed, "this is the one day of the year when I regret having taken this assignment and get homesick. I used to love Christmas in Sweden; the family all together, the laughter, the food and the present giving under the tree. I'd always set aside a few minutes to stand at my bedroom window and gaze out at the snow covered fields. I know we're doing the best we can here, but it's just not the same. If only there was some snow it would improve things."

I patted him on the shoulder. "Maybe in a few years' time there'll be settlements much further north where there is snow in the winter. Then we can go there for a proper Christmas holiday." I thought it best to change the subject before we both got too nostalgic. "Tell me, will you go back to Earth when you retire?"

He took a while to answer. "I just don't know. I've never spoken much about family before, but we have two sons. Both were at college when we left and there was much talk about them joining us here. If they do then our roots will be firmly planted and there'll be very little to go back for. If they don't come then yes, we probably will return. How about you?"

"I've nothing to go back for," I said decisively. "You know something of my background so you'll understand why. Christmas was never much fun for me. My parents were never there for a start. My aunt did her best, but while my sister Aileen was still at home we spent the day squabbling and fighting. Once she left Aunt Eleanor and I went to a restaurant for our Christmas dinner. No, I'm here for life. All that's important to me is right here, my friends, Donna, Moira and hopefully the children that are still to come."

CHAPTER SIXTEEN

It was the third Sunday in January before Nils finally managed to arrange a meeting of the four directors. I didn't have to ask him for a parallel meeting of the biologists: he insisted that we and the chief engineers and four bankers also got together. Athens was judged to be the most central point for the assembly, so early that morning we set off. Thankfully it was a dry day, not particularly warm but blessed with some crisp winter sunshine. Arriving just after nine we split up. Kristina welcomed me to her office and within twenty minutes Roger arrived from Helsinki and Denise five minutes later from Verona. They insisted that I chair the meeting. I started off by taking reports from each centre on progress to date. These were encouraging. Kristina and Denise had both been surprised by how quickly everything had grown and the latter insisted that growth was still strong over the past month. When we compared temperatures at the four towns the reason was obvious. Verona's readings were between four and ten degrees higher than anywhere else.

At noon Kristina's two assistants arrived with a cold buffet. Afterwards we toured Athens. Kristina had made rapid progress. She'd managed to wheedle three fairly large plastipods for use as greenhouses and was bringing on a wider variety of plants than we'd managed to do in Stockholm. Other than that she'd copied my approach almost to the letter and the gardens of all the houses appeared well stocked. Then it was back to the office for a general discussion which quickly developed into a question and answer session as the others wanted to know my future plans. Their particular concern was the timetable for introducing livestock to the world. I'd expected something of the sort and had my response ready.

"As you know, we're bringing in bees, cows, pigs and chickens to Stockholm in small numbers later this year. I believe the first ship will arrive in March or April and they'll be on that. I suggest that you order similar numbers to arrive two years from when you first set up camp. But before you do, make sure that there's enough pasture land for the cows. Don't be railroaded by the farmers, who are sure to want them as soon as possible. Remember that once the animals are here we can't send them back. If the pasture runs out all we can do is kill them off for food. If you're in any doubt at all err on the side of caution. There shouldn't be a problem with the bees. By next year you should all have plenty of flowers for them. If you judge that you've enough to feed them, pigs can arrive with the cows."

"What about sheep?" Denise wanted to know.

"I want to wait another year or two before bringing sheep in," I replied. "Even then I would only advocate bringing half a dozen or so and letting them multiply naturally. We just cannot risk running out of pasture."

"Fish?" queried Roger. "The plankton and stuff seems to be spreading pretty rapidly."

"I want to be over cautious with them. The plankton may be spreading but remember fish multiply very quickly. Don't forget they'll have no natural enemies here apart from Man. For the moment I'm not planning on bringing any in for at least another four years, though I may revise that estimate next year."

"Surely there'll be enough food for them before that," commented Kristina. "How much does a fish consume?"

Her question triggered off a memory from my days at university in Riccione. One of the girls asked that same question of our lecturer during a marine biology lesson. He'd given her a long hard look.

"A hell of a lot," was his reply. "And that's the most accurate answer I can give you. Despite all the research that has gone on nobody has been able to come up with a formula. It varies enormously from fish to fish." I repeated that anecdote.

"Will you bring them in as young fish?" was Roger's next question.

"No. I propose to use spawn. Seemingly it can be cryogenically frozen just as humans and animals can. We'll have to do that with the salmon anyway. Remember they always return to the location where they spawned. We don't want them going psychotic on us and swimming round in circles because they can't get back to Earth." That drew a laugh.

"What other fish will you go for?" asked Denise.

"Trout for the rivers and lakes, possibly even some sea trout as well. For the open sea I thought cod, haddock, herring, plaice, sole and halibut to start with. Later on we can think about the likes of bream, bass, hake, whiting, turbot and mackerel. But I stress again I'm not going to be rushed into this. We simply cannot afford to over stock and run the risk of the fish dying for lack of food." I don't think any of the three were happy with my decision, but there was no further argument. If there had been I was quite prepared to pull rank.

The final query came from Kristina and centred on plans for birds, insects and wild life generally. I had my answers ready for that as well.

"Again this is a few years down the line and something we have to be very careful about. We need to find a balance for everything as we go along. Probably it will be possible to bring in some butterflies and moths in a couple of years. The trees and bushes should be advanced enough to give them a natural habitat. Hopefully we can introduce a few small birds in about three years' time. For the sake of colour I was thinking of the likes of canaries and budgies at first, followed by sparrows and robins. As far as insects are concerned I'm still unsure. The danger of any species reproducing too rapidly is ever present. We don't want flies because they carry disease. Ants would overrun the world in just a few years. Mosquitoes and midges are out for obvious reasons, as are cockroaches. Beetles are a possibility, so are ladybirds. If you can think of any others please tell me. The same goes for other wild life. We don't want rats or mice, rabbits breed far too rapidly and do too much damage, as do foxes. Maybe in time a few badgers, stoats and weasels, but the woodlands will need to develop considerably. I'm afraid we have to accept that we'll never be able to have the variety of wild life that there is on Earth and the other colonised planets."

Bernard Stocks

The meeting broke up shortly thereafter and I discovered Nils, Hans and Herr Klost were awaiting me. There was very little conversation on the way back to Stockholm. Each of us was busy with our own thoughts. For my part I considered that it had been a day well spent. Just before we got home Nils announced that we would be holding similar meetings on the third Sunday of every month from that point on. He also arranged for the four of us to meet the following afternoon so that he could brief us on future developments.

The session began at two o'clock in the office that Nils had set up for himself. He took brief reports from each of us regarding our own discussions and then took the floor.

"You all know the programme for this year," he began. "In April the two hundred for the new settlement north of Helsinki will arrive. I can't give you an exact date as I'm not yet in contact with the ship that's bringing them. This new group will be constituted in the same way as the previous ones. Then in May the six hundred for the industrial, mining and drilling section are due, followed in June by the Oval Lake four hundred. Now these last two groups will be somewhat different in composition. There'll be a director and a banker, but no biologist or chief engineer. There'll be a small number of agricultural workers under two or three experienced farmers and they will be responsible for the planting of grass and trees, etcetera. Although the directors will join our governing council they'll have full autonomy to make their own decisions. That could raise one or two problems for you, Alex. For instance, they could decide to bring in livestock almost immediately. How serious would that be to your plans?"

I didn't need to give it much thought. "Very little. Both of them are far enough away, so they won't encroach on our grazing land. If they do overreach themselves and run out of pasture then it's their problem, not ours."

"Good," Nils went on. "So that's this year taken care of. Now yesterday was a significant day in the history of Cara IV. Up to now the decisions have all been taken by our control group back on Earth. They've planned how many people to send and where to send them to, according to the original schedule for colonisation. The final clause of that schedule stated

116

that when a proper government was established here the decision making would be passed to that government. Such a government is now in place. From now on we decide on the scale and location of immigrant groups and send our requirements to Earth. Of course we have to give them notice, usually two years in advance to give them time to assemble the personnel. We planned our programme for the coming two years yesterday, and I'll be relaying our decisions to Earth tomorrow morning via one of the ships in transit in the usual way. Next year there will be four intakes of two hundred. Two of them will double the population of Stockholm and Athens. The other two will be set down at new sites inland, one due west of here and one due west of Athens. The following year there will be five intakes, of which three will go to Helsinki, Verona and the new township north of Helsinki and the other two to new inland locations."

"Can we find jobs for another two hundred here in Stockholm and can we feed them?" Hans asked.

"My view is yes in both instances," Nils replied. "As far as jobs are concerned we've asked for as many agricultural workers as possible. I want to see a massive extension to the areas that we have under cultivation. As to food, we haven't used nearly as much as expected of the rations we brought with us and the new arrivals will be bringing more tinned and dried items with them. Which brings me to another point. As well as arranging numbers I have to order more food and other materials." He turned to me. "I've got the estimates you gave me just before Christmas, Alex. We're well ahead of schedule in the matter of cereal and vegetable production. Is there any chance that meat and fruit supplies could be accelerated?"

I shook my head. "You all know my thought processes. I simply will not risk all that we've accomplished by trying to do too much too soon. I know I'm being over cautious, but the penalties if anything should go wrong are too severe to take chances. I stick by my original forecasts. It will be twelve years at least before we are totally self sufficient in meat production and around fifteen as far as fish are concerned. The provision of fruit will increase rapidly year on year after next year. There will be a small amount this year, but I will have to hold all of that back for seed purposes. Next year some will get on to the market and from then on it's all plain sailing. Sorry, Nils, but that's the way it is."

I guess I must have spoken a bit heatedly, for he held up his hand palm outwards. "It's O.K. Alex. I accept your findings. After all, you're the expert and I think you're right to be cautious. I just wanted to be sure, that's all. Incidentally, I'm ordering four of the new high speed hoverbuses. Even though the mining lot and the Oval Lake crowd will be working independently we all need to keep in touch. As you know, the new models are capable of speeds over two hundred and fifty kilometres per hour, so journey time to each location will be just over an hour. Right, so much for future plans. There were one or two more matters arising from our meeting yesterday. Now here's some good news. A small factory has been set up in Helsinki to manufacture glass and glass products. As you know, one of our major problems has been the lack of containers. If all goes well there should be a steady flow of jars and bottles coming on the market within the next few months, not to mention glass dishes. I've sent a message asking for large preserving jars to be a priority. Most of the gardens are likely to have a surplus this year and it would be a bonus if we could preserve this instead of letting it rot. I gather, too, that they will be able to produce glass oven ware. One of the complaints I get frequently is the shortage of saucepans and the like. That reminds me, Hans. Another regular complaint is about the state of the streets. When it rains they become a bog. Is there any way of providing some sort of paving?"

Hans scratched his head. "The problem is the lack of stone locally. We had to go over seventy kilometres to find something suitable for the monument. Leave it with me for the moment. We're well up to date on our other projects, so I can spare half a dozen of the team to look at the possibilities. Thankfully there's a couple who are skilled stone masons. But we won't be able to do too much, possibly just one line of paving slabs down the middle of each street."

"That would be a bonus," Nils smiled. "Well, I think that's all, gentlemen. We'll meet again once a month after full council meetings. If there's anything you want Earth to send us next year, please let me know within the next hour. I'll be sending the signal off at five o'clock." Hans and Herr Klost left immediately, but I stayed seated.

"I've a couple of requests," I said thoughtfully once they'd gone. "I think we can bring in the first sheep next year, say with the third group to arrive. Let's say six ewes and two rams. If they come in July or August that will give next year's growth of pasture a good start. I'd also like to bring forward the beginnings of bird and insect life. The trees are growing faster than I expected. Most of them doubled in size again last year and many are around six feet in height already. The bushes have also doubled in size. Small numbers again, say six female and two male canaries and the same numbers of budgerigars. There's also enough foliage for a few butterflies and ladybirds, so maybe one clutch of eggs for the latter and three for the former. No cabbage whites, for obvious reasons. Let's start off with small and large tortoiseshells and Red Admirals. We can add different species as we go along."

"I'll put all that on the order," Nils promised. "Talking of birds, you haven't forgotten that we have a few cats and dogs arriving in April."

"No. The dogs are no problem. Hopefully the cats won't roam as far as the woodland. We'll have to make sure there's plenty of seed and other food handy for the birds, but with the bees arriving Julie, Maria and I won't have to spend so much time pollinating everything by hand. That will give us enough leeway to look after the birds. Oh, and one other thing. I was speaking to Sean a couple of days ago. He reminded me that once the cows arrive in April there'll be a daily yield of up to thirty gallons of milk. He has twelve five gallon churns which came with the initial cargo, but as the herd grows he'll need more. I'd say another couple of dozen at least."

"It shall be done," Nils pronounced. "In fact I'll order three dozen just to be on the safe side."

That January was appreciably colder than the previous year. We even had a slight frost for a couple of nights in mid month and Julie's records showed a temperature low of minus two degrees. Roger phoned me one morning to say that they'd had a few flakes of snow. We all hoped this would prove an unusual winter. The only heating we had in the houses and buildings was one small convector heater apiece. But in the last couple of days of the month the thermometer started to rise and by the end of the first week in February the first shoots of new growth were evident. The winter bulbs that had been planted in the gardens had already made their appearance and the white, yellow and blue of snowdrops and crocuses gave our surroundings a welcome touch of colour. I began to think about transplanting the remaining fruit trees and bushes that were growing in our second greenhouse.

The problem was that there was little free space left around the town. I didn't want to use up any of the area set aside for housing. It was certain that our population would not stay at the four hundred or so that next year's intake would bring. After working out how much to set aside for the incoming two hundred I consulted with Eamonn, who suggested starting a new orchard between his own area of farmland and the fields where the Lemaire brothers had sown cotton and sugar beet. Julie, Maria and I started this task in the third week in February, the frequent rain showers notwithstanding. Once the greenhouse was more or less cleared we planted the remaining seeds that we had.

One other event of note occurred that month. True to my promise I'd laid down two football pitches the previous July, one on North Park and one on South Park. Hans managed to cobble together four goals and some corner flags from odd lengths of metal piping left over from other tasks. Painting the lines was a major problem and in the end we had to settle for using light coloured sand instead of paint. As soon as the pitches were ready for use two clubs were formed. For most of that winter they played each other, but by the time February came around they were hosting teams from Athens and Helsinki as well. Discussions then took place about forming a league the following season. Athens, Helsinki and Verona expected to have pitches ready by then, so with two clubs from each town an eight team league was agreed. This put pressure on me from the tennis players to provide courts and I had to promise to have at least two ready for the beginning of April. The golfers too were getting restless, but I had to point out that it would be another couple of years, maybe more, before we had enough grassland to lay down even a nine hole course. Hans was among the golfing enthusiasts and he came up with the idea of setting up a driving range. The suggestion was received warmly and two of his gang volunteered to undertake the work and run the finished product.

CHAPTER SEVENTEEN

By the end of February Nils was in radio contact with all three of the incoming ships and was able to give us more information. The director of the new settlement north of Helsinki was a Spaniard, Jose Manuel Gonzales, and he was naming his town Malaga. Neither Nils nor myself recognised his name. The mining and drilling group was led by an Englishman, Nigel Lancing, also unknown to us. The mining town would be called Manchester and the drilling area Salford. Wolfgang Haltenberg, an old friend of Hans Friedland's, would take charge of the Oval Lake group and their town would be Hanover.

The ship bringing the Malaga contingent arrived on the sixteenth of April. Once again our intrepid foursome set out at the crack of dawn but this time we had company. Alastair Baird had borrowed a small van and was coming to collect his three hives of bees. Two men and two women drove lorries which would transport the pigs and chickens back to Stockholm. Another van would pick up the dogs and cats. Finally Sean, Eamonn and two assistants had hit on a tried and trusted method of getting the cattle back home. Among the transport we'd brought with us initially were half a dozen altabs—advanced land travel auto bikes to give them their full name. With these the four men would copy the old wild west cattle drives, taking two days at least to get the beasts the hundred miles or so they had to travel. The altabs were battery powered and had been used extensively in early colonisation. Prototype models had only had a range of some fifty or sixty miles but in the last forty years newer models could manage up to three hundred miles on one charge. It promised to be quite a spectacle and I made up my mind that if my work schedule permitted I would drive out a couple of times to watch the event in progress.

Jose Manuel Gonzales turned out to be almost a carbon copy of Salvatore Celli. He was roughly the same age, heavily built and with similar features. The one difference was that Gonzales had a thick head of pure white hair.

He welcomed us warmly before pointing out the various people that we needed to meet. My opposite number on this occasion was a Dutchman, Pieter Van Jonk. The name meant nothing to me but I recognised him straight away as yet another of the students that had been on the same course as myself at Riccione. Denise and Kristina had decided not to make the long journey north, but Roger from Helsinki had arrived a few minutes ahead of me and the two of us introduced ourselves to Pieter.

"I'm really glad to see you two guys," were his opening words. "Unlike you I've had no practical experience since leaving university so I'm going to rely on you both for guidance."

"We'll give you all the help we can," I promised. "You'll be on the radiophone within a week or two so we'll be able to keep in close contact."

"In the meantime," Roger chipped in, "come down and see me whenever you've got the time. I've done just about all my long distance work, so I'll nearly always be somewhere around town. So what have you been doing up to now?"

"As soon as I finished the course I got a vacancy in the procurement department at Space Headquarters in Switzerland." He half turned towards me. "After you took off, Alex, all requirements were passed to us and we did all the purchasing. I found it interesting at first, settled well in Switzerland and married a local girl. But after a while I got bored and restless sitting at an office desk all day. I talked it over with Lola, my wife. She was fed up with her job in a supermarket and liked the idea of relocating to one of the colonies. The first two jobs I applied for were on Mars station and Persephone, but I didn't get them. Then this post on Cara IV came up; this time I was lucky and here I am."

Roger and I spent the next hour giving Pieter some sort of timetable for the work needed. Thanks to the efforts Roger had put in there wasn't a lot to be done in the way of sowing grass, so he would be able to get started quickly on tree and other planting. He took copious notes. We met Lola, his wife, briefly. She was small, dark, pretty and just showing the signs of pregnancy. When the second cargo ship arrived with the housing components they had to leave us. Roger decided to head back home, but

I was curious to see our livestock, which had come in the passenger ship. Alastair had already loaded his three beehives and was ready to move. The pigs were just being offloaded, still unconscious from the cryogenic chambers. A forklift truck carried them one by one from the ship to the waiting lorry.

"They'll wake up on the journey," Sean told me. In response to my query he added: "they're all around one year old as far as I can make out. I haven't picked up the paperwork yet. The chickens will be out next and they're very wide awake. I had a look at them half an hour ago, as I did with the cattle. Incidentally, they've sent ten cows instead of the eight we ordered. According to one of the crew cattle don't travel through space as well as other animals so they always put in a couple extra just in case. It's not a problem. The grazing will stand it and it will give us extra milk for butter and cheese making."

"Are you sure you're going to manage the drive O.K.?" I asked him.

"Barring unforeseen emergencies it should be a doddle," was his answer. "We've checked the route a couple of times. There's plenty of water, reasonable grazing most of the way and we've picked out four or five spots where we can bed the herd down for the night. It won't be like the cowboy movies, you know. There are only twelve beasts after all. In the old days they used to have anything up to two hundred with about half a dozen men to handle them. The altabs are more manoeuvrable than horses, too. We're aiming to cover about twenty miles today, then with luck fifty on day two and arrive on day three around midday."

I watched the chickens being brought out but by then Nils was impatient to get started on the return journey. By that time the erection of the houses had started. I found out much later that one of the innovations for the groups after us was to train people in how to erect the housing units before leaving Earth.

Despite being in her seventh month of pregnancy Donna was still coping easily with her work in the bakery, so about two o'clock the following afternoon Maria, Julie and I piled into one of the cars and set off to see if we could intercept the cattle drive. Sean had told me the route that they'd be following and with the land being flat for most of the way I reckoned we should have no difficulty in spotting them. It had been dry for most of the previous week anyway, so even if we didn't get a sight of the herd itself there was likely to be a considerable dust cloud accompanying it. Sure enough, that's what happened. We were driving some ten miles inland from the coast and had just come level with Helsinki when Julie spotted dust rising into the sky on our left hand side. A couple of minutes brought us level.

It was an awesome sight. The cattle were in four groups of three abreast and moving at about six miles an hour. Two altabs flanked the leaders, the other two brought up the rear. Eamonn was in the front and gave us a wave. Sean at the rear stopped his machine as we drew alongside. I asked him if all was going well.

"Fine and dandy," he beamed. "The first four or five miles the bulls wanted to stray and the cows tried to follow them. But once we got the knack of heading them off it was easy to keep them in close formation. We're just about on schedule, too. Our proposed camp for the night is thirty-five kilometres ahead. We'll make that with time to spare and be home between eleven and twelve tomorrow. In two days' time you'll be drinking fresh milk." We followed a discreet distance behind the herd for twenty minutes, then waved to the modern day cowboys and headed home.

The demand for pets was overwhelming and in the end all we could do was hold a ballot for the lucky twelve owners. Forty-five names went into the hat for a dog and thirty-nine for a cat. Nobody was allowed to enter both draws. Donna and I were among the few not to enter. With a young child in the house and another on the way we deemed it inadvisable to bring in an animal at this stage. The draw was held in public and turned into something of a carnival. When the lucky ones were announced you'd have thought they'd won a fortune in the lottery.

The arrival of all these animals posed a problem. Nowhere on the world at that time did we have a vet. I discussed the matter with Nils and discovered that, like myself, he hadn't given the matter any thought. Sean and Eamonn we knew could deal with simple afflictions to cattle and poultry, but anything more serious would be beyond their knowledge. We could only think of one solution. Accordingly I broached the subject to Nico, our doctor, one evening when we were visiting.

"I'd be happy to take it on until a proper vet arrives," he declared. "Obviously quite a bit of our training as doctors involved animals. But if anything serious came along, like an outbreak of foot and mouth disease, I'd be useless. The sooner you get someone the better." I told him that Nils had already sent a request back to Earth, but that it would be a year at least before a vet would arrive.

As with any small community news travelled fast in Stockholm. Three days later I was working in one of the greenhouses with Maria just before noon when Teresa came in. "We've all to take containers to the grocery store," she burst out breathlessly. "There's milk from the farm." I went home quickly to get one of our few precious plastic bottles and walked round to the main street. A queue had formed at the door of the store. When I reached the counter some ten minutes later I received a full litre from a large churn. The ration was, as previously agreed, half a litre per person per day. We didn't have ration books and no checks were ever made, but as everybody knew everybody else there was never any cheating. Donna was at the bakery with Moira, so I called round there and we solemnly drank our first fresh milk for three years. Moira was a little doubtful at first. She'd mainly been breast fed up to ten months and then gradually converted to dried and tinned milk. After a couple of tentative sips she decided that she liked it and soon was looking for more.

The arrival of the livestock led to a certain amount of rearrangement. Sean felt that living in the town left him too far away from the farm, so Hans and his gang dismantled their house and re-sited it some three miles away. Eamonn decided to follow suit. From left over bits and pieces Hans managed to construct a rudimentary milking shed capable of taking four cows at a time. There were no machines; all the milking had to be done by hand. The original intention had been for Sean and his family to handle the butter and cheese making as well, but a change of mind saw these activities set up as separate businesses. Only three families were now relatively unemployed and two of these took up the opportunity for regular work. The remaining two factory units were brought into service and the somewhat antiquated machinery installed. Sean's wife oversaw operations for the first few weeks until the new owners were sufficiently knowledgeable to carry on by themselves. Within the month home produced butter started to appear on the shelves of our food shop. The cheese had to mature and would not be on sale for at least six months, though small amounts of soft cheese appeared from time to time.

The next lot of settlers due was the mining and drilling outfits. Their arrival date was the third of July. I decided not to join the welcoming party on this occasion. With no biologist in the group there wasn't really any need for me to be there. The main reason, though, was that Donna's time was getting near and I was back to working a minimum twelve hour day between the bakery and my other duties. I also tried to make time to keep in touch with the progress of our newly arrived livestock. Alastair's bees were thriving and it gave me a homely feeling to see and hear them buzzing about the gardens and in the greenhouses. The cattle seemed none the worse for their change of scene and the chickens were laying regularly. There were no eggs for consumption, though. Sean was keeping them all back for breeding purposes. His aim was to at least treble his flock within twelve months. Even the cats and dogs appeared happy in their new surroundings.

The morning after the arrival of the industrial crowd Nils sought me out to give me the latest news. "I had a long chat with Nigel Lancing yesterday," he began. "A really pleasant fellow and younger than I expected. I'd put him around the thirty mark. The first thing I learned was that they haven't brought any animals with them and the Oval Lake crowd won't be bringing any either. They intend to wait and buy from the rest of us when we have enough livestock to sell. They have brought plenty of seed and young trees, mainly conifers. One interesting point is that they won't be setting up home on the seafront like the rest of us. Manchester will be about eight kilometres inland in a small valley in the foothills of the mountains. A river runs through the middle of it to provide their water supply and they plan to build on both sides. I didn't go up to see where Salford will be situated, but I understand that it will also be in the foothills close to a small lake and about six kilometres from the sea. You should try and find a day to visit before the winter. Manchester should be a very picturesque sight when completed. Nigel is all in favour of keeping closely in touch with the rest of us and promises to attend all the monthly meetings. He knows Wolfgang Haltenberg very well and reassured me that he is just as keen."

"Did you get any indication of how soon we can expect results from the mining and drilling?" I asked.

"According to Nigel it will be a year at least," Nils replied. "Their first few months will be spent in exploring the surrounding areas and finding out what they've got. Then they'll work out the best way of digging it out. The original survey team only reported that there were deposits of various metals; they didn't give any indication of quantity or accessibility. Oil may be a little quicker to come on to the market. He reckons that the first well should be on stream in five to six months. That will open the door for a number of new industries. Talking of industry, we called in at the glass factory in Helsinki on the way back. They're now in full production and are taking orders. We can open up another shop right away. The Poulsen family are still looking for something to work at, so I'll offer it to them."

That decision meant that there were no unemployed left in the town and I began to see the wisdom of Nils wanting to double the size. We had an expanding economy and we needed the larger labour force to keep it growing. In fact we could have done with more people there and then. With the harvest about to start Eamonn was looking for more help and there was little available. In the end he had to rely on those already employed to give up whatever spare time they had during the day. So much of the work carried out by machines on Earth had to be done by hand here on Cara IV. Even the potatoes had to be lifted using spades.

The Oval Lake party arrived on the nineteenth of July. Again I absented myself from the welcoming group, but I learned next day that they had landed safely and were busy erecting housing and settling in. Their town of Hanover was situated on the eastern shore of the lake at about the midpoint. Hans was plainly envious of the materials his opposite number had at his disposal.

"Over three thousand five hundred kilometres of piping alone," he exclaimed. "One cargo ship was completely full of it. Mind you, the whole project will probably need that and more. Lief, my opposite number, showed me the plans. They'll be linking the lake with all the existing towns and are routing them past the next twenty or so proposed settlement areas so that quick connections can be made once people move in. We'll have a fantastic water supply system when it's all completed and still have our local sources as backup. I almost forgot. Wolfgang asked me to thank you for laying down the grass and young trees around the lake."

I laughed. "It's really Roger Beasley he should be thanking. It was his idea. I only went along for the ride. I'll give him a call and tell him his efforts are appreciated."

CHAPTER EIGHTEEN

Both Donna and I had hoped our second child would be a boy, but it wasn't to be. Hannah Jane Dunsmuir came into the world at twelve minutes past three on the afternoon of the twenty-eighth of July. As with Moira, she was born in the hospital with Nico and Jennifer in attendance. It was an easy birth, though Donna nearly broke my hand in the preceding few minutes, so tight was her grip. As a concession to my Scottish habit of ignoring metric weight Nico told me gravely that Hannah was seven pounds two ounces, one ounce lighter than Moira had been. Moira had wanted to be in at the birth, but we thought it inadvisable and she waited in the next room with Teresa. Now fifteen months old, she had developed into a sturdy and determined child. She'd started crawling at eight months and walking soon afterwards. Her first words, predictably mummy and daddy, were uttered shortly after her first birthday. She now spoke clearly and with confidence, though she still had trouble with the letter 'r'. Her own name came out as Moya, and Teresa was Auntie Twees. I was holding Hannah when Teresa brought Moira into the bedroom.

She studied her sister gravely and then held out her hands. "Moya hold."

From the corner of my eye I saw Donna give an almost imperceptible shake of the head. I decided to ignore it. I gently lowered the baby into Moira's arms, making sure that I was still taking most of the weight. For a long moment Moira looked at Hannah. Then she bent forward and solemnly kissed the baby on the lips. "Moya love Han," she said softly.

"We'll give Hannah back to Mummy now," I instructed. "We have to go to the bakery and work."

Moira looked again at her sister. "Bye, Han. Moya go bake."

After she and Teresa had left the room Donna took me to task. "You were taking a chance, letting her hold the baby."

"I thought it was important," I told her. "It would be easy and natural for Moira to be upset that she now has to share our love with her sister. By letting her hold Hannah the two of them have bonded, possibly for life. In any case I was taking most of the weight. Now, you've got the phone at your side, so call me if you need anything. Maria's coming in to sit with you for the next couple of hours or so."

"I'll probably go to sleep for a while," said Donna. "If you remember I slept for four hours after Moira was born." I kissed her and left. Maria had already arrived and took my place in the room.

We'd been taking Moira to the bakery with us almost from birth. She never seemed to tire of watching the bread being made. For the past month or so we'd given her little pieces of dough to knead, enough to make two or three rolls and that had kept her amused and happy. In a way I suppose it took the place of the toys that we couldn't give her.

I'd have liked to have visited the two new settlements, but the next two or three months were busy in the extreme. The bakery and the children took up a lot of my time and though Julie and Maria covered most of my other duties there were still a number of things that required my personal attention. As I'd predicted at the beginning of the year we'd had a very small amount of fruit from the bushes we'd reared in the greenhouse. According to my diary our total yield amounted to twelve gooseberries, fourteen blackcurrants, nine redcurrants, eleven strawberries and five raspberries. The latter two types of berries we replanted whole. For the rest we dissected the fruit to separate the pips for planting. The tiny bits of flesh that were left over we divided between the three of us.

Maria was disappointed that the grape vines that she and her partners had planted had borne neither flowers nor fruit. Their vineyard was an impressive sight. Set on a rise in the ground that almost formed a terrace, there were twenty rows each of thirty vines, with some nine feet between rows. It was tended with loving care. Unless the weather was bad Maria's two partners spent time every day weeding out the odd shots of grass that appeared on the site from time to time. No doubt on Maria's instructions each small root was replanted on a bare spot in the vicinity. The vines were healthy and nearly three feet high by now. I was sure that the following year would see the first fruit appear.

The newly formed football league soon proved to be a boon for more than just the players. This link with leisure time back on Earth attracted interest from everybody and Saturday afternoons saw most of the non playing population spectating. The bus services found their weekend revenue rising sharply as supporters started to travel to away games. Perhaps the only people in our world who weren't happy were the doctors. Their workload more than doubled through dealing with injuries to the players. The four tennis courts that I'd provided were also popular and before long we had to set up a booking system for Sunday play. Thankfully science had long ago provided footballs, tennis balls and rackets that hardly ever wore out.

Our third year on the planet drew to a close with a flurry of wet and windy weather. With two young children to look after Donna and I didn't go to the Christmas or New Year dances, though we preserved the Hogmanay traditions of first footing with the other Scots in town. Moira was still fascinated with her baby sister and spent hours at the side of her cot chattering away. By now she had mastered the letter 'r' and was speaking quite plainly, even forming simple sentences. New Year's Day 2243 brought a welcome surprise. Teresa announced that she was getting married at the end of February. The lucky man was none other than Pablo, the Spanish lad who had had a crush on Maria in the early days after our arrival. He was still quite shy, though he'd gradually become more confident during his courtship. Love must have been in the air that winter. Roger Beasley had become a frequent visitor to Stockholm for the previous three months, though I saw little of him. I didn't think much of it at the time and it took Maria to tell me that Julie was the reason. As yet there'd been no talk of marriage, but I suspected that that would not be long delayed. I was happy for the two of them, but realised that it would cause me a problem. Should they marry Julie would go and live in Helsinki, leaving me an assistant short. With full employment in the town it would not be easy to find a replacement.

My first vital job of the New Year was to discuss possible additions to our livestock with Sean. Nils had set our next committee meeting for the third Sunday of January and would need a list of what to order from Earth for the following year. Cattle and poultry had settled in well to their new surroundings, as had the pigs. By now there was ample pasture land available, even allowing for the sheep that would be coming in the spring. It didn't take us long to agree on a list. Samples taken from rivers, the lake and the sea were encouraging and I decided the time was right to introduce fish to the world, albeit in small quantities. By the day of the meeting I was fully prepared. As usual Nils began by giving us news of the year's incomers.

"The first arrival will be the extra two hundred to join us here in Stockholm," he began. "The ship is none other than the *Ural Star*, still under our old friend Captain Petrovic. They expect to be here the last week in March. Early May another two hundred will set up the first of the inland towns, the one due west of us. This is to be called Lisbon. Two months later the reinforcements will arrive for Athens and a month after that the second inland town group will be here. Their town is to be called Ballymena. So much for this year. As you know, we had a meeting of the overall council last week and we formulated our plans for next year. We're asking for five groups at six weekly intervals from early March. Three of the five will bring Malaga, Helsinki and Verona up to four hundred plus. The remaining two will locate inland due west of Helsinki and west of Verona. Once again the emphasis will be on farm workers. The powers that be on Earth are anxious for us to be self-supporting in food as soon as possible, so that they can reduce the number of cargo ships per expedition. I believe you've some good news for us in that direction, Alex."

"Indeed yes," I replied. "Progress on all fronts has been faster than I expected. I've got a bigger order list for you than I would have believed six months ago. Sean and I are agreed that we can at least double the herds and flocks, so you can put down another ten cows, ten sheep and twelve pigs for a start. Add to that another thirty chickens. We will be asking for the same for the year after that, by the way. With the offspring from our present livestock that should give us decent sized herds within five years. Even allowing for the increase in population we should just about be producing enough for Stockholm. The other settlements will follow year on year. It's time now for horses to come. Six mares and two stallions about nine or ten months old, please. I'm also ready for the first fish to come in. This will be in the form of small quantities of spawn, say not more than an eighth of a kilogram of each. We'll start with herring, cod, plaice and haddock for the sea, plus trout and salmon for inland waterways. After that we can add to the marine varieties. No fishing will be allowed for at least three years after the spawn is placed in the water. That will give the fish time to grow and multiply. It may be an even longer ban than three years depending on how things go."

"All noted," said Nils. "Anything else?"

"Yes. I want to add a few more birds and insects. Alastair tells me he can use another four hives of bees. I'd also like to introduce some sparrows, starlings, blue tits, wrens and robins, say a dozen of each. Finally four more species of butterflies and a couple of moths would be welcome. I'll leave it to the suppliers back on Earth to decide which will be most suitable for our climate."

Nils had been taking notes. "I've got all that, thanks. Hans, I'll discuss your requirements with you after the meeting."

February and March proved to be the warmest since our arrival with average temperatures more than two degrees above the previous best. Growth everywhere was little short of phenomenal. When we held our biologists' meeting in late February everyone else had the same good news to impart. After the meeting Roger stayed behind. I suspected right away that he wanted to talk about Julie and I wasn't wrong.

"We'd like to get married sometime in June," he announced, "but if that puts you into difficulties we would be willing to postpone it. However, I have a suggestion to offer. I've spoken to my two assistants and one of them, Marta Levski, would be quite happy to relocate here to Stockholm to take Julie's place. She's Bulgarian, by the way, and very good, though obviously not as experienced as Julie. To be perfectly honest I think she'd be only too pleased to make the change. She's having problems with one of the men on the construction gang. He keeps pestering her, despite the fact she's told him a dozen times that she's just not interested."

I thought for a moment or two. "In that case, why don't we make the switch in the next few days? That would let you and Julie be together and save you both a lot of travelling. Of course I'll be sorry to lose her; she's done a fantastic job here, but I don't want to stand in the way of true love." I said these last few words with a smile on my face. We called Julie in there and then. She was overjoyed. Arrangements were quickly made. Marta would move to Stockholm the following Tuesday and spend the rest of the week working with Julie and Maria and generally finding her way around. Julie would transfer to Helsinki on the Saturday. My only worry was that Maria and Marta wouldn't get on together but my fears were groundless. By the end of Marta's first day the two were firm friends. Though small and slim Marta proved to be very strong physically and soon showed that she could handle heavy lifting almost as well as Julie had done.

The next important item on the agenda was Teresa's wedding. It was tacitly accepted that Donna would be the bridesmaid and I was very flattered when Pablo asked me to be his best man. Teresa also insisted that Moira should be a page and we had a hilarious few days coaching her in her duties. Like all weddings in Stockholm everyone turned up, those who couldn't get into the church itself listening outside through the open doors. The whole town attended the meal afterwards. We never did find out where the happy couple went for their twenty-four hour honeymoon. Donna did her best to learn the secret, but for once Teresa was giving nothing away and Pablo never did have much to say for himself.

The *Ural Star* was due on the ninth of April. Nils was by now in regular contact with Captain Petrovic. Seemingly the latter had promised a few surprises for us when he landed, so by the middle of March the level of excitement began to rise. On the appointed day most of the town rose at six in the morning in order to get as much of their day's work done as possible. We all wanted to be at the landing site, which was some two miles to the north-west. Thankfully it was a dry and warm morning. As the *Ural Star* came into sight high above us I was standing in a group with Nils and Hans. Donna was by my side with Hannah in her arms while I did my best to control a wildly excited Moira. It was her first sight of a spaceship. Nils and Hans were accompanied by their wives. Our doctor and his family were a little way off in the company of Teresa and Pablo. Most of my fellow biologists had decided not to attend, but Denise made the long journey up from Verona. Her excuse was that, unlike the rest of us, she had never seen a landing.

The ship touched down at ten to eleven. The main hatch opened, but to our surprise Captain Petrovic came out alone while a uniformed First Officer stood framed in the hatch. The captain stood for a moment looking all around before walking across to our little group. He and Nils embraced and said a few inaudible words to each other, then he came straight to me.

"Alex, my friend," he smiled. "You have done as I requested."

"What was that, captain?" I asked, puzzled.

"You have turned the brown into green. I was so impressed as we came in on the final orbit. The difference from our last visit was nothing short of amazing. I have some pictures showing then and now on board. You must come and have a look at them and see the miracle that you have worked."

I waved a deprecating hand. "It's not all down to me. My two assistants and the other biologists have done just as much."

He turned back to the rest of the group. "And now my friends you must forgive me for being a little theatrical and stage managing the disembarkation." He turned and made a sign to the officer at the hatch. Seconds later two families came through the opening, four adults and three youngsters under the age of five. Suddenly Nils let out a whoop. "My children," he shouted and rushed forward, his wife not far behind him.

Captain Petrovic chuckled and signed again. This time it was Hans who got the surprise as two couples emerged. He was more restrained than Nils. "My brother and sister and their spouses," he announced in a matter of fact tone as he went forward in his turn.

"One more surprise," Captain Petrovic was obviously enjoying himself as he gave yet another signal. A single young man appeared and Donna gasped. "I don't believe it. It's my brother Patrick." Thrusting Hannah into my arms she sprinted forward followed by Teresa.

The captain turned to me. "That's all the surprises for today," he said with a broad smile. "But I see you have been busy apart from turning the world green." He was pointing at the children.

I laughed. "It hasn't all been hard work," I told him as he made much of the two girls. "But while I have you to myself may I ask a favour?" He nodded. "Of course. Ask away."

"Eighteen months ago I and my opposite number in Helsinki had the use of a lifeship and pilot for a few days. We planted around the Oval Lake, then crossed the mountains inland and sowed grass and trees over a wide area. I'd very much like to visit and check progress if you could grant similar facilities."

"With pleasure," he replied. "See your old friend Bert Larrabey and make arrangements with him. He'll be out once all the immigrants have disembarked." He made his way back to the ship.

Arms round each other, Donna, Teresa and Patrick had made their way slowly back. Donna made the introductions as she took Hannah back from me. Patrick was about my height, slightly slimmer, with sandy rather than red hair. In looks he was closer to Teresa than to Donna. His handshake was firm and his smile broad.

"Already I'm glad that I came," he said, his accent broader than those of his sisters. "I take it these are my nieces," he added as he embraced Moira, planted a kiss on Hannah's forehead and shook hands with Pablo. "I never expected to find the two of them married, let alone one of them with a family. We'll have a lot to talk about later, but now I have to work."

By this time the rest of the passengers had left the ship and were forming up in groups around the cargo hatch. The crew were preparing to unload the housing components. As many of the current townsfolk as could be spared would help in setting up the new homes, including myself and Pablo. A few days previously Hans and his team had marked out exactly where these were to go, so we expected to have everything in place well before nightfall. At that moment I spotted Bert Larrabey among the unloading party, so excusing myself I went across. As I approached I noticed that he had the insignia of a First Officer on his uniform. He had his back to me, so when I reached him I tapped him on the shoulder.

"Congratulations on your promotion," were my opening words.

He swung round and a smile lit up his face. "Alex! It's good to see you. How are you?" I brought him up to date in a few short words and then broached the subject I had mentioned to his captain.

"No problem," he assured me. "I'm going to be busy for the next three days as are all in the crew. After that I'm at your disposal. Come to the ship on Friday evening and we'll make arrangements then."

I found that I hadn't forgotten the way to put up houses despite the three year interval. I was part of a team with Pablo and Maria's two vineyard partners. We completed our first house in a respectable forty minutes, then took a couple of minutes off that time for our next two. Not all the newcomers were to live in the town. Nils, in agreement with Sean and Eamonn, had agreed that the two new head farmers and a dozen or so of their farmhands should live on the new farms themselves. It made sense as the two additional farms would be around four miles inland.

The next three days were busy ones for Maria, Marta and myself. We had been saving a goodly number of plants and a quantity of seed to give the hundred or so new gardens a head start. We had to break off on the second day as the birds and ladybirds were offloaded. We took them straight to the southern woodland and turned them loose in the middle, having already laid down seed and breadcrumbs. Though we knew that they would eventually find their way into the town we hoped to discourage them as much as possible. Cats will be cats and we didn't want to risk losing any of our small number of feathered friends. Already I'd asked everybody to save suitable scraps of food and leave them for us to take down to the woodlands. But we'd underestimated the attraction that the first birds on the world would prove. In the evenings and occasionally during the day people would take their offerings to the wood, often spending up to half an hour just watching the birds feeding. They soon became very tame and with care could be tempted to perch on the hand and feed from that. I'd have taken a bet that these were the best fed birds in the entire universe.

CHAPTER NINETEEN

Three cargo ships had arrived with the *Ural Star* carrying a wide variety of cargo. The most intriguing was a large food freezing plant. This came with its own self assembly factory plus a manager, three operators and a maintenance engineer. The manager was a cheerful Dutchman, Edgar Vermoot. I pointed out to him that it would be two or three years down the line before there was any worthwhile surplus to freeze.

"We know that," he smiled. "We're all going to become farmhands in the meantime. Though if we can persuade the farms to sell us some milk we can at least make ice cream in small quantities. We can also guarantee a supply of ice cubes from now on."

The produce from this new addition to our resources would initially be very different to that we'd been used to on Earth. Packaging was virtually non-existent on our world and would be for some time to come, so there would be no nicely labelled one kilogram bags of frozen produce. The plant came supplied with a number of flat plastic packs capable of holding twenty kilograms of frozen produce each when expanded and filled. Adjacent to the plant would be a frozen food shop with refrigerated compartments. Customers wanting, say, half a kilo of frozen peas would have to bring a container and would have them weighed out and supplied loose. Assuming packaging was still unavailable when meat and fish products became available for freezing then these items would be served unwrapped. It didn't sound very hygienic to me.

By far the most popular item among the newly delivered cargo was a fully functional laundrette. The original planners in their wisdom had decreed that washing machines for every house would be both too expensive and too heavy a burden on the space available in the cargo ships. Hence up to that point all our washing had to be done by hand. Admittedly none of us had much in the way of clothing anyway but those of us with children spent a lot of time washing the bits of cloth which we'd had to substitute for proper nappies. We also had little in the way of baby clothes. Parents were issued with two cotton smocks for each child and of course these had to be washed almost on a daily basis. As the children grew the smocks had to be handed in before bigger ones would be issued.

On the Friday evening I made arrangements with Bert to visit the far side of the Rocky Mountains the following day, with a stop at Oval Lake on the way. With his approval I included Maria and Marta in the excursion and phoned Roger with an invitation to join us and bring Julie. I thought it would be a reward for the three girls for all the hard work they'd put in. The newly arrived cargo ships had brought more tree nuts and seeds and, again with Bert's permission, I proposed to plant some new woodland beyond the mountains. It was a beautiful warm and sunny morning when we took off. Oval Lake presented a different scene from the one that Roger and I had encountered the previous year. Along a five mile stretch from the eastern shore excavations were proceeding apace. A two storey building, the first such to be seen on Cara IV, bordered the lakeside. To the south lay the township of Hanover. We received a warm welcome from the few people in the town itself and the information that the building we had remarked on was to be the main pumping station. Morning coffee appeared as if by magic and we received an invitation to tour the site and stay for lunch. Regretfully we had to decline.

For the outward leg of the journey I'd sat in the co-pilot's seat next to Bert while we discussed the programme for the day. During our stay at Hanover Bert and Maria had paired off immediately on landing and spent the time there deep in conversation. I was the last to board for the next hop and I noticed with some amusement that Maria was firmly ensconced next to Bert. Roger and Julie had commandeered one of the rear portholes and sat with arms entwined. Marta gave me a rueful smile as I joined her.

"Romance seems to be in the air," she whispered. "What a pity you're already married." Then we both laughed.

Even though I'd seen it before the flight over the mountain ranges was just as breathtaking as the first time. Being earlier in the year there was more snow in evidence than when Roger and I had last come this way. Over half the slopes were covered in white and all the higher small lakes displayed a sheen of ice. Bert shouted back that the outside temperature was minus fourteen degrees. Soon we were descending on the far side and Roger and I gave a muted cheer when we saw patches of green everywhere. Our previous efforts had obviously borne fruit. We landed close to a grove of small trees. In eighteen months they'd grown to well over a foot high and looked strong and healthy. A nearby patch of grass was also more than a foot tall and just beginning to show signs of spreading. For our first task we planted enough to double the size of that particular wood. Next we planted some one hundred trees in a line about a mile away from the lake. We lunched on the shore in warm sunshine. While the rest of us relaxed after the meal Marta and Julie took off their footwear and went paddling for a few minutes. They reported that the water was cold but not excessively so. While they were in the water Roger got them to take samples for analysis. He was keen to see if the aquatic material he'd deposited was thriving. Then it was off to half a dozen new locations to plant the rest of the material we'd brought with us.

I deliberately left the co-pilot's seat to Maria for the return journey. She and Bert had their heads close together for the whole time and it was easy to see that the attraction was mutual. In a way I felt sorry for them, particularly Maria. Service on a space ship and romance were difficult bedfellows. There was no way that Bert could simply leave the ship and settle on Cara IV right away. At the very least he'd have to return to Earth to resign and then apply to come to us as a colonist. That would mean a minimum of a two year separation and probably much longer. I said as much to Marta in an undertone.

"I think Maria will be very unhappy," she agreed, also speaking quietly. "We'll need to watch over her closely."

One of the first things that Nils did after the arrival of the extra colonists was to appoint three new assistants to the bakery. This meant that Donna could take on more of a managerial role, giving her more time to look after our children. It also took some of the extra work off my shoulders. Brother Patrick had settled quickly. Like nearly all Irishmen he was outgoing and made friends easily. As a trained electrician he'd been co-opted into Hans's squad. For a week or two he worked all the hours of daylight but thereafter spent nearly all his spare time with us. He loved the children and Moira adored him. One of his delights was to babysit, which gave Donna and I more leisure time together. From then on we went visiting more often and got into the habit of going for long walks in the summer evenings when we weren't working.

Ten days after its arrival the *Ural Star* left on its return trip to Earth. Maria was in tears as it rose into the skies. She and Bert had been inseparable since our flight over the Rockies. His other duties had been negligible so he constituted himself Maria's assistant and helped her in all her work. The previous day Bert had confirmed to me that he intended to resign as soon as they reached base and apply for emigration to Cara IV.

"I'll be at the end of my service contract at the end of the year, so I won't have any problems," he told me. "My main worries will be how quickly I can get accepted as a colonist and whether I can be transferred to Stockholm from wherever I'm sent."

"Don't fret over the latter point," I advised. "When the time comes I'll have a word with Nils. He's still pretty much the head man in the world and I'm sure he'll be willing to pull a few strings on your behalf."

Marta and I kept a close watch on Maria without making it obvious. She was quiet and withdrawn for a week or so after Bert left, but thereafter her usual sunny disposition asserted itself and she slowly returned to normal. The one thing we did notice was that she flung herself into her work with even more vigour than before and spent all her free time at the vineyard.

A couple of days after the cargo ships followed the *Ural Star* I was invited to a meeting between Sean and Eamonn and the two new farm managers. The purpose was to agree farming policy for the future. I had a right to be there anyway, as I still had the final say on the allocation of land around Stockholm, not that I had any intention of asserting my authority. Little could be done to implement changes that year because Eamonn had already planted his crops. It was decided that the two new farms would plough their respective areas and duplicate Eamonn's work for that year. Thereafter they would go their separate ways. Eamonn would concentrate entirely on cereals, which were his speciality anyway. One of the new farms would grow main crop vegetables only, while the other would be responsible for all fruit and salad items such as tomatoes, lettuce, siboes and beetroot. Until Sean had sufficient livestock to demand his full attention he and his hands would help out the other three farms as required. I wasn't overly happy at having several square miles of my lovingly tended grassland put to the plough, but I realised it was necessary for the general good. Eamonn suggested rounding up some mainly unemployed people to strip as much of the grass as possible from the affected areas and replant it on bare patches elsewhere. I accepted the offer with gratitude, though it would only save a small percentage.

The remaining three intakes for that year came at six weekly intervals. Lisbon was set up at the end of June, Athens received its additional two hundred settlers early in August and Ballymena came into being in mid September. The result was that by the end of autumn extensive new areas had been seeded with grass and trees and several new farms had been ploughed ready for the following spring. When I made a lightning tour at the end of October I calculated that within two years nearly half of the area bounded by Verona, the two northern towns and the Oval Lake would be grassed, forested or under cultivation. Not bad going in four years. I thought.

The director of the Ballymena settlement was a woman in her mid thirties, Bridie Garrity. She was small and slim and came complete with a husband and two teenage sons. The biologist was from Slovakia, Leandra Sikosky. She'd been on the course following mine at the university in Riccione and though she hadn't quite made the top half dozen had been high enough in the rankings to be assigned to Cara IV. Apparently our growing world was still regarded as a plum posting. Leandra had two somewhat surprising pieces of news for me.

"I'm to be the last biologist that will be sent here," she informed me. "According to what I've been told the top brass back on Earth reckon that there is little or no need for any more in view of the progress the rest of you have made. Secondly, as you've seen, we have a female director here in Ballymena. The next six directors due to come will also be women. Equality being such a big political issue on Earth there was the fear that Cara IV was becoming too male dominated. So now they're trying to redress the balance."

Fertility wasn't confined to the plant world that year. Nineteen new babies saw the light of day, five of them in Stockholm. Our animal kingdom had expanded significantly. In total we gained four calves, eighty-two chicks and no less than twenty-five piglets. The pets had been busy too with ten kittens and nine puppies seeing the light of day. These were quickly snapped up. On the food front yields of fruit, particularly soft fruit, were much higher than we'd expected. Between the farms, our greenhouses and people's gardens I reckoned that each person had at least a taste of fresh fruit for consumption even after we'd put aside what we needed for seeding purposes. Maria was overjoyed when her vines produced over three pounds of grapes. Rather than make a limited quantity of wine she and her two partners decided to expand their acreage. They took possession of two more fields adjacent to their existing holding. Generously she shared the small quantity of fruit left over with Marta and I. Our fledgling deciduous trees had also produced flowers and seed for the first time. When it was all gathered in I realised that we would be able to plant nearly two hundred new trees the following spring.

Donna and I had been trying for another child since early summer and with great joy Christmas brought confirmation that she was pregnant again. Our two girls were a source of constant joy to us. At eighteen months Hannah was following in her older sister's footsteps. Like Moira she was a sturdy child and very determined. The two of them were inseparable. In our spare moments Donna and I were teaching them to read and write and we'd even got Moira on to simple sums. Everything that we taught her she gravely passed on to Hannah though the latter hadn't as yet got around to recognising letters, words or numbers. It had been decreed from our early days on the world that primary school would start from the age of four, with provision being made for three year olds to attend a kind of pre-school class. There'd been half a dozen teachers among that year's new arrivals, so class sizes would be minimal right up to secondary education. As yet no decisions had been taken on what form eventual qualifications should take. Nils and the other directors intended to set up some sort of education board to decide on this and other academic matters.

Once the festive season was out of the way I had to give thought to what to bring in from Earth in twelve months' time. By now all the communities that were more than eighteen months old were ordering their own livestock so I only had to worry about Stockholm's needs on this occasion. This necessitated a long discussion with Sean in the first instance. It didn't help matters that he was in two minds himself.

"On the one hand, Alex, I'd like to double the number of birds and animals we have already," he confided. "But I'm not sure at all if we have sufficient food for them and for our present expanding herds. Maybe we should do what you've preached all along and err on the side of caution. After all, we are getting more of just about everything coming in later this year. A few more cows would be useful as they don't multiply as quickly, say another ten or twelve. We don't need any more pigs. Those we've got and those that are coming will multiply in sufficient numbers. Probably we could do with more sheep, but let's leave that for the year after next. I'd also like to bring in some ducks, geese and turkeys, maybe about a dozen of each. I can find food for them all right. By the way, have you given any thought yet to getting in some game birds such as pheasants, partridges, grouse and wood pigeon?"

"I've given thought to it, Sean," I told him. "But the woodland isn't anywhere near advanced enough to accommodate them yet. It'll be another five years at least before we can even consider it and then only in very small numbers."

The January meeting of what we were beginning to call the world's parliament was postponed for some unknown reason until the last week of the month, so it was early February before we had our own local planning session. Nils started as usual by detailing future plans.

"We're asking for five intakes again next year. There'll be three new inland towns set up and Lisbon and Ballymena will be doubled from the other two. The new towns will be south-west of Malaga, south-south-west of Lisbon and due west of Verona. I gather from Nigel Lancing that he will be requesting another four hundred for the north-east area. He intends to keep Manchester solely for mining and refining and set up a new town on the coast to handle the subsequent manufacturing. This will be called Stockport. There'll be no addition to the Oval Lake colony. The two new settlements this year will be roughly sixty kilometres west of Malaga, on the river Finn, and seventy kilometres north-west of Verona. The former has been named San Sebastian and the latter Oslo, so you can guess the nationality of their directors. I asked specifically about any new industries that might appear this year but nobody seems to have any major project on the drawing board. The best I could get was that if sufficient cotton was produced this year there might be some sort of textile output late in the year from Verona. There is some good news from Manchester though. Nigel tells me that they have discovered large deposits of iron, copper, aluminium, tin and chromium, plus smaller quantities of a number of other metals. There are even traces of gold and silver. Mining operations are due to start in earnest next month and manufacturing in late summer. The prospectors have also found an extensive seam of pure china clay and plans are being laid to get some sort of pottery industry up and running. So much for that. Hans, I've already got your orders, so I just need you, Alex, to give me yours."

I told him the gist of the deliberations I'd had with Sean and he noted them down. "In addition to that there's only one other item and I'm doing this with some trepidation. In fact I'm throwing caution to the winds as it were and taking a chance. I'm assuming that the fish we're getting this year will thrive and also that the plankton stocks will cope with the demand on them and continue to multiply. So I want to add variety and bring in a small quantity of spawn to give us sole, bream, bass, mackerel, turbot and whiting. Depending on how the first arrivals settle this year I plan to add hake, skate and some shellfish the following year. Add to that more trout and salmon spawn so that we can stock other rivers and lakes around the whole countryside. Oh, and I'd like three more species of butterflies and two of moths as well. Earth can decide which."

Nils had been busy writing as I spoke. "All noted. One final point. The first arrivals this year will be the party to reinforce Ballymena. That means less travelling to collect our incoming goods. Alex, you might let Sean know if you see him before I do. He'll want to make arrangements for picking up his stock. At least he won't have so far to drive his cattle this time."

The last two weeks in January were mild and spring like and wherever I looked growth was strong. By the second week in February Alastair's bees had awoken from their winter slumbers and were happily buzzing around the winter blooms in the gardens. Morale throughout our town continued to be high. Though everyone worked long hours and many of us were engaged on physical labour outdoors in all weather we all took great satisfaction when we saw the results of our labours. There is something eminently satisfying about the simple life. In effect we had regressed to the kind of existence lived by our forefathers back in the nineteenth and early twentieth centuries. We had no manufactured entertainment other than our personal computers. We made our own leisure pursuits and enjoyed them all the more. Everyone, in Stockholm at any rate, glowed with good health and there wasn't a single person, male or female, that looked overweight. Doctor Nico often complained that he hadn't enough to do, even though he had to cope with half a dozen or more injuries sustained by the footballers every week.

CHAPTER TWENTY

The second conference we had that year produced one piece of news that I had been expecting for some time. As usual Nils had given us the gist of the directors' meeting held the day before and taken reports from Hans, Herr Klost, Nico and myself. Then he moved on to the final item on his agenda.

"At the end of our meetings we always jot down a few points that we either want to leave for the next session or want to discuss with others in our towns. This is one that I'd like to have your views on. There have been three or four formal requests from individuals to move from one town to another. In the main it's to be nearer to friends or relatives and it's probable that there will be others in the near future. What do you think?"

"I don't see how we can refuse," Hans reflected. "After all, this is a free world, not a prison camp. Every town has spare housing, so there are no problems on that front. I suggest you make it policy and invite applications, with the proviso that permission won't be automatic but depend on local needs and circumstances."

"I agree with Hans, but with one reservation," I contributed. "Because we were here a year before anyone else we are marginally better off here in Stockholm in the way of food and amenities. There may well be some people who'll want to come here for that reason and no other. Any such application should be discouraged."

"I agree," said Nils. "Are there any difficulties on the banking front, Herr Klost?"

"None at all," replied the banker. "It will only take a day to set up the mechanism for transferring an account from one town's bank to another."

"In that case I'll be voting in favour," announced Nils. "What's the position with vacant houses just now Hans?"

"When I checked last week there were sixteen two roomed units and eleven three roomed units empty. Those figures should still be correct as I've had no notification of any moves since then."

While that particular matter didn't come as a surprise to me there were shocks just around the corner. The next director's meeting was held on the last Tuesday in March. It had been arranged for Hanover to give the directors a first-hand look at the progress being made in the water supply scheme. I had my first inkling that something was afoot when I got a phone call from Nils at five in the afternoon.

"Alex, I've been unable to contract Ingrid," he said. "She must have gone out and not taken her phone with her. Could you slip round and tell her that I won't be home tonight. If she's not in leave a message. We have so much still to discuss that we've decided to stay overnight here." I promised to do as he asked and before I forgot wrote a short note on a piece of scrap paper. Ingrid still wasn't in when I called at their house so I slipped my letter under the door.

In the end the directors spent a second night at Hanover. Hans and I talked the matter over at length and came to the conclusion that something vitally important was being considered. We weren't wrong, as we found out the following day at our local meeting. Nils had a lot to tell us.

"We spent part of the time inspecting the installation there," he began, "but the reason for the long session was that we were taking some important decisions regarding the immediate future. It's become apparent in the last few months that government of our world is fast becoming a full time job. We propose therefore to establish a capital city which as near as possible will be at the centre of the area bounded by the new town to be set up south of Verona, Oval Lake and the Manchester complex in the north. We've settled on the exact site. The town thus created will be called Europa and when we send our requirements next January they will include six hundred settlers, housing and all the allied paraphernalia. Any questions so far?"

Hans took the words out of my mouth. "I've always assumed Stockholm would be the capital. We were first here and we're centrally placed."

Nils smiled. "We're centrally placed as far as the coastal towns are concerned, but a hell of a long way from Hanover. Don't forget too that all the expansion in the next ten years will be inland."

"Does that mean you'll be going to leave us and live permanently in Europa?" was my question.

"Oh, no, nothing like that. We'd all continue to live in our home towns and commute daily. With the new high speed hoverbuses the longest travelling time for anyone would be under an hour and a half. In any case, at the beginning we'd probably only need to meet two or three times a week. Incidentally, once the official parliament is up and running we'll be holding elections. I may not even be our representative after that."

"I'll be very surprised if you're not," Hans commented and I nodded agreement.

"There was another main decision that was taken," Nils went on. "We managed to get copies of the large scale maps that the engineers at Hanover are using and we've settled the location of every new town that will be set up in this phase of colonisation. Including the present settlements there will eventually be forty-eight towns in this segment of the world. Once they're all functional future immigrants will be used to increase gradually the population of each town to between two and three thousand. That will take anything up to twenty years. When that's accomplished we'll consider whether to expand further north and south or cross the mountain range. The latter option will depend on what transport we'll have at our disposal by then."

One part of my mind was considering all that Nils was saying while another was turning over an idea I'd been working on for some time.

"Do you have one of those large scale maps with you and if so can I get a copy please?" I asked. I didn't want to go into details at that time as my thoughts were only half formed. "It would be tremendously useful in my own future planning." I knew that the maps Hans had only covered the narrow strip of land bordering the coastline and though we had been given maps of the whole eastern seaboard before leaving Earth these were on a very small scale.

"I've got one at home," was the answer I got from Nils. "I'll get it copied and drop it in to you. Meantime the other important issue we agreed on was that Europa would become the distribution centre for all goods. Everything produced, food, machines and all other items will be sent to Europa. All orders will be sent there and the goods supplied from there. There will be a few exceptions, mainly items moving between two adjacent towns where it's more convenient to send direct. Now I know there are objections that can be raised. In many cases it will mean double handling and extra transport miles. But Nigel in Manchester assures me that when his factories are up and running they'll want to concentrate on the manufacturing side and not be sending small consignments here there and everywhere. The same applies to other industries elsewhere. It will also save work on the ordering side. Supposing Hans here needs two or three different machines and other components. Instead of ordering each item separately all he will need to do is send one order to the despatch centre in Europa. His goods will come in one consignment and not in dribs and drabs."

The map that Nils gave me proved to be exactly what I needed and over the next few days I worked out my proposed course of action. First of all I used some of our meagre ration of paper to make six copies, then I called a meeting of the six other biologists for the following Sunday. I picked Sunday because I was able to get the use of the school building. I needed plenty of space for what I intended. One by one they drifted in, with Denise the last to arrive at half past ten. Maria and Marta, who were to stay for the meeting, served coffee and then we got down to business. To ensure I didn't forget anything I'd made a few notes beforehand and I consulted these before I started.

"I think I've mentioned to some of you that our trees here in Stockholm have produced seeds this year," were my opening words. "In fact, we've got enough to plant nearly two hundred new trees. Over the next two or three years your own trees will follow suit in ever increasing quantities."

Kristina interrupted me at this point. "I've already had a dozen or so acorns."

"There'll be a lot more next year," I assured her. "Now I hardly need to tell you that the more trees we can plant the greater the benefit, if not for ourselves then certainly for the next and future generations. Therefore I've formulated what I'm calling my ten year plan. In reality it could take anything up to twenty years to complete but my poor brain can't think that far ahead. Basically I want to lay down forests in all the vacant land between the towns. I've been able to get detailed maps of where every town will be located and I have a copy for each of you. I've coloured in the area which each of you will be responsible for. As we're a year ahead here we'll be taking two sections; the ones covering the square formed by Helsinki, San Sebastian, Lisbon and Stockholm and that to the south bounded by Ballymena and Athens. Your own areas will be to the south or north as appropriate and the west. Now before I go any further would anyone like to make any comments?"

There was silence for a moment or two and then Denise put up her hand. "Do you want me to carry on planting more tropical trees or will I bring in some temperate ones?"

"Stick to the tropical trees," was my advice. "We want as much variety as we can get. But if the seeds are there give preference to those which will achieve a future supply of timber. You know what's required: teak, walnut, mahogany, bamboo, etc. One of the things you might consider as well is to plant date and coconut palms all the way down the coast to the new town that's going to be set up south of you."

There were no other comments, so I continued my discourse. "You'll notice that I've drawn a ten mile circle, that's about sixteen kilometres, around every town. That's to allow for farmland and future expansion. So far it sounds very straightforward but there is one snag. There will be hoverbus services between every town sooner or later, so we'll have to leave a passage for them between the trees. I've fixed that at half a kilometre wide. I'm hoping that our engineers will be able to come up with some kind of lighting around the edges to give directions. We'll have to leave this space diagonally as well as straight across, so basically each

151

forest will consist of four parts. I haven't shown this on the map. It will be up to each of you to work out the details for yourselves."

The problem with the hoverbuses had only occurred to me the night before. At that time they only ran during the hours of daylight. Though they were fitted with headlights these were not too far reaching, having been designed for use on Earth where street lighting and roads were clearly marked. It was considered too dangerous to use the vehicles at night. Even with no obstructions in the way it would be only too easy to stray off course and head out to sea or into uncharted country. Scientists back on Earth were working on the dilemma and it was hoped that some solution could be found. Whether this would be stronger lights or some sort of installed radar or deflectors in the buses nobody seemed to know.

Maria and Marta had organised a cold buffet early in the morning, so we had what Roger described as a working lunch. We spent the rest of the day going over the fine details of the plan and I was pleased to see that everyone was enthusiastic. The meeting broke up just after three. I felt it had been a worthwhile day.

A few days later the ship arrived bringing the extra two hundred settlers for Ballymena and our additional livestock. It also carried three veterinary surgeons, an addition to our world that was much overdue. In fact we could have absorbed a dozen quite easily. The directors divided the settled part of the world into three roughly equal portions and allocated one vet to each. In the north San Sebastian was to be the headquarters and in the south Verona. I'd hoped that the central area HQ would have been Stockholm, but Ballymena was chosen as the most suitable. As Nils explained to me when I questioned the decision we had to bear in mind the new towns that would be set up inland. Of course we hoped that more vets would arrive in due course but we couldn't be certain that they would.

The most exciting aspect for me was the receipt of our fish spawn. With Maria fully occupied between her normal duties and her vineyard I gave Marta the responsibility for marine matters. The spawn was still frozen when it was unloaded, so we took it back to the office and left it overnight to defrost. The next morning Marta and I took a hovercar and headed up the coast to a point some ten miles south of Helsinki. We then drove southwards as slowly as we could looking for suitable places to deposit the now thawed spawn. What I was looking for were places where a piece of land jutted out into the sea. I wanted to place the spawn in water at least three feet deep: one where the supply of food would be more plentiful than at the water's edge. We'd travelled fifteen miles before finding the first suitable spot. This was a triangle of cliff that had its sharp edge in about six feet of water. A narrow ledge on one side made the traverse possible but somewhat hazardous. We managed it with care and I gave Marta the parcel of haddock spawn to drop carefully into the calm water below.

Our next halt was six or seven miles south of Stockholm. Here a finger of sandy beach protruded some thirty feet into the water and Marta placed the cod spawn on the surface and we watched it sink slowly to the bottom. Another twenty-five miles south and we found the perfect location for the plaice. I'd been hoping for some kind of bay or inlet and was beginning to despair of finding one when Marta gave a cry and pointed to a small cove enclosed by low rocks. We scrambled down to the shore and Marta insisted on taking off her shoes and socks and wading out about twenty yards to lower the spawn gently into the water. By now it was past lunchtime so we headed back home for a meal. I'd considered leaving the trout and salmon 'planting' till the following day but Marta insisted on carrying on. She was so full of enthusiasm that I hadn't the heart to say no. Accordingly we went up to Lake Gothenburg once we'd eaten. I'd divided the trout spawn into four sections and we put them in the lake at equal distances apart. The salmon I'd split into three and these went into the River Sverige at roughly four mile intervals.

I'd intended to visit the various sites once every four or five days but Marta forestalled me. Every morning she rose at six o'clock just as it was getting light. I'd been able to get an altab for our permanent use and on that she visited all the locations, returning between ten and eleven to carry on with her normal duties. It was about two weeks later, a Thursday morning if I recall correctly, that she came bursting into the office at half past ten.

"Alex, come with me," she said breathlessly. "I've something to show you." I had a pretty good idea what it was, but I played along. We took the car to where we'd left the cod spawn. Proudly Marta pointed down into the water. Sure enough, there was a froth of tiny wriggling fish. I said a silent prayer that nothing would hamper their growth. Within the week most of the other spawn both at sea and inland had hatched. Marta still kept up her daily inspection and I accompanied her once every few days as the fish grew. After about three weeks those in the sea started to move out into deeper water, presumably to find richer sources of food, and we didn't see them again. But we were able to watch the trout and the salmon. The former too had moved out from the shore, but Hans had a small boat on the lake and we often went out for an hour in that. It became a competition between Marta and I as to who could spot the most baby trout in that time.

While I enjoyed working with Marta and liked and respected her very much indeed I never had the easy relationship with her that I'd had with Julie and still had with Maria. There were hidden depths to her that I never managed to plumb. She had no interest in the opposite sex and was often rude to any man who tried to flirt with her. Yet I was fairly certain she wasn't gay. I often discussed her with Donna, who was just as puzzled as I was. The best suggestion she could come up with was that Marta had been hurt badly at some time in the past. One thing we were certain about. Marta would have made a wonderful mother. She often babysat for us if Patrick wasn't available and she was brilliant with the children. They loved her too. There were times when Moira or Hannah or more usually both were being cheeky and naughty, but as soon as Marta came in the door they were as good as gold.

It was just about that time that I made some slight alterations in the functions of the biology department. Hitherto we'd concentrated on growing plants in our greenhouses and either planting them out in the gardens ourselves or giving them to the householders. From then on I decided that we would put all our efforts into producing seed. There were none in the community who were fully unemployed, though around twenty only found part time or casual jobs. A trawl among these produced Flora Kuyper, a middle-aged Dutch lady who had had experience in the tulip growing industry. She readily agreed to open a new seed shop, the original one having closed after just a few months. Hans had managed to use some left over units from the housing components to build four extra two-roomed shops along our growing main street. The arrangement we made was that we would pass on to her all the seed we grew without charging and that she would then sell it on to the householders. With so little in the way of entertainment nearly everyone in the community had become keen gardeners and there was even talk of holding competitions for the best flowers, fruit and vegetables. Somehow that scheme never got off the ground, but the desire for attractive gardens remained strong. In the beginning we extracted the seeds ourselves in the greenhouses, but very soon Flora insisted she had more time than us and we simply passed everything over to her. We couldn't spare any of our meagre stock of paper for seed packets, so Flora ordered up a quantity of large glass jars, selling the seed loose at so much a gram. I can't remember now exactly what she charged, but I do know the price was very low. The farmers all continued to produce their own seed but passed on any surplus to Flora.

In June Helsinki, Athens and Verona took delivery of their first livestock. By now the grass was spreading rapidly through the countryside and I issued a directive saying that for the future every new settlement could bring in animals and poultry one year after arrival. This would make ordering easier. They would simply indicate their requirements before leaving Earth. In the meantime our own additional cows in Stockholm doubled milk production and rations were increased. From the first of June onwards the daily allowance per person of milk doubled to a litre per person and butter went up from fifty grams to seventy-five per person per week. The cheese ration remained unchanged at fifty grams, but with a promise that it would increase in the following year. Much of our cheese stock was still maturing.

CHAPTER TWENTY-ONE

On the eighteenth of July our hopes were fulfilled and Donna gave birth to a fine healthy boy. We named him Eoin George and he weighed in at a massive nine pounds eight ounces. The bonding moment between Moira and Hannah had been so successful we repeated it with Eoin. Once again the baby was delivered in one of the two new tiny hospital wards that Nico had set up and the two girls came in about twenty minutes later. We allowed each to hold the baby in turn, Moira first. As before, she kissed the baby gently on the lips and told him she loved him, then Hannah gravely did exactly the same. Because this had been a much more difficult and taxing delivery Nico insisted that Donna and the baby should stay in the hospital for three or four days. Donna was rebellious.

"I can't leave Alex on his own to look after the two girls," she protested. "It'll be far too much for him."

"Don't be silly," I told her sternly. "They'll be no problem. I'll take them to work with me and they'll love it. In any case, Moira is at pre-school every morning and Patrick and Marta are always around and willing to step in if needed. So just do what Nico says and have a good rest."

"I can rest just as easily at home," she objected, though less forcibly.

"Aye, I know your idea of resting," was my response. "You'll only be on your feet nine hours a day instead of twelve. Anyway, Nico's the boss. If he says you're to stay here then here you'll stay and no more arguments." She gave in with ill grace and I was sure I'd be getting an earful when she eventually returned home.

That summer was the hottest and wettest we'd had since coming to Cara IV. The result was even faster growth than normal. For the first time we had enough fruit for all without the need for rationing. In fact we had a surplus of gooseberries and strawberries. Two middle-aged sisters from Bulgaria bought up all they could and set up a homemade jam business. They ordered a supply of three hundred gram jars from the glassworks in Helsinki and that autumn everyone in Stockholm got one jar of the product. The woodlands benefitted from the hot weather too. By the end of autumn we had enough material to plant another six hundred trees. The first few cones appeared on the coniferous trees as well. It never ceased to amaze me how quickly things grew on Cara IV. It was as if the planet regretted the millions of years that it had lain barren and was determined to make up for lost time.

At the start of September Denise paid a flying visit, bringing with her a couple of melons of different varieties, a pumpkin and three pomegranates. Up to then we hadn't tried growing any of these. I knew that melons would grow well in temperate climates though I wasn't sure about the other two. While Denise admired the baby and settled down to some woman talk with Donna I headed off to the greenhouse, extracted the seeds and planted as much as I could. There were plenty of seeds left over, so these went to Flora's shop.

Another Christmas and New Year passed and it was time once more for our annual order to Earth to be discussed. The main item on the agenda was the establishment of Europa. After discussions with Sean my own agenda was fairly small and predictable. I wanted more trout and salmon spawn plus three additional species of fish and three more types of butterflies. Sean wanted a dozen more cows, the same number of sheep and more poultry. He also suggested getting another four horses, all mares and half a dozen goats and donkeys. Hans wondered whether we should bring in more dogs and cats, but I vetoed the suggestion.

"The ones we've got are multiplying nicely," was my view, "and the other towns have started to bring some in. We don't want them overrunning the world in ten or so years' time."

With the increasing output of cotton from the southern towns and the first small quantity of wool from the few sheep around we finally got some new baby clothes and joy of joys some proper nappies. These had to be bought in from Verona and Athens. It seemed common sense that as these were the areas that grew the raw materials they should also specialise in the manufacture. Hans raised a point at our monthly meeting in April.

"We're getting the beginning of organised trade on the world; clothing from the south, metal products from the north, glass from Helsinki. So far we're not producing anything worthwhile for export to the other settlements. There must be something in which we can corner the market, but I can't come up with any ideas."

Nils looked at me. I took my time to consider the matter before speaking. "All being well there should be a considerable surplus of fruit this year and we'll be the only town that has one. If we turn the extra over to jam making there should be plenty for us and enough to sell elsewhere. We might just be able to make enough to corner the market for the next couple of years. After that, though, I'm afraid other towns will have their own surpluses. But if we can keep things ticking over for, say, another five years we can be the leaders in the fishing market. I suggest we order a couple or three small fishing boats from Earth next year. That will give us a head start on everywhere else. Apart from supplying fresh fish we can set up processing plants. Tins should be readily available by then; there'll be fish oil products if we can build up a market for them, not to mention offal that can be used as manure and pet food. There is one other possibility. As you know, Maria has her own vineyard and with her partners has set up a facility for making homemade wine. Small quantities of the first of the wines will be available this year. None of the other towns, not even Verona, is anywhere near as advanced. By the time the jam boom comes to an end we can supply reasonable quantities of wine to others."

"In the meantime," Nils summed up, "we can keep thinking about this and see if we can come up with any more ideas." And there we left it.

Three new townships were set up that year. Tilburg was some forty miles south-west of San Sebastian in what had hitherto been a fairly isolated area. The other two were in what we called the 'deep south'. Rotterdam was on the coast some fifty-five miles south of Verona, while Sofia was situated on the shore of a small lake eighty miles due west of Verona. We wanted, or should I say the council of directors wanted to increase substantially the production of tropical crops, especially cotton, dates, pineapples and bananas. A few miles inland from Rotterdam was a low lying area of around forty square miles. Several engineers, including Hans and one of the team from the Oval Lake had surveyed the site and reckoned that it could be flooded without too much trouble to provide the conditions suitable for growing rice.

All this time work had proceeded apace at and around Oval Lake. By the summer the forecast was that the whole project would be completed within the next four years. That estimate covered a supply to all forty-eight proposed settlements. Water to the existing towns should be running within three years. At the request of the governing council the supply to Europa was made a priority as there was little in the way of rivers and lakes in that vicinity. Meanwhile Hans was in regular discussions with his fellow engineers centred on setting up a similar national grid for electricity supplies.

"Don't hold your breath, though," he told me with a grin. "We're sorting out the ways and means and how much material we'll need, but if we get started within three years I'll be surprised. Sure, we'll get started some time, but allow ten years at least for completion."

At the beginning of September Nils asked Hans and I to accompany him on a trip to the site of Europa. He wanted our views on matters affecting the setting up of the township. I was delighted to be asked. Although I'd almost certainly flown close to or over the locality on my trips to the other side of the mountains the area was unfamiliar to me. We set off by hovercar, Hans driving, early on a Wednesday morning taking packed lunches with us. The one hundred and thirty mile journey took us just over two hours. As we were approaching our destination the ground began to rise ever so gently until I estimated we were about two hundred and fifty feet above sea level. Beyond the slope lay a huge natural bowl, almost circular in shape and at a guess some ten miles in diameter. A couple of narrow streams flowed through the bowl and there were a few microscopic patches of grass in places, otherwise it was bare. In the middle of the bowl a metal stake had been driven into the ground. We stopped beside this and got out of the car.

"I've brought the two of you along to come up with some ideas," Nils broke a half hour of silence between us. "We have a design for the layout of the town, but the environment needs attention. I also want you both to be involved in the actual setting up of the town when the new group arrive."

"What's the timescale?" Hans wanted to know.

"The ship bringing the six hundred colonists is due to arrive around the second week in June," said Nils. "Wolfgang assures me that the water supply from the Oval Lake will be installed by then." He gave a light laugh. "If he's wrong we're in dead trouble. Right. Let's have any thoughts that occur to you."

I continued to look around me while Hans took up the invitation. "Actually it's an ideal situation as far as a power supply is concerned. We can put as many wind turbines as we need anywhere around the ridge top. If you let me have a copy of the proposed layout I can place the generator and control unit somewhere suitable. You'll need four or five bridges over those streams, but they'll only require to be small ones so we can fabricate them ourselves. The only thing I'm not sure about is whether we can get hold of sufficient stone to put slabs down in every street. With up to five hundred houses plus shops and offices, not to mention a parliament building it all adds up to a lot of individual streets."

By the time Hans had finished I'd made up my own mind and was ready when Nils looked towards me. "I presume there'll be farms here as in every other town. The first priority is to get some grass sown. I'll need to find out if any of the other towns have any seed left as we have none. If not it will be a case of scouring the countryside. There's plenty of grass going to seed at the moment, but that method will be time consuming and the sooner we get planting the better the grass will have grown by next June. I'd like a copy of your plan as well, please. Once I know where the open land is going to be I'll plant some fruit trees and bushes, plus a few more trees here in the bowl to break up the bareness of the landscape. Then if Hans tells me where his turbines will be sited I propose a ring of trees around the rim of the bowl. That will suffice for the first three or four years. After that, as you know, we'll be working towards foresting the whole area around. Once all the houses are up and occupied we'll come and put a small amount of stuff in the gardens. After that, though, it will mainly be up to the householders, as we'll be charging for the seeds and plants."

We spent a little over two hours discussing matters in more detail while we had our lunch. It was a warm dry day with just a hint of a cool breeze. In my mind I tried to visualise what the town and its environs would look like in a few years' time and I came to the conclusion that it would be a pleasant place to live, though a small lake somewhere close would have improved the outlook considerably. I said as much to the others.

"It wouldn't be too difficult to put in a man-made one," was the comment from Hans. "They've got plenty of excavating equipment at the Oval Lake. Once their job is complete we'll be able to use it for all sorts of other projects."

We arrived back in Stockholm at four o'clock and I spent the next hour and a half phoning round in search of grass seed. There wasn't a lot on offer, but in the end I located twenty-two sacks, which was more than I'd expected. I drove many miles the following day collecting them from far flung places. The next day Marta and I took a van and drove out to the Europa site. I managed to persuade Eamonn to come along as well as I wanted an expert opinion as to the best areas for crops and for pasture land. He followed us by car and for company brought along his daughter, fifteen-year-old Siobhan. On arrival he spent an hour or more walking round with a spade in his hand, digging into the soil at intervals. Eventually he made up his mind.

"There's not much difference," he concluded, "but I'd say that the south of the town would be best for crops." I expected him to return home after he'd delivered his verdict but both he and Siobhan insisted on staying and helping to scatter the grass seed. We were glad of the help and had the job done in little more than an hour. Siobhan seemed to be enjoying herself and whenever she was in range asked Marta and I a whole string of questions. I'd brought along a few dozen acorns and horse chestnuts and we finished our days' work by planting them at intervals around the ridge top. Hans had given me a rough plan of where his turbines would be going. Once we'd completed that part we took a rest and while the girls sat and chatted Eamonn and I walked around. I had an idea that I wanted to put to him.

"I take it Siobhan will be leaving school at the end of the year or early next year," I began. Eamonn nodded and I went on. "She seems to be keen on this sort of thing. I could use another assistant, so unless you have full time work for her on the farm I'd like to take her on. It's up to you, though. The farm has priority."

"Oh, I can find plenty of work for her," Eamonn replied in a dry tone. "The trouble is that I won't be able to pay her for it. If you can give her a job and she's keen on the idea then take her with my blessing." A brief question established that Siobhan was very keen on the idea indeed.

In fact I hadn't been entirely honest, but at that time I didn't want to betray a confidence. Maria had approached me the previous week to ask if she could be relieved of her duties by the following spring. The vineyard was prospering and she and her partners were proposing to buy more land and extend further.

"Of course I wouldn't leave you in the lurch," she promised. "If you can't get a replacement I'll happily stay on. But the vineyard needs more and more attention and I'd like to involve myself more in the wine making side of things." She sighed. "I thought I'd got the wine business out of my system when I came here, but I guess it's still there after all. Then when Bert comes back and we get married I intend to move my house to the vineyard."

I moved quickly thereafter. Arrangements were made for Siobhan to spend any spare time she had before the end of the year with Maria. Once she left school she would come in full time, shadow Maria for a month and then take over. I had no worries about her being unqualified. She was a bright, intelligent girl, quick to learn and in any case most of the work she would be doing was routine. In many ways she reminded me of Julie. She was built along the same generous lines and physically immensely strong. Like Julie she had a very outgoing disposition and a real appetite for hard work. The main difference between them was that Siobhan had long auburn hair as opposed to Julie's short and severe brown locks. Most important of all, she and Marta liked each other and soon became friends.

I called another meeting of all the biologists towards the end of November. Though they were constantly in touch with me individually to report progress I wanted everyone to know what everyone else had achieved during the year. We held the meeting in Ballymena, a suitable central point, with Leandra Sikosky acting as hostess. It was an upbeat assembly. Production everywhere had exceeded expectations, in some cases by as much as forty per cent. Progress around Verona was little short of phenomenal. Denise was of the opinion that she would be able to send several varieties of tropical fruit to other towns in the next year and they had already taken fruit off the ration in the town itself. Cotton and sugar output too was well in advance of previous estimates. Once we'd finished patting ourselves on the back we discussed plans for the coming year. Most of my colleagues were now in a position to make a start on my plan for forestation. When we added up the seed available we found that we would be able to plant upwards of one thousand two hundred trees in the following twelve months.

CHAPTER TWENTY-TWO

The previous winter had been the warmest since our arrival. Just to balance the books this one was the coldest. The new year brought with it sub zero temperatures and on the fifth snow blanketed the east coast as far south as Athens. The Manchester complex was very badly hit, with almost eight inches. In Stockholm we had three. Worse still, it lay for a full ten days before thawing. Even then temperatures remained low with occasional night frosts until the end of January. Day after day was cold and cloudy. Julie was still keeping her weather watch despite her marriage and move to Helsinki and she told me in a phone call on the thirty-first that there'd only been thirteen hours of sunshine during the whole month. I thought wryly that we had congratulated ourselves too soon at our biologists' meeting. Not surprisingly morale was affected. For just about the first time most people walked around with long faces. Even Jennifer, the doctor's wife and normally the most cheerful of souls, greeted me one morning with a glum look.

"If I'd known it was going to be like this I'd have stayed in Edinburgh," she grumbled.

"No you wouldn't," I retorted. "You're forgetting that in Scotland it was often like this for most of the winter. Anyway," I added with a grin, "you'd never have let Nico come here by himself with all these beautiful young girls around." She gave me a sour look and walked on.

Inevitably things improved and by the end of February I reckoned that growth was only about ten days behind that of the previous year. My main concern was the welfare of the farm animals, but Sean assured me that all was well. He was too good a farmer to be caught out by bad weather and had stockpiled plenty of hay and other cattle food. A considerable acreage had been given over to turnips and swedes over the past two years and there was more than enough to feed to the animals. I checked frequently on the birds in our woodland, but they too seemed to have coped and were still being fed and fed well by the townspeople.

Despite the low temperatures neither rivers nor lakes froze over. Marta and I kept a close check on them and the growing trout and salmon seemed none the worse for wear. Early that month we took a boat out to sea but we failed to find any sign of fish. I crossed my fingers and hoped for the best. Maria finally gave up her post at the end of the second week of February and Siobhan officially took over. Within days I noticed a change in Marta. While she and Maria had been on good terms and worked well together they'd never been close friends. Maybe the fact that Maria was older and more senior had something to do with it though I may have been wrong. But a very strong friendship had already evolved between Marta and Siobhan. After a fortnight Siobhan left the farm and moved in with Marta, while the latter lost much of her serious demeanour and smiled and laughed far more often. Donna from time to time asked me if the two of them were lovers. I told her I didn't think so, but in any case it was none of my business. They were happy, they worked hard and well and that made me happy. What they did with their spare time was up to them.

It was in that spring that the pattern of life began to change on our world. People generally had more leisure time than hitherto. Very few now worked on Saturday afternoons or Sundays and travelling between the towns increased. Roger and Julie became frequent visitors. Their first baby was due in August. After lunch, while our wives talked about babies and other matters of female interest Roger and I would tour the greenhouses and the woodlands north and south of the town talking shop. Roger was a restful companion; in many ways the opposite of myself. He had a prosaic attitude to life and a methodical approach to everything. I was more impulsive and prone to improvise. We would have made a good working team. Kristina and her family from Athens were other regulars, as was Denise and her partner. Naturally we returned these visits, much to the delight of the children. There were more parties too. What few sports facilities we had were in constant demand and the desire for a golf course was ever present. Finally I bowed to pressure and Hans and I sat down one day to design one.

The major problem was finding sufficient space for a course that wasn't too far away from the town. I began to regret my original decision to plant the two areas of forest so close. It meant that there was no suitable area within two miles. Though there were a fair number of vehicles around we were still a long way short of having one car for every family. Eventually we picked out a site three miles to the north, just beyond the coniferous wood. The area along the coast and for several miles inland was by now well grassed and wasn't used for grazing. Over a period of several weeks we worked out a plan for a nine hole course which could in time be extended to eighteen holes. Construction would start in the autumn and would be carried out by Hans and a small squad. I would be responsible for preparing the greens and for planting trees along the fairways. Initially there would be no clubhouse, but the word from the north was that manufacturing of building components would start in less than eighteen months' time. When these were available Hans would then add a clubhouse. In any case it would take the best part of a year before the course was completed and probably another few months before it was playable.

Another milestone was reached on our anniversary day of the sixth of April. Sean had been fattening up the surplus male pigs from the previous year's litters and he slaughtered four of them for the occasion. Each adult was allowed five hundred grams of meat and each child two hundred and fifty. As a special concession even babes in arms were allocated a child's ration. Single people living on their own got chops or loin steaks, families got joints. With an allowance of one hundred and seventy-five grams, or two and three-quarter pounds in real terms Donna and I got a shoulder joint. I'm ashamed to say we made beasts of ourselves and had very little left over after our midday meal. Though a little doubtful at first the girls soon got the taste too and consumed their fair share. Donna took some of the cooked meat, shredded it, pulped it and added the result to Eoin's mashed vegetables. He digested it happily and was none the worse for wear afterwards.

The second Saturday in May dawned warm and bright and on the spur of the moment I decided to take a trip out to the Europa site to see how the grass was progressing. We made it a family outing. Donna put together a picnic lunch and we set off around ten. Thankfully the children all enjoyed travelling by car and we didn't need to stop once. As we came over the top of the ridge I was pleased to see a swathe of green on the right hand side of the bowl. I was so busy admiring this as I drove slowly to the centre and parked the car that I didn't notice anything else. Only when Donna drew my attention to it did I see the big water tower rising above the western side of the ridge. Pipes with no visible connections snaked out from this. Wolfgang had kept his promise and Europa would be connected to the supply from the Oval Lake within days of the colonists arriving.

Naturally enough the children fell in love with the place and all the open space they had to play in. Even Eoin, though only just beginning to walk, had a ball, alternately crawling and staggering around in circles. The girls wandered off on their own though the nature of the ground meant that they were always in sight. Almost inevitably Hannah fell into one of the small shallow streams. Donna and I were laying out the picnic and the first we knew of it was when her screams rent the air. The girls were some two hundred and fifty yards away and I covered the distance in what must have been close to record time. When I reached them Moira had already pulled Hannah from the water. The two of them were soaked. Hannah gave me a beaming smile and said happily: "I fell in." I hugged her tight with one arm, gathering Moira into the other for an even bigger hug and told her she was brave and had done well. By the time we got back to the car I was soaking wet too. Thankfully Donna had thought to bring a couple of towels with her and we soon dried off in the sun. The rest of the day passed without incident. On the way home I toured round the rim of the ridge to check on the trees I'd planted. Nearly all were showing above ground, but the tallest was only about four inches high.

Our yearly supplies from Earth arrived a fortnight later. After releasing the new birds and butterflies Marta and I, occasionally accompanied by Siobhan, got down to distributing the fish spawn. As far as the sea species were concerned it was difficult to find suitable places with three feet or more of water. In the end we had to resort to standing at the water's edge and lobbing or throwing the spawn as far as we could. I didn't think any damage would be done, but I crossed my fingers every time to be on the safe side. The next couple of days we toured huge swathes of the countryside dropping small quantities of salmon and trout spawn into every suitable river and lake that we could find. Finally Marta and I took the long trip out to the Oval Lake and put the last of the trout spawn into four separate locations. Throughout the three days, whenever we were near a town we called into the police office there and warned the staff to be vigilant and enforce the fishing ban rigidly. That included children wanting to fish for minnows.

Every arrival I'd attended up to that point had been blessed with fine weather. Perversely, when the settlers for Europa appeared the conditions were horrendous. I'd gone with Nils and Hans. Salvatore Celli had made the long journey from Verona, picking up Bridie Garrity at Ballymena on the way. It was just after eleven o'clock when the *Fleur de Lys* appeared through the lowering clouds and touched down in pouring rain. Remarking that there was no need for all of us to get wet Nils splashed his way across to the ship. Some fifteen minutes later he returned.

"Captain Asarne has decided not to offload the passengers until the rain stops," he informed us. "By the look of it that won't be today. In the meantime he's invited us all to lunch. We'll drive as close to the entry hatch as we can."

We got to within three yards, but we still got wet before we entered the ship. Captain Asarne was a tall thin Frenchman of Algerian descent. He greeted us warmly before leading the way to the wardroom. Here we met Therese Dupres, the director of Europa. On the small side and slightly plump with grey hair I initially estimated that she was in her early fifties. I later learned that she was in fact forty-one, having gone prematurely grey in her late twenties. Hers was a sad story. She had married at twenty-four and on the last day of the honeymoon her husband had been drowned while swimming. The post mortem was inconclusive, but the theory was either that he had had a sudden heart attack or been struck down with cramp. After a period of mourning she had immersed herself in politics and had been a government minister in France when she was appointed to the directorship of Europa.

We lingered over lunch. Madame Dupres wanted to know all about our progress on Cara IV and we were all hungry for news of Earth. After we'd eaten the directors went off to a private cabin to talk business while Captain Asarne took Hans and myself on a tour of the ship. He was the second most senior captain in the Space Fleet and an interesting companion. He'd made more than a dozen trips carrying colonists to the outer worlds and was loud in his praises for the progress made on all of them. On his retirement in five years time, he told us, he would not go back to Earth but would settle on Persephone.

All three of the accompanying cargo ships had touched down when we finally got back to the car well after three. The rain was still incessant and it was obvious that nothing would emerge from the ships that day. I didn't go back next day, although it was dry and sunny. The convoy carried nothing for Stockholm and I'd done all I could to help the environment until the town was properly installed. Poor Nils was left to travel on his own as Hans had taken a lorry and a large squad to help with putting up the houses and other buildings. It was a full three weeks before I visited the site again, taking Siobhan with me. We took a lorry load of small trees and bushes with us to plant in the gardens, plus a variety of flower and vegetable seeds for distribution. It was a long hard day and we didn't get back to Stockholm until half past nine.

Two months later saw the first meeting of the World Parliament. Nils invited Donna and I, along with Hans and Herr Klost and their wives, to the opening ceremony. Leaving the children with Marta we set off early in the morning of a hot, sunny and cloudless day. Formal clothes were unknown on our world but we did the best we could as a mark of respect to the event. I wore my best uniform, sadly now a little threadbare, while Donna looked radiant in a pale green dress that she reserved for special occasions. It was a simple ceremony, with short speeches, first from Nils and then from several other directors. Then came a blessing from representatives of the Protestant, Catholic, Muslim, Jewish and Russian and Greek Orthodox churches, after which the parliament was officially declared open for business. Then we were given a tour. It was by far the largest building yet erected on Cara IV. There were sixty-four seats in the debating chamber arranged in four semi-circular rows facing a main desk. Behind a low wall there was accommodation for some forty spectators. Four smaller committee rooms were in the rear, plus a canteen, two large store rooms, a bathroom and three additional toilets. There were four fully furnished en suite bedrooms for anyone needing or wishing to stay overnight. A further three rooms were bare, ready for use for any purpose that might be decided at a later date. A large car park at the rear completed the establishment.

After a buffet lunch we were taken to see the second biggest building in our world. The Capital Hotel was the first such venture on Cara IV. Boasting eight bedrooms, a restaurant and a cafeteria, it sat in an acre of land at the edge of the town, giving plenty of room for expansion in the future. I wondered aloud to Hans whether such a facility was necessary.

"Maybe not for a while," he admitted. "But in time there'll be people visiting to make submissions to parliament and there'll be sightseers wanting to see government in action. Europa itself may become a tourist centre. I don't suppose for a moment that the population will remain at six hundred. Very soon it will be the largest town in the world and that alone will attract interest."

Before leaving for home I drove round part of the area that I'd left bare. There must have been plenty of labour available for farming as field after field was sprouting green shoots. I spotted corn, maize and potatoes growing among other things. Three large plastipod greenhouses housed tomatoes, lettuces and courgettes. I gave silent congratulations to whoever had organised matters. They'd accomplished a great deal in two months.

I did a fair amount of travelling that autumn. Marta and Siobhan were more than capable of dealing with the daily workload and the bakery practically ran itself so for the first time in five years I had time on my hands. Apart from visiting all the other biologists and inspecting their kingdoms at first hand I also made my first trip to the far north. Arriving in Manchester the first person that I ran into was Nigel Lancing, the director. He recognised me immediately and insisted on giving me the grand tour, not only of Manchester but of Salford and Stockport as well. I saw two or three of the separate mining operations that were going on as well as the processing plant. An adjacent building was making blocks out of the rock left over once the metals had been extracted. At Salford I got a glimpse of the two drilling rigs that were operating about two miles from the town itself. But the most interesting place was Stockport. The layout of the town was similar to all the others, but a quarter of a mile away was a miniature industrial estate. Small factory units, about twenty of them in all, were being set up to produce a variety of metallic goods.

"The first factory goes into production next week," Nigel told me proudly. "That will concentrate on tins suitable for canning food and for general storage. The biggest unit you see over there will make housing components identical with those we've been bringing from Earth up till now. Over the next six months we'll start making things like ploughs and farm machinery, plus the batteries to power them. Within two years we'll be turning out our own transport vehicles and possibly even washing machines. The sky's the limit. One of our architects has even designed an old fashioned aeroplane similar to those on Earth in the mid twentieth century. There's oil in abundance in the wells around Salford so we'll have the fuel to propel it. Mind you, that's a good few years down the line. By this time next year we'll be making all the pipes and all the electrical cable that we'll need too. We'll even be making our own wind turbines and generators by the end of next year."

His enthusiasm was infectious. I plied him with questions for a full half hour. All metal products would be centred on Stockport, but Salford would concentrate on plastics. Both these towns were getting another two hundred newcomers early the following year, bringing each up to the six hundred mark. I pondered all I'd heard and seen on the way home and came to the conclusion that in ten years' time the only shortages in the world would be of wood and paper. There was nothing that could be done about that, however. I was determined to give the trees at least forty years of growth before we started cutting any down. Even then I would be setting a strict quota to ensure future generations were protected against shortages.

In the beginning our new World Parliament sat for two days a week, on Tuesdays and Thursdays Nils continued to keep Hans, Herr Klost and myself updated on everything that went on. The first matter for discussion was the forthcoming elections and the general policy regarding future polls. It was decided that each parliament would serve a four year term. One member would be elected for each town. There was a minority among the directors who wanted that amended to two per town but they were outvoted by a large margin. Although Nigel Lancing officially held the directorship of all three northern towns it was unanimously agreed that each town should have its own member. There were now eighteen townships in the world but members would be added as this number increased. Once convened the new ruling body would elect a president and vice-president but no other officers. Every meeting would be chaired by the president or in his absence the vice-president. If they were both absent discussion could take place but no firm decisions taken.

It took a while and much thought to come up with a suitable method of conducting the poll. Paper was in short supply and we simply couldn't afford to use the normal method of voting slips. After much discussion a very ingenious plan was adopted. Among the accessories used by the engineers were a large number of coloured bolts around three inches long. These were commandeered. Each candidate in places where there was more than one was assigned a colour. As each voter arrived at the polling centre one bolt of each colour was placed on a shelf in the polling booth and the voter was given a sealed container with a suitable sized slot in the lid. The voter selected the appropriate bolt and placed it in the container. He or she then took the container back to the overseer's desk and took the remaining bolt or bolts in tightly closed hands and put them in a sack, being careful not to show them to the polling clerk or any other bystander. It sounded clumsy but in operation it worked like a charm.

I wasn't surprised to see Nils returned unopposed. He was immensely popular in Stockholm and rightly so. In the other seventeen towns eight directors were also returned unopposed. This left only nine, eight with two candidates and one with three. Nigel Lancing had decided to represent Manchester, so two of these nine were Salford and Stockport. All the other directors were also successful, most with large majorities. The only one who was made to sweat was Minos Sousopolis in Athens. He wasn't too popular in his home town. He had the reputation of being autocratic and overbearing. In the end he just scraped through by one hundred and twelve votes to one hundred and ten with many abstentions. At the first meeting of the new body Nils was unanimously elected as Cara IV's first ever president, with Salvatore Celli as vice-president. On a visit five days after the election Kristina told us that she had had serious thoughts about putting herself forward as a candidate, and was already thinking about doing so in four years' time. I saw a little light go on in Donna's eyes and when Kristina had gone my wife blandly suggested that I should become a politician.

"You are joking, I hope," I said to her. "I've no intention of making a fool of myself, which is what I'd do if I got elected. Thanks all the same, but I'll stick to growing plants and rearing fish. That's the job I was trained for and that's the job I'll stay with for the rest of my life. Apart from anything else it will soon be a five day a week job being a politician and I want to see my children every day and as much of the day as possible." The look on her face suggested that she was prepared to argue the point, but I glared at her and went out to the garden to play with the children.

Yet again our output of food items increased substantially. I reckoned it at fifty per cent over the previous year. A small amount of jam and wine was available in October for 'export' to other towns. We had a surplus, too, of tomatoes. An enterprising young Belgian and his wife perfected a way of making tomato ketchup and went into business. He did a roaring trade. Our food freezing plant was working full time from the middle of July until the end of October. Their main output was of peas, all kinds of beans, cabbage, broccoli and swedes. With the poultry herds expanding the egg ration was increased from one to two per person per week and the cheese ration increased by fifty per cent at the end of November.

CHAPTER TWENTY-THREE

The next five years seemed to pass very quickly. Year on year our standard of living improved. By 2250 only meat was still rationed worldwide. We were still working mainly on the dried and tinned meat that had come from Earth, but stocks of this were running low. I lifted the ban on sea fishing in June of that year. Nils had taken my advice and brought in two small but fully equipped fishing boats a couple of years earlier. They were the only ones on the planet and our industrial centre in the north had not yet got round to shipbuilding. Thus we were able to corner the market. The boats were only allowed out for two days a week to conserve stocks. The government decided not to ration fish, but insisted that equal quantities of every catch must go to every town. In practice this worked out at around half a pound of fish per person per week. In rivers and lakes there was an abundance of trout and salmon but once again I erred on the side of caution and wouldn't lift the ban there for another year.

Thirty-three of our planned forty-eight townships were now established. As each new one appeared its director took his or her place in parliament. A second general election had been held and once again Nils had been returned unopposed. In fact there were only two changes from the previous assembly. The representative from Salford had decided not to stand again and was replaced. In Athens Kristina Olsen had carried out her threat to stand and in a two horse race had defeated the unpopular Minos Sousopolis by over thirty votes. Europa itself had grown to become the largest town in the world with over one thousand inhabitants. Total world population had passed the seventeen thousand mark. The amount of goods coming from Earth with each new arrival grew less and less and mainly consisted of manufactured items that we still hadn't been able to make ourselves. Only one cargo ship now accompanied each incoming batch of passengers.

There'd been something of a baby boom over the intervening years. As conditions improved and more people got married or lived together thoughts naturally turned to starting a family. Donna and I had extended our own family to five with the arrival of Andrew Patrick and finally Lynn Teresa. We often talked about extending our brood further, but in the end decided that five was enough for us to handle. Thankfully they were very close to each other. Squabbles were few and far between: in fact most of them were settled by Moira, who was emerging as the leader and disciplinarian of her younger siblings. Our wider family was growing too. Teresa and Pablo had three children with another on the way and Patrick was also married with one son.

Three and a half years after leaving Bert Larrabey came back to claim his bride. Initially he was in the intake for one of the new towns, Plymouth I think it was, but he very quickly organised his transfer to Stockholm. He and Maria were married within a fortnight. They did me the honour of asking me to be best man. Maria abandoned the idea of moving into the vineyard. The difficulties of providing water and electricity to such a remote spot proved insuperable so they stayed in town. Bert's original plan had been to take a job as a hoverbus driver but between the vineyard itself and the winery there was enough work to keep him fully employed. Maria and her partners had formed themselves into a company, the Stockholm Wine Corporation. They now owned eight fields and had plans to add another two in the near future. Crops increased every year and they were now selling large quantities of their product to other towns.

Within the past year beei had appeared on the market. The first brewery had been set up in Malaga two years previously and had been followed by one in Lisbon and one in Oslo. The product was weaker generally than the beer we'd known back on Earth, but still drinkable. I'd expected someone somewhere to open a pub but surprisingly nobody did. I think the brewers themselves were surprised. They'd jumped the gun by ordering a large number of thirty gallon metal kegs and then found they couldn't dispose of them. In the end they had to send most back to be melted down and recast into smaller kegs of six to nine gallons which they sold to householders. Small cafes and the odd larger restaurant had also appeared here and there. A restaurant opened in Stockholm and was well patronised. The absence of television, theatres and cinemas had so restricted leisure activities that people welcomed a chance to get out in the evenings. The lack of meat and fish led to restricted menus of course. It became almost a competition between such establishments to come up with something novel in the way of vegetarian soups and main meals.

So far there had been no moves to distil spirits on a commercial basis. There had been some laboratory experiments carried out but these were inconclusive. The absence of peat in the water precluded any attempt to make recognisable whisky. Some was produced but proved bitter and tasteless. I had neglected to include junipers among my purchases so gin was out of the question. Brandy would have been a possibility but despite the rapid increase in the cultivation of grapes the growing wine trade took care of all production. The same applied to rum. The sugar was there to make molasses, but was needed for more general purposes. That left vodka, for which there was little demand. A small amount of cider was being made, but again I had not provided for cider apples so this wasn't a great success. Two new types of wine did gain a following. The pears we were growing fermented into a very drinkable perry. Bees had adapted well to life on Cara IV and with few natural enemies had multiplied rapidly. The excess honey was converted into mead. Surprisingly very few people seemed perturbed at the lack of hard liquor. I could only assume that everyone's life was so fully occupied and there were so few real worries that they felt in no need of the stimulation that strong drink could offer. Nils offered another explanation.

"Hardened drinkers applying for passage to Cara IV were told in no uncertain terms that spirits would not be available for a long time. That put nearly all of them off the idea of coming here. They applied instead for the more advanced colonies like Paladia and Persephone."

Donna was still nominally the manager of the bakery though she took little part in the operation. Teresa carried the day to day responsibility, now with five employees. Ample supplies of flour, sugar and other ingredients had allowed the shop to branch out into cake making, as well as five or six different kinds of bread and rolls. Once meat came off the ration she planned on a further expansion into pies of various kinds. There was much speculation as to when this would happen. My original estimate had been fifteen years and it looked as though I'd been about right. I certainly couldn't see it happening in the next two or three.

My grand plan for forestry was coming on apace. By my rough calculations we now had between fifteen and twenty per cent of the proposed area planted. I was often asked what I would do when the project was completed and my answer was always the same.

"If there's suitable transport available by that time we'll start on the other side of the mountains. If not we'll go further north and south."

The other question I had to field regularly was the obvious one: when could we start felling trees for timber and for paper making. I don't know how many times I had had to make it plain that the absolute minimum would be forty years from planting and the more likely assessment would be fifty years. Timber and paper were really the only major shortages on the world now. We were able to bring in small supplies with every arrival from Earth, but not nearly enough to meet the demand. This was a handicap to the schools in particular, though the problem had been marginally overcome. The discovery up north of large deposits of slate fuelled the manufacture of the old-fashioned slate boards used in schools back in the nineteenth and early twentieth centuries. Useful though this was it didn't make for good writing skills and we were all worried that several generations would grow up unable to express themselves on paper. It was crude, but it fulfilled its purpose. Of even greater concern was the lack of books and especially new books. Again, some had been sent from Earth and each town had a pitifully small library. The government was keen to encourage growth of the arts, but without the raw materials those of a literary or artistic bent were stifled. It would have been rewarding to have a day to day account of life on Cara IV for future history books, but the best we could do was to keep some kind of diary in the memories of our computers. I wasn't one of the meticulous ones, my diary entries normally being restricted to two or three lines. Donna was slightly more conscientious, keying two or three paragraphs a day. Her contributions were mainly about the children though and shed little light on the overall history of the world.

April of that year had seen another step towards normality with the introduction of income tax. This had become a necessity. Police, street cleaners and other public sector workers had to be paid, as had teachers. Thankfully the government took the sensible approach and made the system as simple as possible. Everyone would pay tax on the whole of their income, whether small or large. Initially the rate was set at five per cent, with the warning that increases were inevitable in the years to come. There was a suggestion that an excise duty should be levied on wine and beer and a committee was set up to consider ways and means. Their conclusion was that it would be too costly to implement such a levy and that the return would thus be negligible. The proposal was defeated, though the government issued a warning that any large scale outbreak of alcohol abuse would result in duty being brought in at a punitive rate.

We wanted to do something special in Stockholm that year to celebrate the tenth anniversary of our arrival. It was Sean who came up with the idea: an open air barbecue for the whole town. He would provide an ox, three pigs and two dozen chickens free of charge to be spit roasted over open fires. A committee was quickly organised to arrange the provision of vegetables. Teresa volunteered to make a huge celebratory cake or cakes, sufficient for everyone to have a generous portion. Next someone suggested having an afternoon of sport for the children and soon adult competitions were added. By the time the big day arrived all that was missing was a merry-go-round and donkey rides! I mentioned that to Sean by way of a joke and he solemnly promised that next year he'd bring two or three of his donkeys down for that purpose. I asked him if he would lay on a merry-go-round as well. I have no intention of writing down his reply! The day was voted a huge success, with the roasted ox the biggest of the attractions. Everyone present insisted that this should be a central feature of subsequent celebrations.

There had been one step forward that pleased everyone and did much to brighten up our lives. A small facility in Stockport started manufacturing paint. Dyes were limited in availability, so there were only five basic colours: white, red, blue, green and yellow. Of these red wasn't very successful, being more of a brick red than scarlet or crimson. By judicious mixing a range of tints could be made. As supplies became easy to obtain there was a frantic outburst of activity everywhere and within a few months each town resembled a rainbow. Donna's favourite colour was sky blue, mine was yellow so our house walls became the former and the doors the latter. Some people even went the length of painting the inside walls as well, though we didn't.

One thing that caused me some slight perturbation was that people were becoming very insular throughout the world. Most were interested in what went on in their own town but were indifferent to what was happening elsewhere. No doubt the absence of TV and newspapers was a major factor. Some news appeared on the rudimentary internet that had been set up but few bothered to read it. The habit of visiting other towns at weekends died out fairly quickly as people realised that one town was very similar to every other town. Any visits made were for specific purposes connected with work or calling on friends. Conversely nothing in one's own town was hidden from view. Of course, what we called our towns were nothing more than small villages where everyone knew everyone else. It was virtually impossible to keep a secret for long. I discussed the matter with Nils more than once and I believe it was mulled over in parliament but nobody could come up with a solution.

For this reason among others I'd got into the habit of visiting Stockport once or twice a year just to find out what progress was being made on the industrial front. Nigel Lancing had been so welcoming on my first time there and had invited me to come back at any time so I felt no qualms about keeping others away from their work. On my second visit he'd introduced me to Peter Pringle, the industrial scientist in charge of the forward planning group and latterly he'd been my host on such visits. The forward planning group by this time consisted of fifteen scientists and engineers and their mission was to work out manufacturing processes for a wide range of essential goods. Apart from the paint they had already progressed to such things as cars, washing machines and fridges plus a host of smaller items. According to my diary it was late August that year when I went to see him. It had been a full twelve months since my last trip and he had a lot to tell me.

"We've made one really major advance since you were here last," he told me. "We can now manufacture the rechargeable batteries that we need for so many things."

"I thought these were supposed to last forever," I countered.

"That's the theory," he said with a slight smile. "In practice they do wear out or lose their potency eventually. In any case we've started to turn out cars, washing machines and ploughs among other things and we'll need a regular supply for them."

I changed the subject. "I know I've asked you this before, but it's the one question I get from everybody when they know I've been to see you. How long will it be before radio and television becomes a reality?"

He smiled again. "I'll give you the same answer as before. Radio soon, television several years. In fact we've already experimented with some basic radio sets. We've only got a small supply of components at present, so it will be a year at least before we can make sets in any quantity. Say two to three years before everyone will get one. TV I'm afraid is going to take at least five years to develop. We're still short of materials for some of the working parts and we haven't yet worked out the broadcasting details or where we'll site the transmitters. It's not going to be easy providing coverage for an area larger than the British Isles. We have a team of three working on that right now, but they're finding it slow going."

Peter's unit was divided into five groups of three with each group of three comprising a scientist and two engineers. As I'd been told, one team were investigating TV and radio. The others covered subjects such as aeroplanes and other methods of transport, household items like refrigerators, cookers and freezers, heavy plant for large scale manufacturing and heating and lighting appliances. The one piece of really good news that I was able to take back home with me came from the last named. Electric radiators and water heaters would be going into production within three months. Though the climate, certainly in Stockholm and to the south, was seldom really cold we felt keenly the absence of hot water and the means to keep our houses warm in winter. Among future projects Peter listed sports equipment, toys and children's games.

Hans had spent two years working on his plan for a single electricity grid throughout the area that had been colonised. He was now in the process of putting teams together to make a start on the actual work. This in itself was a massive feat of organisation. Squads in various locations would carry out the installation in their particular area. Hans himself would mainly function as an overseer, monitoring progress, dealing with problems and queries and generally slotting each piece of the project into place. It wasn't a role that he relished. He was a hands-on manager much keener on getting his hands dirty with the nitty-gritty day to day work than just issuing orders.

"There are times when I envy you, Alex," he said to me one day when I asked him how things were going. "You have the double benefit of making the plans and then being able to get involved in the grass roots, if you'll excuse the pun. I'm becoming little more than an office boy. As to how things are going, the best I can say is that we've made a start in half a dozen places. And before you ask, it will be ten years at least before we're anywhere near completion. I've just been told it will be another two to three years before we can get enough cable. We're going to put all the wiring underground, so that means a lot of digging and there's only two or three earth moving machines on the planet right now. Thanks to your forestation project we're not going to be able to work in straight lines in many places either. I'm almost sorry I put forward the idea in the first place."

"Think of the benefits when it is in place," I consoled him. "As for our forests, it's going to be the best part of ten years before they grow to any height. There's no reason why you shouldn't go straight through them. Even if you have to displace some trees we can soon replant them." He cheered up a little at that.

Apart from my trips to Stockport I'd got into the habit of making an annual inspection visit to the 'deep south' to chart progress. In view of the travelling involved I always took two days over these. Verona boasted a small hotel, one of only four towns to do so, and I stayed there overnight. I drove down in the morning and spent the afternoon and evening touring the area with Denise. The following day I'd leave early, pick up Denise and head on down to Rotterdam. We'd spend the morning looking round, have a fairly late lunch and then I'd drive home, dropping Denise off on the way.

I really enjoyed these excursions and they became something of a holiday for me, though I felt a bit guilty at leaving Donna to cope with the children on her own. Denise was a delightful companion and it was like visiting another world to see the tropical flora instead of our own temperate varieties. In both towns date and coconut palms had been planted along the coastline for some four or five miles north and south. As seed became available Denise planned to cover the whole of the coast for the forty or so miles between the towns. Near to the town walnut, brazil nut. pecan and mango trees were now over fifteen feet tall and producing ever increasing quantities of fruit. Further out the cotton fields extended for mile upon mile. Plantations of banana trees and sugar cane occupied several square miles of land to the north and south of each town. There were fields devoted to sweet potatoes, pineapples and different types of melon and groves of orange, grapefruit, lime and lemon trees, not to mention more usual vegetables and fruit. Farm animals were still fairly small in number, but herds and flocks were growing year by year and both towns were already self-sufficient in dairy products as well as fruit and vegetables. A start had been made on flooding the area that would eventually become paddy fields for the growing of rice.

Although Rotterdam was less than two hundred miles south of Stockholm the difference in climate was noticeable as soon as one reached Verona. While not studying the subject as meticulously as Julie had done Denise took an interest in meteorology and kept detailed records. The mean temperature in that area of the world was almost ten degrees higher than at Stockholm. Even during my visit at the beginning of October I found the heat oppressive. The previous year there'd been a thunderstorm on my first day, the first I'd experienced on Cara IV, and the rain came down with tropical ferocity for over an hour. Denise told me that these storms occurred on average once every two months and pointed out the lightning conductors on the roof of every building. I was glad that those who'd planned the initial settlement had settled on Stockholm and not one of the southern sites. I'd tried and failed to get an explanation for this climate variation. There were no professional astronomers or meteorologists on Cara IV. The former were deemed unnecessary as any further venture into space would be hundreds, if not thousands of years into the future. Why we had none of the latter was a puzzle. They would have been of immense value on a new world. I recalled my knowledge of Scotland. The distance between Stockholm and Rotterdam was roughly equivalent to that between Inverness and Berwick. I was sure that while there may have been occasional daily variations of up to ten degrees between these two places, the average over a year would not have been more than two or three degrees, if that. In Rotterdam Denise had introduced me to the chief engineer, a middle-aged, soft spoken Czech named Pavel Volkov. He too had what he called a morbid interest in the weather patterns in the south.

"I know a bit about climatology," he told me one day, "and I've done a lot of research and I still can't come up with an answer."

Pavel explained that his main passion was for camping and had been since his early boyhood in the Czech Republic. Most weekends if the weather was reasonable he packed up his tent, took a few supplies, jumped into his car and headed off into the country.

"My favourite spot is a little cave near the shore and about a hundred and fifty kilometres due south of here," he went on. "I've been there on many occasions at different times of the year. I always take a thermometer with me and note the readings every couple of hours during the day. When I come back I check them against the records here. I can tell you that there is less than half a degree of a difference, yet my cave is almost as far away as we are from Stockholm." A dreamy look came into his eyes. "You know, Alex, I sometimes think that this planet is alive in some way and has feelings. If this is true it must have been very lonely for all those million years. Now that it has company it is doing all it can to make us welcome." He raised a deprecatory hand. "But maybe I'm getting foolish as I get older." I assured him that he wasn't and told him about my theory of the rapid growth in plant life. It had been an interesting conversation, but had got us no further forward with the problem we were trying to solve.

Sport continued to grow in extent and popularity. Every one of our thirty-three towns had at least one football ground and the league now boasted two divisions. Once building components became more available changing rooms were added and at some of the grounds an attempt had been made to put in some rudimentary terracing. Every town had tennis courts within two years of arriving and gymnasia were beginning to appear along with badminton and squash courts. Our golf course in Stockholm was being extended to eighteen holes and nine hole courses had been laid out in Europa, Athens, Stockport and Lisbon. Other towns had plans to follow suit. Some sports requirements were already being produced in both Stockport and Salford as metal and plastic became more plentiful.

CHAPTER TWENTY-FOUR

I'll never forget my fiftieth birthday. It was the third Thursday in August and started out as a normal day. I rose as usual at seven thirty and brought Donna her morning cup of tea in bed. We had a leisurely breakfast together. The children were all away by then, with the four oldest married and with families of their own. Lynn had moved in with her boy friend just three weeks before. I'd planned to work as normal that day, and afterwards a large family party had been arranged. We'd hired one of the plastipods and some two dozen friends had also been invited. Though it was supposed to be a secret I knew that Donna had baked a huge birthday cake for me. Around ten o'clock I was working in one of the greenhouses along with Marta and Siobhan, when the former announced she was going to the toilet and left. Within ten seconds she burst back in.

"Alex," she cried, "come and look. There's a spaceship preparing to land."

I was mystified. There were no arrivals scheduled until the end of September and they were for northern towns and should have been nowhere near Stockholm. Siobhan and I followed Marta outside; where she pointed to the north. Sure enough a ship was in plain view about two thousand feet up and floating slowly down to land. By my reckoning it would touch down some four miles from town inland from the golf course. The three of us jumped into a car and headed in that direction, arriving at just the moment the ship settled on the ground. With even more surprise I realised that it was the *Ural Star*. Two or three minutes passed before the exit hatch opened and Captain Petrovic stepped out. I walked towards him with a smile on my face and my hand outstretched. As we came together he shook my hand firmly but did not smile in return. He looked both stern and sad at the same time.

"Alex," he said and paused for some seconds. "I bring grave news. Earth has been destroyed."

I looked keenly at him, wondering if this was some elaborate practical joke. I couldn't really take in what he had said. Eventually I found my voice. "How. when. what happened?" I stuttered.

"About eight months ago," he replied, his tone still sombre. "A huge meteorite more than two thousand kilometres in diameter, crashed into central America. The impact caused a massive explosion and Earth was knocked out of its orbit. It started falling inwards towards the sun and burnt up in a matter of days. Sadly most of the inter-planetary ships were in transit at the time and not more than a handful of people escaped in those that were left. Six billion people must have perished and in the most horrible way."

I heard sobs from behind me and when I looked round I saw Marta and Siobhan were both crying unrestrainedly. I felt close to tears myself. But Captain Petrovic was speaking again and I turned back to him.

"I have some pictures of the holocaust, taken by the nearest ship. The *Vesuvius* had only taken off two days previously and stopped to observe. We were en route to Paladia when it happened with two thousand new colonists. Once I was sure that no hope remained I decided to bring them here instead. Cara IV is by far the least populated of the colonies and I figured you had a greater need of some extra settlers. As the senior captain I've also ordered three other ships to come here instead of their authorised destination. Two of them were headed for Magna and one for Garant. Of course there'll be some people who were joining relatives on the other planets. Between the four ships we should have enough fuel to take them to their preferred destination once things have settled down. As you know our ships use little in the way of fuel. Now I should report to Nils. Is he around?"

"No," I replied, still in a state of shock. "He's a full time politician now and he'll be at the parliament in Europa. In fact he's the president. But he should know as quickly as possible. Can you arrange a lifeship to take us there?"

"Yes indeed. I'll get my senior first officer to pilot us. Wait here, it will be about ten minutes." He headed back into the ship.

Bernard Stocks

Some twenty other people had seen the ship land and made their way to join us. I gave them a quick summary of what the captain had said, then turned back to Marta and Siobhan.

"Marta, will you find Donna and tell her what's happened. I'm going with Captain Petrovic to Europa and I don't know when I'll be back. Tell her we'll have to postpone the birthday party for the time being. Siobhan, you can go round the town and break the news to as many as you can. Do it gently. Almost everyone will have had family and friends still on Earth. See the various religious leaders first. They'll almost certainly want to organise memorial services and there will be many in need of immediate comfort." The two nodded their agreement and set off back to town in the car.

It was ten minutes to the second when a hatch at the rear of the ship opened and a lifeship crept out and stopped. I went across as the entry door opened and climbed in. I nodded to the captain and then looked towards the pilot, a woman. She looked familiar but I couldn't place her immediately.

Captain Petrovic made the introductions. "First Officer Natasha Validze, Alex Dunsmuir."

Recognition dawned on both our faces. "I should have known you," I said. "You took Roger and I on the first ever trips across the mountains."

"That's right," she said with the familiar cheeky grin that I recalled so well. "As you can see, I've risen in the world since then." I asked her how long she'd been with the *Ural Star*. "Since I got my promotion six years ago. I wasn't the most senior second officer on the *Viva Espana* and the powers that be thought it diplomatic to move me in case my promotion caused any resentment."

Quickly I gave her directions to Europa and moved to a seat in the rear, where Captain Petrovic soon joined me. He had with him the photographs and videos taken by the *Vesuvius*. The former were very clear and sharp and the last few of the thirty or so showed Earth twenty-four hours after the collision as a giant fireball. I was near to tears again as I tried to picture

186

the agony that the billions of victims must have suffered. It was beyond imagination.

There was a glorified car and lorry park in Europa mainly used for the distribution network, but it was a good two miles away from the parliament building. I directed Natasha to land in the square outside instead. Leaving her with the ship the captain and I hurried into the building. Luckily one of the support staff who knew me was on duty in the lobby leading to the main chamber.

"Something dreadful has happened, Francois," I said. "It is vital that the captain here speaks with Nils Anderssen and Salvatore Celli at once. Please summon them immediately; it is most urgent. We will wait in the anteroom at the side."

For a moment he seemed disposed to argue but when he looked again at our faces he decided against it and went into the debating chamber. Within a minute Nils and Salvatore emerged and came into the room. I made hurried introductions and left them to it. I would like to have stayed, but I realised that I had no place in the grave discussions that would follow. I passed the news on to Francois but told him not to mention it to anyone else until Nils gave permission. Then I rejoined Natasha in the lightship. A couple of the local police were eyeing it up when I got back, but I explained that a vital matter had arisen and that delay would have had serious consequences. Again I was lucky that one of the constables knew me by sight. At the same time I didn't want too much attention drawn to the ship just then so I told Natasha to move to a nearby open space. She elected to stay with the ship; I went back to the parliament building to await further instructions.

It was some twenty minutes before the three men emerged from the anteroom. Captain Petrovic had orders for me. "I will need to stay here for some time, probably two days or more. You and Natasha head back to Stockholm. I ordered that the passengers should not be resuscitated. Tell her that order still stands. She can authorise shore leave for two of the crew at a time. I will communicate with her when my movements become clearer."

Nils also had a word or two with me. "I'll almost certainly be staying overnight as well. There are many decisions to be made. I'll give you a

Bernard Stocks

full rundown as soon as I get back home. Meantime thanks for acting so promptly."

On the way back Natasha and I deliberately avoided any discussion of the tragedy that had befallen. She insisted that I gave her an account of my activities since we had last met. I complied as concisely as I could, then asked her if she was married.

"Oh, no," she replied decisively. "Marriage and the Space Service are not good bedfellows. I have no regrets. As for the future, much depends on what Ivan decides." Ivan was Captain Petrovic. "If we are to settle here maybe I'll get you to introduce me to some nice middle-aged men. I'm well over forty now, you know. It may be too late for me, but we'll see. If I'm honest I'm not too worried either way." I didn't say so but I was sure she'd have no difficulty finding a husband. She was a very attractive woman.

When I got back home I found the whole family crammed into our house. Moira and Hannah were serving endless cups of tea and coffee, but managed to find a scratch meal for me. Donna had gone to the bakery and after satisfying my hunger I went to join her there. Both she and Teresa had red rimmed eyes and it was obvious they had been grieving for those of their siblings who had remained in Ireland. It made me feel guilty. I had given no thought to my own family and friends. Over the years Earth had become a very remote and distant memory. I found it very difficult to even recall faces and names and of course I had no idea whether my parents and Aunt Eleanor had still been alive. They would have been close to ninety by that time. After making sure that Donna was all right I checked on Marta and Siobhan. They'd both gone back to work, stating that only by working could they keep their minds off what had happened.

My next move was to track down Hans. A couple of phone calls brought the information that he was checking a fault in the power supply close to Lake Gothenburg. I found him there. He was aware of the situation and I told him all that had happened in Europa.

"We won't know much more until Nils gets back," I concluded.

He agreed and became practical. "If we're going to take in another eight thousand bodies I'd better check on housing availability. As far as I can recollect we only have eight or nine empty properties in Stockholm so it might be an idea to order more components right away before every other town gets the same idea. Let's see. Forty-eight towns and eight thousand people means roughly an extra one hundred and seventy per town, anything between ninety and a hundred and forty houses."

"Parliament may decide to authorise more new towns or even extend beyond the mountains," I pointed out.

Hans was doubtful. "Unlikely, I would think. Anyway, more housing stock wouldn't come amiss. The birth rate is still high and those born here since we arrived are leaving home for their own accommodation. The only difficulty is where to put more houses. We've just about used up all the space in town. That's your problem though, so I won't lose any sleep over it."

When I returned home Moira and Eoin were with Donna. By this time I had completely forgotten about my birthday. I was quickly reminded. Moira came over and sat on the arm of my chair. She was so like Donna in looks, though taller and broader than my wife and much more decisive.

"We've cancelled the party as you wished," she began. "But we're not letting the occasion go unnoticed." I started to protest but she placed a finger on my lips. "Shush. Just for once Dad you're going to do as you're told. This is what we've arranged. The children will be coming in at half past six to wish you happy birthday. We'll cut the cake then and give them each a piece. Then they'll leave and at eight o'clock we're having a meal just for you and Mum and the five of us."

I looked helplessly at Eoin. Our oldest son topped me by a good three inches. His hair, red at birth, had faded over the years and was now a light sandy colour. It was a standing joke in the family that he bore very little resemblance to either Donna or myself. He was heavily built with a square, almost pugnacious face that belied a gentle approach to life and people. I put on a hurt expression and asked him, with the barest fraction of a wink: "Are you going to sit there and let your big sister bully your poor old dad?"

He laughed. "Just for once, yes. I don't often agree with her, but on this occasion she's right." His statement actually was something of a lie. Our five children were and always had been very close to each other and rarely disagreed. "If you try and talk your way out of it Hannah, Andrew and Lynn are waiting in the wings to add their voices to ours." I could see argument would get me nowhere so I gave in as gracefully as I could. I still didn't feel at ease with the situation, though. In a remote sort of was I thought it was disrespectful to the memory of the billions on Earth who had died to be celebrating something as unimportant as a birthday. But as Donna pointed out when we were alone again, Earth meant little to children who'd never lived there or even seen it.

Our seven grandchildren duly paraded at the time fixed by Moira. Their ages ranged from two to eight. Their parents must have given them strict instructions before leaving home as they were all well behaved and quiet, even when the birthday cake was handed out. The occasion must have been a bit strange to them. Birthdays on Cara IV had always been fairly muted affairs. The shortage of paper products meant that cards were unknown and with few luxury items around the giving of presents had also died out. Donna had surpassed herself with the cake. It was a full fifteen inches square, with yellow icing and the words 'Happy 50th Birthday' inscribed in blue.

Hannah had taken charge of the cooking. The previous day she'd been to the farm and persuaded Eamonn to sell her a goose. With help from Moira she prepared the whole meal and brought it across to us promptly at eight o'clock. Though the mood was sombre I enjoyed myself in a quiet way. It was seldom that the seven of us were alone together and memories of the past quarter of a century kept recurring to me. Donna and I were very proud of our family and I think we had every right to be.

CHAPTER TWENTY-FIVE

It was late Saturday afternoon before Nils returned to Stockholm along with Captain Petrovic. The latter went straight to his ship while Nils took time out to change and have a meal. He then called Hans, Herr Klost and I to a meeting.

"You all know the outline of what's happened," he began, "but there are certain aspects of the situation that affect us personally. I'll deal with those in a moment, but first here are the arrangements we've made to accommodate the new settlers. Parliament has set up a small sub-committee to assess housing availability and allocate those who will be staying. Some, as I believe you know, will be wishing to join friends and relatives on the other colonised worlds. They will be given temporary accommodation. Once the remaining three ships arrive Ivan, Captain Petrovic, will make arrangements to take them onwards. All those staying will be absorbed into existing towns. We did discuss setting up more new towns but in the end we decided against it for the time being. We've made a survey of food and other resources and there is a sufficient surplus of everything to cater for an extra eight thousand people. Ivan will start resuscitating his own passengers on Monday. On present calculations we will need at least another three hundred houses worldwide, but parts are in stock at Europa and as you know only too well it doesn't take long to put them up. Engineering teams in Hanover and Manchester are standing by to undertake this. The next incoming ship isn't due for two months and I would hope by that time we will have the necessary extra houses ready."

"That takes care of the general picture. But unfortunately the catastrophe affects us personally: even Hermann is involved indirectly. From day one three of us have been employed and paid by the Space Service. Now that body no longer exists we are effectively out of work and cannot be paid. The method by which we were paid in the past, and Hermann will correct me if I'm wrong, was that the equivalent of all Service personnel's

191

salaries was remitted to Cara IV once a year in the form of banknotes and coins." Herr Klost nodded his agreement. "From this allotment Hermann was authorised to pay all salaries. Without the incoming capital he can no longer do that."

"That is correct," said Herr Klost. "It was an excellent arrangement. Although on the surface it appeared that the Space Service was responsible for your pay, in fact it cost them nothing apart from the expenses involved in printing the notes and striking the coins. Without the annual supply of these there is no money to pay you all. I'm sorry, but that's the way it is."

"I haven't got the figures of the number of people involved," Nils continued, "but at a guess it shouldn't be more than a hundred or so." He looked directly at Hans and I. "Unfortunately the two of you and your staff are among them. As far as the members of our parliament are concerned, most of whom were service employees, we will be taking a small, and I mean small, salary from now on. This will be paid for by a rise in income tax to eight per cent. Now I know you haven't had much time to consider the matter, but I'd like to hear your immediate thoughts."

I looked at Hans and he looked at me. I nodded to him to go first. I needed more thinking time.

"As you know my staff has dwindled in the last few years since the electricity grid was completed. Most have set up their own businesses. There are only four left apart from me that are still employed by the Space Service. Sorry, I should say were employed. I'll need to talk to them before making any firm plans, but we will probably form some sort of co-operative and go into business for ourselves. There is still plenty of work to be had. I might even retire. I'm past sixty and have saved enough to generate an adequate private income for my wife and myself. I'll be more than happy to spend my time fishing or on the golf course."

Nils turned to me. "Whatever your own plans are Alex, I hope you'll continue to oversee rural development even though you won't be paid. In practice that simply boils down to forestry nowadays. I and the rest of parliament want to be sure that no trees are felled before they should be and that the projects that you have in hand continue. Would you be willing to do that."

"No problem, Nils," I replied, more cheerfully than I felt. "Nowadays I do very little of the actual planting. I just tell other people where to plant and by some miracle it gets done. As for myself, like Hans I've got reasonable savings providing Herr Klost can guarantee that the interest rate stays at no less than three per cent. The bakery still belongs to Donna, though she only takes a very small percentage of the profits. The children are all away from home and earning their own living. My main concern is for Marta and Siobhan. I'll need to discuss things with them right away. We may follow Hans and set up our own operation, though with the surpluses throughout the world I'm not sure if it would sustain the three of us."

Herr Klost had another point to make. "The situation affects the banks in one other aspect. In future we will have to make our own notes and coins. I estimate that the notes that we have in hand should last ten years and the coins at least twenty and probably more. Now without supplies of paper in the foreseeable future the notes are going to be a problem. It may well be that we will have to dispense with them and use coins only once the current stocks are worn out. I have had discussions recently with the Forward Planning Unit in Stockport and they assure me that the making of coinage will be a simple matter. There are plentiful supplies of the metals needed, including gold and silver, and they have the technology to make the presses and to produce coins that cannot be copied by the layman."

"One last item before we close," said Nils. "Ivan and his first officer would both like to make their homes here in Stockholm. Can you fix them up, Hans?"

I broke in before Hans could answer. "The house next door to me has just become vacant. The lad who was there got married last week and moved away."

"That's one I didn't know about," Hans admitted. "I'll add it to the allocation list."

After the meeting I went for a walk along the beach. I wanted to get my thoughts in order and to try and make some plans for the immediate future. But try as I might my thoughts kept reverting to the past few years. As Nils had mentioned our world was very close to being self-supporting. The only real shortages were of timber and paper products. We were producing more food than we consumed; rationing was a thing of the past. The last item still rationed had been meat and that shortage had disappeared some eight years before. Our factories could manufacture just about anything, no matter how big or complicated. We now had many of the benefits of a modern civilisation including radio and television though the latter was limited to one channel broadcasting for nine hours a day. We had ample transport for our current needs and if one or more of the space ships was to remain and the lifeships could be kept running we would now have easy access to the other side of the mountains. True, there wasn't much in the way of luxuries. No precious stones had yet been discovered on our world so jewellery was virtually non-existent. One enterprising person had been making imitation jewellery out of coloured glass and was scraping a living out of it, but we had become so used to existing without such luxuries that sales were small. I had brought in some oysters over the past ten years, so there was a possibility of pearls coming on the market eventually.

As I'd mentioned at the meeting my own and my wife's circumstances weren't too bad. The children all had jobs. Moira and Hannah had taken over the manufacture and supply of cakes, leaving Teresa with the bread making side of the bakery. Eoin had apprenticed himself to an electrician at the age of fifteen and now ran his own business. Andrew had taken up teaching and Lynn ran the local library, such as it was. Small quantities of books had filtered through from Earth over the years, but Lynn proved resourceful and had turned part of the space she had into a modern day museum charting the history of Cara IV. It proved a big attraction to both locals and visitors to our town. My main concern was for Marta and Siobhan. Though they would have no difficulty finding other jobs they loved their present positions. I wasn't looking forward to giving them the bad news the following morning.

It was close to eleven when I finally got back home and more than two hours later before Donna and I got to bed. First I had to tell her what had passed at the meeting. After that we took stock of our options and discussed various plans, none of which seemed viable on closer examination. At one o'clock Donna yawned.

"We're just going round in circles," she complained. "There's no immediate hurry anyway. We won't starve for a year or so and something may turn up. As long as we've got each other that's all that's important." I couldn't argue with that.

Despite our late night I rose as usual at seven thirty. My first port of call after breakfast was the cake shop to thank Hannah once again for her culinary efforts on the evening of my birthday. Then I went in search of Marta and Siobhan. I ran them to earth in one of the greenhouses and suggested we repaired to the town's only cafe as we had things to discuss. Over coffee I gave them the unwelcome news. They took it stoically. While I was talking I studied the two of them. Neither had aged much over the intervening years. Marta had put on some weight and the first lines had appeared around her eyes and mouth. Siobhan's hair had faded somewhat. She had married five years previously and now had a son and a daughter. Marta still lived a solitary existence, apparently quite happily. I reflected yet again how sad it was that someone who was so good with children should have none of her own. Nowadays she spent much of her spare time babysitting for Moira and Hannah.

"We don't have too many options," I said when I'd given them pause for thought. "I'm assuming that we can keep possession of our three greenhouses and the additional land we have and that we won't have to buy them. I'll check that with Nils in the next couple of days. But the stark fact is that there's no way three of us can make a living from it. Supplying seeds to all and sundry, even if we sell them instead of giving them away won't provide an income for one, let alone three. Our small orchard isn't a viable proposition either, nor is the land that we have. Given the surplus production worldwide anything we grow will fetch low prices even supposing we can sell it in the first place. As I see it we have only two choices. We can abandon everything we have and give the land and greenhouses back to the government for future sale, or we can take part time jobs somewhere and run our holdings as a hobby."

Both of the women were near to tears and there was silence for more than a minute. It was Marta who pulled herself together first. "I'd hate to just let everything go after all we've put into it over the years. If we're voting on it I favour the second option. Surely we can change our direction and find some things to grow that aren't readily available or in surplus?" Siobhan was quick to agree with her.

I'd been thinking and had another suggestion to put. "Look, Donna and I have saved quite a bit over the years and we still have an income from the bakery. Maybe I should drop out and leave the whole thing to both of you." That drew strong protests from both of them and they insisted that I should stay in control. I was flattered and accepted the verdict gracefully.

"One thing I insist on." I continued. "Whatever profits we make I'll only take twenty per cent, leaving forty each for you. Now that's settled let's decide what we can grow that's likely to make a profit." That was easier said than done and though we talked for more than half an hour we couldn't come up with any solution. I then switched the subject and talked about possible part time jobs. Other than seasonal farm work there wasn't a lot on offer.

There's an old saying 'cometh the hour, cometh the man'. In this case it was a woman. We had been alone in the cafe all this time, then suddenly the door burst open and Maria came hurrying in.

"Alex," she burst out. "I've just heard the news. I'm so sorry. What are you all going to do?" Like my two companions Maria seemed to have aged little over the years, despite the fact that she was close to fifty. Her features were a little more finely drawn and there were strands of grey in her hair, but that was all. By now she and Bert were one of the richest couples on Cara IV. The expertise of her and her former partners, both now dead, plus the fact that they were the first in the field, ensured that Stockholm wines stayed ahead of all opposition and were in high demand. Their company now operated three wineries, one devoted entirely to champagne. Wine was by far the most popular tipple throughout the world. Further attempts to make palatable whisky had failed. Some brandy and vodka had been produced but there wasn't a great demand. Of the spirits rum was the most popular. Mead, the result of fermenting honey, also sold well. I recounted our discussions to Maria and told her of the conclusions we'd come to.

"In that case I may be able to help," she stated decisively. "Bert and I are planning to expand again. We've bought more land and will be planting at least four more vineyards and opening a fourth winery. At present we oversee both the growing and the whole production and it's proving too big a load for us to handle. We've decided to concentrate on the manufacturing side and get someone in to look after the vineyards. Why don't the three of you take over, Alex as manager and you two as assistant managers. We can offer you a good salary. You'll have four full time employees, all with several years' experience, plus part time help during the busy season. You'd still have enough time to devote to your own enterprise if you wanted to carry on with it. If that doesn't appeal to you I can offer you part time employment in one of the wineries. Take a couple of days to think it over and let me know what you decide on Monday sometime." She stood up abruptly, smiled and left the cafe quickly. I looked at Marta and Siobhan.

"Yes or no. Full time or part time?" I asked. "Or do you want time to think about it?"

Marta took the lead again. "Whatever we do I'd want the three of us to work together. We make a good team. Personally I'm in favour of full time, but only if we all want that. I do want to keep our own operation going though."

She looked at Siobhan, who nodded. "Although it's more restricted it's still the kind of job that we've been doing and I'd rather work outdoors than in a winery. What do you think, Alex?"

"I tend to agree, but I'd like to discuss it with Donna before I make a final decision. It would mean working longer hours than we have been doing in the last few years. Perhaps you should have a word with your husband, Siobhan. Remember you've two young children to look after."

Siobhan gave a broad smile. "Maurizio does what I tell him," was all that she said.

Donna raised no objections. "Better working more hours and doing something that you like and are qualified for. Don't worry about me. I can find plenty to do at the bakery if I'm bored, not to mention helping out with our ever increasing horde of grandchildren." I contacted Maria on the Saturday and arranged to start my new job in ten days' time.

CHAPTER TWENTY-SIX

The house next door to ours was bought by Captain Petrovic, or Ivan as he insisted we called him from then on. He spent three days getting it furnished with help from Donna, then we saw practically nothing of him for over a fortnight. He had a further few days at Europa in discussions with parliament, then headed up to Salford for meetings there and in Manchester and Stockport. He called in to see us on the evening of his eventual return. His mood was buoyant.

"I thought you might be interested in what I've been doing," he began. "The *Ural Star* will be staying on Cara IV. Any onward journeys will be taken by one of the other ships that will be coming. When I gave some thought to the matter I concluded that there wasn't much point in just leaving the ship lying about. As you know, we use very little fuel in space flight. I've talked to the oil refinery people in Salford and they assure me that they can produce what fuel we need. Also I've talked to the Forward Planning Unit in Stockport regarding the supply of spare parts with similar positive results. The government are keen to have surveys done of the adjoining planets Cara III and Cara V and are prepared to pay us to do so. There is also a possibility of undertaking an exploration of the west and south coasts of this continent. Once all the new arrivals are here and we've made arrangements to transfer those who wish to go elsewhere we'll make a start with Cara III."

"What about I and II?" I asked him.

"No point," he replied. "We compiled some data on them on a previous visit. Cara I as you know is less than fifteen million kilometres from the sun and has a mean temperature of over three thousand degrees Centigrade. Even in protective clothing it would be impossible to survive on the surface and I doubt if the ship itself could stand up to it. Cara II is forty million miles out, but even there the daytime temperatures are over three hundred. In any case, spectro-analysis shows that both planets are composed of rock and little else. The temperature on Cara III, on the other hand, is equivalent to that in Central Africa. We have little or no data on it, not even photographs in fact. It will be useful to get detailed information about it. All we know for certain is that it has an atmosphere of some sort. The same applies to Cara V, which is approximately fifteen to twenty degrees colder than here. That's just about bearable."

Of the two thousand passengers on the *Ural Star* only forty-four insisted that they wanted to be transferred to Paladia. Around fifty more were keeping their options open. They would sample life on our world until the last of the four ships had arrived and then decide if they wanted to move on. According to Ivan the parliament was quite happy to give them their choice.

In the week prior to taking up my job on the vineyards Marta, Siobhan and I cleared out our greenhouses, disposed of all surplus seed and made ready for planting the following spring. We'd decided to experiment with semi tropical fruit such as melons and figs. On the appointed Monday morning I picked the two of them up and drove out to our new scene of operations. Our first act was to meet the four permanent workers, two men and two women all in their thirties. I'd been worried in case they showed resentment at the fact that we'd been brought in to take charge over their heads but they gave us a warm welcome. They showed us round the existing areas, row upon row upon row of healthy vines stretching over twenty fields, some terraced some not. Then we went to look at the newly acquired land. Here the grass was high, for no animals had been grazing this far from town. It didn't take a genius to work out our task for the next couple of months.

"We'll need to cut the grass before we do anything else," I told the others. "With luck we'll be able to sell it to the farmers for hay. Then we strip the whole area and finally plough it. If we get time before Christmas we can also mark out our planting lines for next spring." Nobody disagreed. Thankfully we were able to get a loan of an industrial sized mowing machine, a bulldozer from Hans and a plough from Eamonn. My mind went back to our early days on the world when all those jobs would have had to been done by hand.

It seemed strange to reflect that I was now working for Maria instead of the other way round. But she was an understanding boss and in any case was so busy at the wineries that she had little time to visit us. In those first three months she came out only twice and Bert once. I formed the habit of going to see her at the close of work every Friday to report progress, though most of the half hour I stayed we spent reminiscing. I missed the freedom of movement that I had had before, also the close involvement in what was going on throughout the world, but I was thankful that I had a job of any sort in the circumstances.

The two ships bound for Magna arrived within ten days of each other at the end of November. They were the *Northern Light*, a Norwegian registered ship, and the *Helveticus* from Switzerland. Both landed at Europa. Through Ivan I learned that the final ship, due in mid January, was the *Hebridean Moon*. That would touch down in Manchester for the simple reason that the bulk of the colonists thereon were technical and manufacturing personnel. Next to ourselves Garant was the least populated of the colonies and still building up its industrial base. Ivan's reasons for diverting the ship were simple: Garant's population was already three-quarters of a million so Cara IV's need was greater.

With parliament meeting six days a week I saw practically nothing of Nils for more than two months. On the Sunday before Christmas he called in just after lunch. He looked weary. Donna made coffee and then left us. Nils asked me first how my new job was panning out. Maybe it was an illusion but I thought he looked disappointed when I waxed enthusiastic about it.

His first words confirmed my impression. "I was hoping that you were fed up with it," he confessed frankly. "As well as making arrangements to accommodate the new arrivals we've been revising our future plans in the light of the situation following Earth's destruction. You probably know that at least two of the spaceships will stay here. I've had talks with the three captains regarding their use. Ivan and the *Ural Star* have an ambitious programme laid out to explore and survey our two neighbouring planets. The other ship or ships are really surplus to requirements but their lifeships will be invaluable. At long last we have the means to cross the mountains quickly and to provide regular transport between both sides.

In fact we can now open up the whole continent. Although we don't plan to establish settlements beyond the mountains for another ten to twenty years we're setting up a programme to get growth going over as large an area as possible. The aim is to cover the whole continent within twenty years, even if it's only small areas of grassland and a few trees every five hundred kilometres. We plan to start as soon as possible with a corridor bounded in the north by a line due west from a point a hundred miles north of Salford and in the south by a line due west a hundred miles south of Rotterdam. As well as planting grass and trees the idea is to introduce fish to the rivers and lakes that currently don't have any. You can see the benefits. As our population grows and spreads out all the amenities will be there for them. It's a huge project and I'd have liked you to take charge of it. There'll be a generous salary, plus whatever you need in the way of assistance."

It was tempting, but it didn't take me more than a few seconds to make up my mind. There were two overriding considerations. Firstly I didn't want to let Maria down, even though I knew Marta could take my place as manager. Secondly and more importantly what Nils was suggesting would necessitate more time spent away from home. My family had become the centrepiece of my life. I had been lucky enough to be with my children throughout their lives and I wanted the same pleasure with my grandchildren. I passed these thoughts on and then came up with an alternative.

"It's really too vast for one person anyway. Here's a suggestion. Why don't you split your corridor into three? Give the northern section to Roger Beasley, the central one to Kristina Olsen and the southern to Denise Mofara. They're just as well qualified as I am to take it on. I happen to know all three are available and I'm sure they would jump at the offer. Based on previous experience they'd only need a couple of assistants each at most. I doubt they'll need any guidance, but if they do I'm always ready and willing to offer advice."

Nils seemed to like the idea and we went on to speak of other things. I gathered that parliament had reluctantly agreed to increase income tax to ten per cent early in the New Year. Ivan and his crew would be employed by the government during the proposed missions to Cara III and Cara V.

One of the other crews were to be commissioned to provide detailed maps of the whole of Cara IV and to expand the information we had from the original pre-settlement surveys. Nils also told me of one other issue which had been under discussion.

"Apart from public holidays there are no official holiday arrangements for anyone. Some members have suggested making a start by allowing two weeks annual leave a year for everyone. Any thoughts?"

I spent a minute or two just considering the idea. "I wouldn't be in favour," I said at length. "For a start most of us have jobs that demand fifty-two weeks a year of our time. That includes all public services. You'd need to bring in extra staff to cover for holidays and that would put the income tax up again, not a popular move. In any case, where would people go for a holiday? You'd need to start building resorts and leisure facilities and staff them. I don't know what the overall employment statistics are, but I suspect that we need everyone working to produce food and manufactured goods and to keep society ticking over. As far as I know there's been no public demand for annual holidays. If there is any discontent add another couple of days for public holidays."

Like Ivan, First Officer Natasha decided to put down roots in Stockholm and she bought the house next door to Marta's. The two of them became firm friends. The remainder of Ivan's crew elected to stay on the spaceship meantime, at least until they'd finished their survey of the two adjacent planets. I gathered that they'd all been offered jobs as lifeship pilots in the future. With a guaranteed supply of fuel and spare parts it had been proposed that the furthest points in our currently populated part of the world should have a daily lifeship service to cut journey times. Even with the high speed hoverbuses we now had it took more than three hours to get from Rotterdam to Salford, whereas lifeships could do it in a quarter of that time.

The arrival of the *Hebridean Moon* at the beginning of February heralded another busy period for Ivan and his fellow captains. They took on the task of ascertaining the wishes of all the eight thousand passengers. After a month of canvassing they reached a total of one hundred and five wishing to go to Magna, forty-eight to Paladia and eighty-seven to Garant. After much discussion the *Helveticus* undertook to convey all of them, ending its journey and staying on Magna. When not in service the *Northern Light* would be based at Rotterdam, the *Ural Star* at Stockholm and the *Hebridean Moon* at Europa. A decision on the siting of the lifeships was deferred until the cultivation of the 'corridor' got under way. The *Helveticus* left on the last day of March.

Parliament authorised our first ever census in April of that year. Shortage of paper meant that it was a very rough and ready affair. Two people from each township were appointed to count the numbers and provide totals of men and women over twenty-one, children from zero to twelve and those from thirteen to twenty. The final results made interesting reading. The total population of our world was just over sixty-six thousand. In the adult bracket men and women were almost equal in numbers, as were the children. Stockholm was now home to one thousand and twenty-five people. The area on either side of the river that I'd originally set aside for housing was now full. With the population sure to increase more houses would soon be needed. Hans started negotiations with Eamonn for part of his land and an agreement was soon reached. Eamonn gave up the eastern half of his farm in exchange for a somewhat larger area in the west.

Lynn, our youngest daughter, had been one of the enumerators in the census and the experience gave her a keen interest in demography, the study of populations. I only became aware of this when I popped in to see her one evening. She was hunched over her computer, flicking through half a dozen or so complicated looking spreadsheets. I asked her what she was doing.

"Although we only passed on the details of three age ranges," she explained, "we did ask the age of everyone and when they first arrived on Cara IV. I called up the enumerators in all the other towns and got them to pass on their findings to me. I'm trying to build up a picture of the present day spread of ages and how it will affect the future. It's a fascinating study. Do you realise we're at the beginning of a population explosion?"

"How do you work that out?" I asked.

"Can you confirm that the early arrivals had a high proportion of people aged thirty and over?" she countered.

"Yes indeed. At the beginning we needed experts in many fields, and it's a fact of life that expertise is mainly in older folk. I'd say that of the two hundred that originally arrived in Stockholm less than two dozen were under thirty years of age. It was the same too for the first fifteen towns that were set up. The colonists only started to get younger when we became self-sufficient in food and other essential goods. That was five years ago, when they started bringing in five hundred to a thousand at a time."

"Just what I thought," she said with a satisfied look on her face. "The last four thousand to arrive under the regular scheme were mostly married couples or single people in their late teens and early twenties, as were most of the eight thousand that came last year. Before that families were averaging close to four children each and there's no reason to suppose the same won't apply to the current crop of young parents. By my reckoning, even allowing for deaths, our population will more than double in the next forty to fifty years. If you don't believe me, just consider you and Mum. You started with just the two of you and look at the size of family you've got now."

"I believe you all right and that's good news," I told her. "With Earth gone and no more colonists arriving we need to expand as quickly as possible. We can produce enough food at this moment to feed more than twice the entire population and our output is growing by the year."

"I've nearly finished what I set out to do," Lynn said as I was leaving. "Do you think Uncle Nils would be interested in what I've done?"

"I know he will," I replied. "And so will the rest of parliament."

CHAPTER TWENTY-SEVEN

It was decided that the *Hebridean Moon* would undertake the survey of our world. I got an unexpected insight into their plans when Captain Hamish McGregor came to see Ivan one Sunday. I'd been next door for a chat and a coffee when McGregor arrived, a big raw boned fair-haired man in his early forties. With his name and looks I'd imagined he'd be from the Highlands or Islands; in fact he hailed from Motherwell. I made to leave but the two captains invited me to stay.

McGregor's plan was simple. Taking the charts and photographs made by the original survey team he'd divided that huge continent into six areas. The spaceship itself would visit each of the six areas in turn, setting down in the centre of the area and then leave the mapping and photographing tasks to the lifeships. The mission was scheduled to take the best part of two years, but at the end of that time we would have a comprehensive map of the entire land area of the planet in far greater detail than the original survey. There would be at least one geologist aboard and apart from geographical features locations which looked likely to contain useful minerals would be pinpointed. I suggested that they also take with them a biologist with seeds and aquatic life to implement the government plan to bring life to as much of the world as possible. McGregor jumped at the idea and asked me to find someone suitable. I spent part of the afternoon phoning round possible candidates. In the end Pieter Van Jonk, who'd been head biologist at Malaga, decided that he liked the prospect. Meantime Ivan was busy with preparations for his voyage to Cara III. He planned to leave in mid July and I asked him about his timetable.

"A spaceship can't travel very fast inside a planetary system," he explained, "so it will take us the best part of a week to get there. Depending on what we find we will probably spend up to two months there before coming back. We're taking a geologist with us, though if the planet's surface is what I suspect there won't be much work for him or her. There's no point in having a biologist. The photos we have already show that there's no vegetation. However, if you can give me a few bags of assorted seeds we can scatter them in various places as an experiment. If they grow, they grow, if they don't there's no harm done. I've no doubt we'll be going back there in about ten years' time and it will be interesting to see if anything has taken."

"What about aquatic life and fish spawn," I queried.

"Not much point," he replied. "As far as we can determine there's little or no surface water on Cara III. There's what looks like cloud cover, but I imagine that any rain that falls evaporates quickly."

Although I was supposed to play no part in the plan to spread vegetation far and wide over the western part of the continent I got drawn into it anyway. Roger, Kristina and Denise had met several times to try and formulate their policy but couldn't agree on a number of points. They stressed that there had been no rancour in their discussions, but they would appreciate guidance from me on the areas of dissent. We met one Sunday at Kristina's home in Athens. After serving two terms in parliament Kristina had decided that politics wasn't after all her metier and had set up a kind of market garden just outside of town. One by one we covered the items on which they couldn't agree The first was where to begin. Roger wanted to start on the faraway west coast and gave his reasons.

"There are two things in favour of that," he argued. "Firstly we don't know how long the lifeships will remain in service. We'll want to go back from time to time to inspect what we sow and maybe add to it. Secondly the predominant wind is from due west, so seeds from whatever we plant will be spread more quickly than if we work from east to west."

That was an easy one for me to field. "I agree with the girls on this one," I told him. "Your reasoning is correct in a way, but flawed in another. I've spoken to two of the captains and there's no reason why the lifeships shouldn't still be operative a couple of centuries from now. We can produce the fuel and any spare parts needed for repair. Yes, the direction of the wind in the far west will spread things more quickly, but don't forget that we'll be colonising from the east. It could be five hundred years or more before we get anywhere near the west coast. Therefore this side of the continent must be the priority. We've already made a start beyond the mountains. In places grass and woodland stretches for fifty miles. Work onwards and outwards from there is my advice."

The next bone of contention was when to begin operations. Denise was all for starting right away, Kristina wasn't sure and Roger proposed waiting until the spring. This time I came down in favour of Roger.

"If you plant stuff now it won't start growing until the spring anyway," I pointed out. "Also you're not going to have too much seed to work with. I suggest you spend from now until the end of November gathering in as much seed of all types that you can and getting underway around the beginning of March."

The other major point on which they hadn't been able to agree was the method of planting trees. Roger and Denise wanted to concentrate on setting up large areas of forest, Kristina wanted to spend time placing individual trees in isolated locations. "If we use trees with winged seeds they'll spread more rapidly," was her logic.

I couldn't agree with her. "If you've got trees with winged seeds they'll spread far and wide even if they're within a forest. Don't forget that we don't know where future generations are going to place their towns and villages. Too many isolated trees could hamper their efforts and be sacrificed in the name of progress. Our aim should always be to provide as much woodland as possible. The larger our population grows the more timber we'll be cutting and we don't want to lose trees unnecessarily. Incidentally, when you're planting new areas don't forget to include shrubs and bushes that normally grow in the wild. Hawthorn, brambles, wild rose, that sort of thing. Add as many wild flowers as you can as well. We want to make as much of the countryside as possible attractive to settlers when they arrive." I had something of a fixation on that last point. Try as I might I had never been able to erase from my mind that first sight of Cara IV and the unending expanse of bare brown earth.

A few other very minor items were cleared up quickly and I left the three of them to get down to some detailed planning. I felt a little bit sad on the way home. The meeting had reawakened my interest in matters of the land and I regretted somewhat my decision to distance myself from it. Not that I was unhappy in my new role working for Maria. After all, it was a job close to the soil and a change from all that I'd turned my hand to before. I was learning a lot, too. In my ignorance I'd believed that growing grapes was no different from growing grass or cabbages. I was just beginning to discover there was a lot more to it than that.

The two spaceships left on their missions within a week of each other. The *Ural Star* was the first to set off on its trip to Cara III and the *Hebridean Moon* headed for the southernmost part of our huge continent four days later. Captain McGregor had decided to tackle the farthest away of his six areas first. Both ships were in radio contact with a hastily established base in Europa, but the staff there were all strangers to me and I got no news of how they were faring. Even Nils was in the dark. His excuse was that he and his parliamentary colleagues had too much to do in other directions. When we met a fortnight later he had some surprising news for me.

"I've two years to run in my present term of office and then I'm going to retire. It's time to hand the baton over to someone younger. After all, I'll be close to seventy by then. Salvatore will go too: he's five years older than me."

"What will you do with yourself?" I asked.

"I haven't decided yet," he replied. "I'll take a few months off, potter around, play a little golf, do a little fishing and think things over. I didn't see as much of my children when they were young as I would have liked, so I'm not going to make the same mistake with my grandchildren. Maybe I'll write my autobiography. Then when paper eventually becomes available and we can have books again I can get it published. I've always maintained that I'd know when it was time to go and I'm sure that I've picked the right time. My job was to set up this world and lay down the organisation for the future. I've done that to the best of my ability and now it's time for the next generation to take over. To be honest I'd like to quit now, but the destruction of Earth has given us new problems to face and I want to deal with them before I go."

"You mention problems," I said thoughtfully. "Apart from the obvious one of getting no more colonists, surely everything else is in hand?"

"There's one very important issue. Knowledge. Up to now if we were short in a particular field we simply let Earth know and an expert would be sent the following year. Now that that's no longer possible we have to make sure that we pass on all the expertise we have, in every field, to coming generations. We're tackling that in two separate ways. First of all we're setting up Cara IV's first university. Initially it will be small, maybe just forty or fifty students. But as the population grows, so will the university. In time there will be more than one. In addition to that we're working on a scheme to provide apprenticeships in specialist as well as manual trades. Remember that we have very few books from which to learn. It is vital that we don't lose the knowledge that we have."

"That's a big step forward," I commented. "Have you any other major changes in the pipeline?"

"Not changes exactly." He smiled suddenly. "Those calculations that your Lynn passed on to me have surprised everybody in parliament. We knew the population would grow, but if she's right, and I'm sure she is, it is going to grow three times faster than our previous expectations. At present there are conflicting views among us in government. Some want simply to let the existing towns grow and grow. Others, including myself and Salvatore, want to limit the size of towns now and in the future and start to set up new settlements. Even those who think as we do are divided in their opinions. Half of them want to spread north and south; the other half want to expand beyond the mountains. Now that we have the use of the lifeships that prospect is perfectly feasible though it could lead to a divided society. There will be much discussion and much argument over the next year or so."

"I wouldn't like to see the towns grow much bigger," I mused. "Right now we have the best of both worlds, town or rather village living but in a rural environment. I would hate to see Stockholm growing into another Edinburgh, much as I loved my home city. I hope your faction wins through."

"I'm hopeful it will in the end," he stated. "Already one or two of the opposition are wavering. We'll work on those. My feelings echo yours. We have a chance to build a different kind of society here, based on small communities in attractive surroundings. No doubt in a thousand years or so the population will be such that big cities will become inevitable, but I hope and pray that moment will be delayed as long as possible."

It was just over two months before Ivan and the *Ural Star* returned from Cara III. I was at work in the vineyards and didn't see the ship land. In fact I didn't even know it was back until that evening when Donna broke the news to me. Ivan had apparently gone straight to Europa to report to parliament, Natasha with him, and it was three days before he came back and called round. I asked him what Cara III was like.

"Have you ever been to Mars?" he asked me. I shook my head. "Have you seen pictures of Mars?" was his next question. I nodded. "You know that Mars is covered in that red soil, with the famous canals but no rivers and no life. Well, change the red soil to yellow and you have the perfect picture of Cara III. Given that, the landscape is so similar to Mars it's uncanny. There are the hills and mountains and the canals which are in fact dry deep valleys. The big difference is that while Mars is fairly cold and has very little atmosphere Cara III is very hot and has an atmosphere similar to ours. Temperatures at the equator were over a hundred degrees Centigrade during the day and around eighty at night. Even at the poles, where we made our bases, daytime levels reached fifty degrees and twenty at night time."

"There is no water on the planet except at the poles and even there it's just a few brackish pools. It does rain everywhere else but the water evaporates as soon as it hits the ground. Humidity is very high and unpleasant, even at the poles. I planted the seeds and stuff that you gave me, but only at the poles. It would have been pointless to put them anywhere else. Whether anything will grow or not only time will tell. No doubt we or one of the other ships will go back in ten years' time or so and we'll find out then."

"I take it there's no chance of colonising the planet, then," I remarked.

"Definitely not. It's far too hot and unpleasant. The only life possible would be under cover and supplies of just about everything would have to be shipped in. We've brought back lots of samples for the chemists to analyse. The yellow soil and dust is a combination of silicon and sulphur plus small quantities of other elements. If we ever run out of the first two there's enough on Cara III to last for hundreds of thousands of years. And now I'm going to have a couple of months' rest before we take on Cara V."

We had word from time to time from the *Hebridean Moon* that their mission was proceeding well. Pieter Van Jonk sent me detailed reports by computer on a regular basis on soil availability and quality and kept me informed as to the materials he had planted. In the extreme south of the continent where the temperature seldom rose above freezing point he'd concentrated on small areas of grass and conifers, gradually bring in deciduous trees as he moved further north. On one of his early transmissions he waxed lyrical about the bareness of the landscape. "I've realised for the first time what it must have been like for you when you landed on that first day," he wrote. "It's an amazing experience. I find the terrain depressing and exciting in equal measure. It's so different from anything I've ever known."

Ivan and his crew set off for Cara V later in the year. This time they were away for four months, which suggested to me that they'd found much there to interest them. I wasn't wrong. As on the previous occasion, Ivan spent his first three or four days back home closeted with the government. When he did return to Stockholm he wasted no time coming to see me. My first question was whether the planet could be colonised.

"Possibly, but in small numbers," he reported. "The atmosphere is breathable, very similar to here in fact. Gravity is slightly higher. It takes about ten per cent more effort to walk or run and despite the time we spent there we found ourselves tiring quickly. The main stumbling block to settlement is the temperature. At the equator where we made our base the highest we recorded was eleven degrees Centigrade. The year on Cara V lasts for about five hundred and fifty days and by my estimate we arrived in early spring. When we left it would be just the start of summer, so it's unlikely that it would get very much hotter. At and around the poles minus forty-five wasn't uncommon. There is plenty of water, though once you get more than fifteen degrees north and south of the equator it is frozen for most of the year. There are four large continents, and unlike here literally thousands of islands dotted throughout the oceans. The whole world is far more mountainous than here on Cara IV but there are large areas of open land with soil similar to that here. We've brought samples back, of course. Most of the seed you gave me we planted around the equator. It will be interesting when we eventually return, as I'm sure we will, to find out how far it has spread. The poles are fascinating as you'll see from the photographs I have here. Huge glaciers extend almost a thousand kilometres from each pole. It's what Earth must have looked like during the Ice Age. To go back to your question I'd say that possibly half a million people could settle there in a belt bounded by two hundred kilometres either side of the equator, though it would be a hard life given the weather. Rain and snow were frequent, as were high winds and gales. There are minerals, though they are not so plentiful as they are here."

After we'd looked at the pictures he'd brought back I asked him what he planned to do next.

"Take things easy," he laughed. "I haven't had a proper break in fifteen years, so I'm going to take at least three months off to relax and look around for a job. I'm not fussy what it is, as long as I will be free to make the return visits to our neighbouring worlds whenever they are."

The night after Ivan's visit Natasha called in to see us. Her news was surprising.

"I've resigned from the ship," she told us. "Even if there are any more trips I won't be going on them. While we were going to new worlds and covering vast areas of space the job was fulfilling, but on these last two trips I've been bored most of the time. Marta introduced me to Maria the other day and I've got a job in the new unit she's setting up to make brandy. I have some knowledge of distilling as my father worked in vodka production back in Russia. When I was young, before I left school in fact, I used to go with him and he explained everything to me. Maria thinks that what I learned and can remember will be of value." For the first time I saw her blush. "There is also a very nice man who will be the manager. He is about my age and single and we seem to hit it off. Maybe marriage is a possibility after all."

Meantime the task of bringing growth to the 'corridor' as Nils had christened it was proceeding apace. As with Pieter the three in charge insisted on sending me updates on all that they were doing. They also made a point of coming to visit me on their occasional days off. Both Roger and Kristina reported that the early plantings that had been made were thriving and that the grassland had spread more than fifty kilometres beyond the mountains. Fish were now plentiful in the lakes and rivers close to the mountains. By the end of that year planting had been carried out to a distance of two hundred kilometres from the mountains. Denise had rather more ground to cover as little had been done previously in her section of the corridor. There was talk of some sheep being transported to beyond the mountains and allowed to run wild, though no decision had yet been taken.

CHAPTER TWENTY-EIGHT

It was seven years and not ten before Ivan went back to Cara III and this time I went with him. Much had changed in the intervening period. Two years previously I'd resigned my job with Maria and joined the recently established university as a lecturer in biology. Marta had taken my place as manager of the vineyards. The university had been set up just outside Europa. It meant a lot of travelling, but the high speed hoverbuses did the journey in under an hour so it wasn't too onerous. At that time there were only just over a hundred students, though as the children born on Cara IV grew to maturity numbers were increasing year on year. My class numbered just five, all under twenty-one. Without paper teaching wasn't easy, but we did the best we could. As one of my colleagues pointed out, what the students couldn't remember they could find out later by experiment. I saw the logic in this. The knowledge that I'd been given had come originally by just such a method.

Nils retired four years ago. His successor was Vera Zivovska, a Russian born woman in her early forties. She had been a staunch supporter of Nils and Salvatore Celli during her time in parliament so policy changed little under her leadership. Though officially retired Nils couldn't escape responsibility entirely, for he was often called upon for advice. The work done in the corridor and throughout the rest of the continent was bearing fruit. Grass was spreading rapidly and miniature forests were springing up in dozens of locations. I'd made a couple of extensive tours to the west and to the south, on one occasion taking my students with me to give them some background to their studies. Increasing pressure was being put upon me to authorise the felling of some of the earliest trees but I remained obdurate. I was determined to wait until we could supply all our needs without imperilling future requirements. I'd set a minimum of fifty years right from the start and I saw no reason to amend that estimate.

One evening towards the end of autumn Ivan dropped in to see me. Donna was out at the time. After the usual light banter he dropped his bombshell. "We're making a return visit to Cara III in the New Year," he announced. "How would you like to come with us?"

I was struck dumb. The boyhood ambition I'd had about going into space had lain dormant within me for many years but had never really died. The prospect excited me. True I'd had that twenty-four hours or so when we were coming in to our initial landing, but the thought of spending the best part of a week on the ship and of exploring a different world was too tempting to dismiss. Meantime Ivan was waiting for an answer.

"I'll need to talk it over with Donna," I responded finally. "But if she has no objections you've got yourself a passenger."

He laughed. "Passenger nothing. You'll be an Acting Second Officer and take your share of the duties with the rest of the crew." That suited me perfectly.

As I'd hoped Donna raised no objections. "Of course I'll miss you," she said, "but if you don't go you'll always regret it. You'd better dig out that old uniform of yours and see if it still fits you. You've put on a bit of weight in the last few years, you know." I hadn't realised the fact but she proved to be correct. Both the uniform jacket and the trousers were tight on me and had to be let out.

We set off in the second week in January. According to Ivan's calculations it would be late autumn on Cara III when we arrived and into winter by the time we left. Observations made on the previous visit had shown that the year there was only two hundred and seventy-eight days. Three of Ivan's former crew had left, Natasha included. The *Ural Star* carried the normal complement of two First Officers, four Second Officers, one of them being myself, and two engineers. The vacancies were filled by crew from the *Northern Light*. My immediate superior and the new senior First Officer was Selma Lubal, a woman in her early thirties of Eurasian origin, born of a Rumanian father and a Pakistani mother. We soon found common ground. Her father had worked as a technical adviser to a large multinational company back on Earth and the family had spent three years in Edinburgh when Selma was in her teens. Although we never found any common acquaintances she knew many of the places in the city that I'd frequented in my young days and she was able to tell me of the many changes that had taken place since I had left all that time ago.

Discipline on the ship was light during our six day voyage. The days and nights were divided into two twelve hour watches comprising one First Officer, two Second Officers and an engineer. Ivan spent six hours with each shift. The two leaders had tossed for the choice and Selma had lost, so we had the night watch on the way out. I soon saw what Natasha had meant when she talked about space flight being boring. Twelve hours spent looking through a viewscreen at unending pure white light tends to deaden the senses, even though the screen was heavily shaded. I only had to bear the boredom for six days, so it must have been soul destroying for the regular crews on the long runs who had to spend nearly a year of such a routine. As one of my colleagues put it: "it's even worse in deep space. There all you see is blackness and if you're lucky a few distant stars once in a while."

Our first sight of Cara III came late on the fourth day when our long range viewer picked up a small dot in the far distance. By that time we had covered three quarters of our forty million mile journey. From then on the viewer was kept trained on our destination. I couldn't tear myself away as the image grew in size almost visibly. Within four hours it had grown from a dot to the size of a tennis ball and we could just make out the yellow colouring. Thirty hours thereafter it filled the viewing screen as we started on our first orbit with Selma in the pilot's seat. Though I'd seen dozens of photographs none had conveyed the appearance of the planet in the way that I saw it now. In pictures the soil had seemed to be of a uniform yellow hue but by the time we commenced our second orbit there was enough detail to see that the colours varied from a pale primrose to a deep gold. About one third of the planet that was visible to us had cloud cover, but even the clouds were light yellow, and a rather dirty looking light yellow at that. Our orbit took us over the poles and here as we crept nearer I saw small patches of blue-gray, which Ivan told me were the water they had come across before. Try as I might I could see no trace of green in the vicinity of these pools. I had brought more material to plant, but it looked as though it would be a lost cause.

We landed on the North Pole and on the same rocky plateau that Ivan had used before. I judged this to be a good two miles in length and almost as wide. It provided ample room for the ship to rest and space on all sides should we need it. It was just beginning to get dark so there was no possibility of going outside immediately. As soon as the engines were turned off Ivan gathered the whole crew around him.

"From now on remember that we're on a strange and possibly hostile world," he began forcefully. "I'm going to give you a few do's and don'ts. First and foremost never leave the ship without notifying myself or First Officer Lubal. Never go out on your own. There must be at least three of you on any outside trip. If you have an accident it means that one can come for help and one stay with the victim. Do not under any circumstances lose sight of the ship. There is a certain amount of magnetic material on this world that renders a compass useless. Remember that while we're here at the pole every way you go will be south. It's easy to get confused. The temperature here at the pole is bearable but the atmosphere is thin so you will need breathing apparatus. When we go to the tropics later on you'll need lightweight heat deflecting suits as well. In this place always wear knee length rubber boots outside as there are areas that are extremely marshy. Always make sure that every part of your body is covered. Winds and gales can arise in a matter of seconds and the sand and soil particles are very hard. They can whip the skin off bare parts of the body in no time at all. Be alert and aware at all times, be ready for the unexpected and watch each other's backs. Finally, if you don't know already, the day here on Cara III is about twenty hours long. I've adjusted all the clocks accordingly. At this time of the year we'll have eight hours of light and twelve of darkness. I suggest we use ten of the latter for sleep. First Officer Lubal will detail one officer to stand watch, to be relieved and replaced after five hours. That's all."

Even though I'd been on night shift the night before I'd stayed up all that day, the excitement of coming in to land proving too much to resist. It didn't take me long to get to sleep that night and for once I didn't dream. Seemingly minutes after going to bed the morning reveille call brought me back to wakefulness. It was eight o'clock and just beginning to get light outside. I was allocated a place on the first team to venture forth along with Selma, another Second Officer and one of the engineers. We dressed in long sleeved cotton shirts, lightweight trousers, cotton gloves and rubber boots. There were some twenty pairs of the latter in the stores. I couldn't find an exact fit among them, so in the end I took a larger size and put on an extra pair of socks. The breathing apparatus consisted of an aluminium and plastic headpiece similar to a diver's helmet and two air tanks strapped to our backs.

"The outside temperature is thirty-three degrees Centigrade," Ivan announced as he opened the exit hatch. "Remember all I told you last night and stay safe. Return in three hours' time at the latest. Good luck."

My first thought on stepping on to the surface was for the rock beneath my feet. It looked to be granite. There was a light wind blowing and grains of yellow sand or soil were swirling about us as we walked. We felt the heat immediately. It wasn't especially unpleasant but it was uncomfortable. On my part I was glad that the time I'd spent in Italy and my forays to the likes of Verona and Rotterdam had acclimatised me to that sort of temperature. At the left hand end of the plateau from the direction the ship was pointing a wide ledge gave an easy passage to the flat ground below. Here it was marshy underfoot and the reason for the boots became apparent. With every step we sank up to our ankles in the moist sandy yellow soil. Selma was slightly in the lead and she pointed ahead. We had full communication through the helmets. It meant that private conversations were out but the advantage was that we always knew what everyone else was doing and thinking.

"The nearest water is just under two kilometres ahead according to my reckoning." Selma's voice through the helmet was loud and clear. "We'll head in that direction. Take it slowly, watch where you're going and shout out if you see anything that may be unusual or interesting."

In the marshy conditions we had no option but to take it slowly. Three of us walked in line some ten yards apart with Selma slightly in the lead. I looked searchingly to left and right as I moved but all I could see was the soggy soil. After ten minutes we could see the sheen of water up ahead and somewhat to the left. Selma signalled and we made a small change of direction. As the details became clearer I saw that the lake, for such it was, was more extensive than I'd expected. It took us another twenty-five minutes to reach the shore, by which time I could see to the other side. I could only make a rough estimate, but I guessed that the stretch of water was some three miles across and two miles wide. From here on the ground it looked more grey than blue. There were ripples on the surface as the wind eddied back and forth but no other movement.

Selma spoke again. "From what the captain told me the crew last time were a good bit further to the right of here. Let's move in that direction."

We'd gone less than twenty yards when the engineer gave a shout. "Look, Alex. Up to your right. There's something growing."

I moved forward to where he was pointing. Sure enough, there were several tufts of grass about two to three feet high. They weren't easy to spot, being yellow like the soil instead of the normal green. The tufts became more plentiful as we continued on our walk. Soon I spotted small trees here and there. Again these blended into the background with leaves and branches as yellow as the soil. Among the items I'd given Ivan for planting on his earlier voyage had been a mixture of perennial flower seeds and a few of these seemed to have survived. It was obvious that they'd borne flowers earlier in the year, but these had been replaced by seed capsules so it wasn't possible to determine whether the flowers had been the correct colour or yellow also. The discovery of plant life gave us all a boost and we pressed on eagerly, but we found nothing more of importance. Before we headed back to the ship Selma took routine samples of soil and water. I made up my mind to take a few samples of the grass and flowers back to Cara IV with me and see how they reacted to more normal conditions. I'd brought a supply of miscellaneous seeds with me and planted them the next day.

We spent four days in all at the North Pole before going to the South Pole. Conditions here were very similar except that there was no rocky plateau to land on. Ivan put the ship down on a large open plain close to one of half a dozen small stretches of water. Grass, flowers and trees had managed to get a foothold here too so I sowed the rest of my stock of seed. With no higher ground visible life at the South Pole was like living in the Sahara Desert back on Earth. After three days we'd done everything we wanted to and Ivan decided to head for the edge of the tropical region.

If I'd hoped for something more exciting there at some twenty-five degrees south of the equator I was doomed to disappointment. True the landscape was different insofar as there were more hilly areas, less open spaces and no water of any kind. Daytime temperatures were in the region of sixty to seventy degrees Centigrade, falling not more than fifteen degrees during the hours of darkness. We could only venture outside for short periods even with the special heat deflecting suits. In any case there was nothing of interest to see. We stayed for four days, during which time there were half a dozen violent rainstorms. At least it was fascinating to watch as the rain evaporated within seconds of hitting the ground, shrouding everything in a thick white mist of water vapour. At length Ivan decided that there was no point in prolonging our time and with general approval gave the order to lift off on the return journey home. In all we'd been away for just over three weeks.

Three months later the *Ural Star* made its return trip to Cara V. Ivan invited me to join the crew once again but my desire for space travel had withered and died and I declined with thanks. Perhaps I should have gone. As both Ivan and Selma told me later it had been much more interesting than the previous trip. Despite the cold conditions nearly all of what the first expedition had planted was thriving. They'd taken more seeds with them and spent over a fortnight placing them in new sites.
Ivan summed up their progress. "I doubt if we will ever want to colonise Cara V unless the sun for some reason starts giving out more heat. Life there would be spartan in the extreme and there would be many hardships. But if the need ever does arise we won't have to start from scratch as you did here on Cara IV."

With no more space flights planned long discussions took place as to what to do with the three ships. Having completed its survey of the southern and western sectors of the continent the *Hebridean Moon* had also become redundant, with lifeships being used for the rest of the mapping operation. No satisfactory conclusion was reached and eventually it was decided to keep the three of them maintained and ready for flight in an emergency. The lifeships would be removed and used separately though such use would be limited until we started settling beyond the mountains. One by one the crew members found other employment. From time to time there was a suggestion that new ones should be recruited and trained but nothing became of it.

CHAPTER TWENTY-NINE

I celebrated my seventieth birthday a fortnight ago. I would have been quite happy to ignore the occasion and treat it like a normal day but when I said as much there was an outcry from the whole family. Even Donna ruled against me. I was left out of the discussions entirely and only on the morning of the day itself did I learn what had been planned for me. The celebrations consisted of an all day open air barbeque. The whole family plus our closest friends had been invited and there must have been more seventy people milling around by early afternoon. I had to admit later that I had enjoyed it but I would have been equally happy having a quiet day at home with just Donna for company. Strangely we'd never resumed the practice of giving presents on special occasions but photography had become a popular pastime and by the time the festivities drew to a close we'd been given over a hundred prints. It was after nine in the evening before we closed the front door on the last of the well wishers and while Donna made tea for us I leafed through the pictures. One in particular caught my eye; the only one of Donna and I alone.

I looked at it critically, then compared it with one on the wall that had been taken on Donna's thirtieth birthday. Not surprisingly we'd both aged. My wife's glorious red hair had long faded to grey, but apart from that she still looked so youthful. Try as I might I couldn't spot one wrinkle on her face. For myself, I was grey too, balding rapidly and with enough wrinkles for the both of us. In spite of these things I reckoned I wasn't doing too badly for three score years and ten. I still had all my own teeth, I was still extremely fit and active and still reasonably slim in build. Above all I was happy. I still loved Donna to distraction as I did all my extended family.

Lynn's prediction of a population explosion, made all those years ago, proved all too accurate. If anything she under estimated. The count at the last census two years ago showed that Cara IV was home to over one hundred and forty thousand people. Clan Dunsmuir had made a major contribution. Donna and I now had seventeen grandchildren and five great grandchildren with two more on the way. Twenty-two new townships have been set up, bringing the total to seventy-four. Six of these are beyond the mountains and three more are planned for the coming year. Twenty lifeships provide a regular daily service to each. A major project, estimated to take more than twenty years, will be getting under way early next year. Industrialists in Stockport have designed and built a massive machine capable of drilling through rock. The plan is to drive at least three tunnels through the mountains at strategic points to enable the passage of road traffic. It's a huge and expensive undertaking, but one that is essential for the future development of our world. The downside is that income tax has gone up another two per cent to pay for it.

Europa remains our biggest town, with a population of over five thousand. It now calls itself Europa City! Oval Lake has become one of the most desirable areas in which to live. Four of the new towns have been situated along its shores. New settlements have also arisen one hundred kilometres north and south of Salford and Rotterdam. I don't envy the people who live in Warsaw, the town furthest to the south, where temperatures reach a hundred degrees Fahrenheit and more during the summer.

The passing years have brought sorrow in abundance. Our biggest tragedy has been the loss of Nils. He passed away eighteen months ago. He never really got over the death of his wife Ingrid the previous year. The outpouring of grief throughout the world was unbelievable. Thousands attended his open air funeral and most followed the coffin on foot as it was carried five miles down the coast to a lovely spot close to the seashore. Within the month a monument had been erected to 'The Father of Cara IV' and the shrine became a constant attraction to visitors. Having been so close to him from day one I felt his loss more keenly than most, but every single person in the world mourned his passing. There were few, from the youngest to the oldest, who hadn't met him and spoken to him at some time. Sadly he never did get around to writing his autobiography.

Herr Klost and Salvatore Celli predeceased Nils by some years. Ivan Petrovic passed away last year at the age of seventy-nine. His going also hit me hard. We'd been neighbours and close friends for twenty years. Natasha was made captain of the *Ural Star*, an honorary appointment as the ship wasn't going anywhere. She had after all found that middle-aged man she'd joked about all those years ago, a fifty year old widower, and got married. All three spaceships have been turned into museums depicting the planet's history and are popular attractions, particularly among the children. I still get embarrassed whenever I visit one to see my picture prominently displayed. Despite their new function the ships are still serviced regularly and could take off in a matter of hours should it ever be necessary.

There had been talk from time to time about sending one of the ships on what the politicians called a goodwill mission to some of the other outworlds. Before the destruction of Earth we'd had regular communications with most of them but never direct contact. All radio messages including those back to Earth had been routed through ships in transit. With no more ships bearing colonists and no trade that we knew of between the other worlds these contacts had ended. For all we knew there might have been some vessels moving between the colonised planets but though some sort of radio watch was kept we never picked up any signals. Personally I thought there was little to be gained by sending a ship elsewhere. Trade would be difficult and expensive and in any case there was very little in the way of goods that we either hadn't already got or could make in the future if we found a need for them. We could certainly have done with more colonists but the same applied to all the other worlds. Despite the massive evacuation programme from Earth the highest number on any one world was on Paladia. The last figure we'd ever heard from there was three quarters of a billion. Considering that habitable land on that world was more than four times greater than on Earth it was doubtful they'd be wanting to lose anyone.

My old colleague Hans is still around and is a frequent visitor, as are Roger and Julie and Nico and Jennifer. Our friendship with the doctor and his wife has never waned. Denise has also become a close friend. She really does have the secret of eternal youth and looks exactly the same as she did on the first day we met. Donna and I are both astounded that she never married. We rib her about it sometimes but she always responds that she is perfectly happy the way things are and has never regretted staying single. The same applies to Marta, another who never seems to age. She is still in charge of Maria and Bert's vineyards and has vowed never to retire as long as she stays healthy. I'm not supposed to know this, but apparently she confided in Donna some time ago the reason for her attitude to men.

"Marta had what she describes simply as a bad experience with a man when she was fifteen," Donna told me in confidence. "She didn't go into details but I would guess that she was the victim of a rape attack. It made her wary and more than a little frightened of men generally. She also admitted one other thing to me. I've been dubious about telling you this because I don't want you to get a swollen head. She said that the only man she ever met that she would have liked to marry was you."

I felt absurdly flattered and I must have shown it. "Now don't go getting exaggerated ideas of your attraction to women," Donna warned with a chuckle. "If your head does start growing I'll batter it back to size with a saucepan."

One couple we see little of unfortunately are Maria and Bert. They still work at least fourteen hours a day in their ever-expanding wine and spirits empire. I bumped into Maria doing some shopping a month or so back and ribbed her about it.

"You must be the richest woman on Cara IV," I joked.

She laughed and shrugged her shoulders. "Could be. But you know, Alex, the money doesn't interest us in the slightest. It's the satisfaction of having built the business from scratch in the first place and watching it grow and keep on growing. As you know Bert and I decided when we got married that we were too old to think about having children. The business is our child."

I put a question that I'd often wondered about. "What's going to happen when you're gone? Or haven't you considered that yet?"

She laughed again. "I guess we won't be worrying much about it by then. But we have talked it over. If she survives us Marta will take over. We made her a full director some time ago. If she should predecease us then we've suggested that the workers form a co-operative and run the business themselves. But that's a long way in the future. Bert and I both get regular check-ups from Doctor Nico and he assures us we're still in our prime. He predicts we'll both survive and stay active well into our nineties. I have to admit though that we are planning to delegate more of our work in the next year or two so that we can take things a bit easier.

I resigned from my job at the university last year but I am not fully retired. Nowadays I travel round giving talks to schoolchildren. It's a highly rewarding experience and I am constantly amazed at how aware even the youngest are of the history of this small world of ours. I'm normally allocated one hour, but I have to leave almost half of that time for questions. When I ask for a response these come in thick and fast. Some of the older pupils ask as much about the future as the past. I try to answer their queries honestly, but I am no longer in close touch with the decision makers and often can only guess at what will happen in the years to come. So far we have been lucky with our ruling politicians. They have deviated very little from the principles set out by Nils and Salvatore Celli in the early days of parliament.

Last month, two years ahead of schedule, I finally gave the go ahead for trees to be felled. At last the two remaining items that we were short of, wood and paper, will be provided. Soon we'll have newspapers and books. I suspect the demand for timber as such will not be too great. We've lived for so long with metal furniture and other artefacts that it has come to be the accepted way of doing things. I've set an annual quota for the next five years that must not be exceeded, but after that there will be sufficient timber to ensure supplies for generations to come. My last official act was to lobby the government and get a department set up to monitor forestry throughout the world. We must not fall into the pitfalls that plagued Earth by using up our resources without making adequate provision for the future. Roger Beasley has been put in charge of this department, so I know it will be in good hands. Typically he is already training his eventual successor, a young woman in her early thirties who was a pupil of mine at the university in Europa.

More than anyone I realise that we have been lucky on this world. Nature has been kind to us. In all our time here there have been no major disasters. Earthquakes and hurricanes are unknown. The worst we have had to face has been excessive rainfall and that only on three or four occasions.

There was some localised flooding in a few inland areas as a result but damage to crops and livestock was minimal and no lives were lost. The generations to come will inherit a world that's pleasant to live in. Crime is virtually non-existent, poverty is unknown and there is ample food for all. Recreational facilities are good and improving year by year. Though I wouldn't trade the last fifty years for anything there are times that I feel I'd like to be twenty-two again and have a further role in developing and expanding our world.

I've always believed that those three events in childhood shaped my life and what I am. But I've long realised that there was one more occasion to add and that that particular event was the luckiest thing that ever happened to me. My mind often goes back to that fateful day at the university in Riccione when Dr. Schmidt pulled the ball out of the bag that assigned me to Cara IV. I'm sure that if I'd got one of the other postings I would have had a fulfilling career and probably got married and settled down. But I would never have met Donna. From the moment I first set eyes upon her she has been the centrepiece of my life; my strength and inspiration. I doubt if anyone will believe this but it's absolutely true: in forty-eight years of married life we have never once quarrelled. I would go even further. Though we have had our disagreements and arguments over the years I can't recall more than two or three occasions when we have even raised our voices to one another. If that doesn't equate to a marriage made in heaven I don't know what does.

I'm not a vain man; at least I don't think so. I'm only too well aware that when it came down to the hard work that brought life to this once desolate world I only played a minute part. But as I travel through the lush green countryside and the huge forests I can't help feeling a certain sense of pride. After all, mine was the guiding hand.

THE END